Michael Egan

The Flying, Gray-Haired Yank

The Adventures of a Volunteer

Michael Egan

The Flying, Gray-Haired Yank
The Adventures of a Volunteer

ISBN/EAN: 9783337342906

Printed in Europe, USA, Canada, Australia, Japan

Cover: Foto ©Andreas Hilbeck / pixelio.de

More available books at **www.hansebooks.com**

THE

FLYING, GRAY-HAIRED YANK;

OR,

The Adventures of a Volunteer.

A PERSONAL NARRATIVE OF THRILLING EXPERIENCES AS AN
ARMY COURIER, A VOLUNTEER CAPTAIN, A PRISONER OF
WAR, A FUGITIVE FROM SOUTHERN DUNGEONS, A
GUEST AMONG THE CONTRABANDS AND UNION-
ISTS, AND FINALLY, A SKIRMISHER AT
THE VERY FRONT AT APPOMATTOX.

A TRUE NARRATIVE OF THE CIVIL WAR.

BY

MICHAEL EGAN,

LATE CAPTAIN CO. B, 15TH REGIMENT WEST VIRGINIA INFANTRY
VOLUNTEERS.

HUBBARD BROTHERS, PUBLISHERS,

DEDICATED

TO

THE GRAND ARMY OF THE REPUBLIC

OF THE

UNITED STATES.

AUTHOR'S PREFACE.

THE title of this book, "The Flying, Gray-Haired Yank," was suggested to the author by a second christening received from his astounded captors, on seeing the rapid flight made by one so gray on the night of his second escape.

The author's reason for presuming to add another volume to the number of works on the late war, is his belief that this little book will find a place in the hearts of the volunteer soldier and the general reader, who never tire of the records of those thrilling scenes.

It seems to him a pity, too, that of all the magazine articles, books and pamphlets lately issued on the war and its history so few are from that great majority who comprised the rank and file of this Grand Army of the Union.

The incidents narrated herein fell to the writer's lot entirely unsought. They are absolutely correct and are reproduced from entries made in his diary at the time of their occurrence. This merit is no trifling one, as it places the narratives before the reader with all the vividness of truth, so often stranger than fiction.

In the mention of engagements in which the writer participated, he has not presumed to give a comprehensive description of events, as would be expected in a general history. He contents himself with telling simply what he saw and how affairs appeared to him from his point of view, thus making the reader share the actual experiences of a soldier at the very front.

The reader will notice, doubtless, the author's constant use of the first person, singular. He feels that in so doing he has laid himself open to the charge of egotism. But he has not been able to eliminate this feature, dealing as he does with occurrences in which he alone participated.

In conclusion, while the writer makes no pretension to the qualifications of authorship, his book has the merit of being entirely his own, as he received no outside aid in its preparation, except from his eldest son, Thomas, who assisted him in arranging the matter for the publisher.

IN MEMORIAM.

CAPTAIN MICHAEL EGAN, of Parkersburg, West Va., died suddenly on Saturday, September 15th, 1888, at Marietta, Ohio, in the sixty-third year of his age. He had been in attendance at the Reunion of the Grand Army at Columbus, and was returning home. Waiting at Marietta for a train, he felt somewhat ill, but kind friends cared for him and he expressed himself as feeling better; but a moment later he dropped from his chair and his brave spirit had departed.

Andrew Mather Post, G. A. R., followed his remains to their final resting-place on Monday, September 17th.

The unanimous testimony of those who knew Captain Egan is that he was a brave, honorable, kind-hearted man. He loved his adopted country and was willing to live or to die for her good.

It is a matter for special regret, that this volume, so long withheld from the public by his conspicuous modesty, was not finished in time for his eyes to behold it.

THE PUBLISHERS.

(9)

CONTENTS.

CHAPTER XI.

CHAPTER XII.

CHAPTER XIII.

CHAPTER XIV.

CHAPTER XV.

CHAPTER XVI.

CHAPTER XVII.

CHAPTER XVIII.

CHAPTER XIX.

CHAPTER XX.

CHAPTER XXI.

CHAPTER XXII.

CHAPTER XXIII.

CHAPTER XXIV.

CHAPTER XXV.

CHAPTER XXVI.

CHAPTER XXVII.

CHAPTER XXVIII.

CHAPTER XXIX.

CHAPTER XXX.

CHAPTER XXXI.

CHAPTER XXXII.

CHAPTER XXXIII.

CHAPTER XXXIV.

CHAPTER XXXV.

CHAPTER XXXVI.

CHAPTER XXXVII.

CHAPTER XXXVIII.

CHAPTER XXXIX.

CHAPTER XL.

CHAPTER XLI.

List of Illustrations.

(17)

Captain Michael Egan,

"THE FLYING GRAY-HAIRED YANK."

CHAPTER I.

VIRGINIA STATE MILITIA IN 1859—RURAL LIFE IN THE STATE AT THAT PERIOD—PROMOTION TO RANK OF MAJOR—STIRRING INCIDENTS OF THE LAST GENERAL MUSTER—STARS AND STRIPES DISCARDED BY A MAJORITY OF OFFICERS—PATRIOTIC, BUT PERILOUS, ACTION OF THE MINORITY.

ABOUT two years prior to the outbreak of the Great Rebellion of 1861, I was in command of a battalion of militia consisting of about three hundred men, in Lewis county, Virginia; a county central to what is now the State of West Virginia.

Having been, previously, subject to the rigid discipline and strict subordination of a military experience in the Dublin constabulary for a period of nine years, the bearing and conduct of these farmer-militiamen struck me as somewhat strange and inappropriate for members of a military organization. They appeared to have no appreciation of the importance of such wholesome and necessary restrictions as those to which I had been accustomed.

With the one exception of the institution of negro slavery, these were the grand old days of true American liberty; taxed lightly and governed little, but wisely, the worthy and industrious farmer was privileged to do what he liked with the

2   (19)

products of his land. He could raise his own
tobacco and work it into any shape desired, or
brew his own "peck o' maut," or apple-jack,
without tax, let, or hindrance.

On "muster days" the boys composing our
battalion assembled at some stated place, generally a central location, and after drill would
usually indulge in horse-trading, or "swapping;"
talk of, and appoint log-rollings, rail-maulings,
house-raisings, apple-cuttings, corn-huskings, and
many other kinds of "frolics," as they were entitled by these sturdy farmers, and each of which
would invariably terminate in the evening, in a
jovial, old-time, "hoe-down" dance.

This rural life in the wilds of Virginia, at the
time of which I write, might well be envied by
even the nabobs and lords of creation. In such
places, above all others, are happiness and godli-
ness sure to be found; person and property were
alike safe in the keeping of those kind-hearted,
industrious, innocent, and religious people. They
were like one happy family in their daily intercourse, cheering and helping each other along
the steep stony path of life; and, finally, when
grim death would step in to claim one of their
number (a rare occurrence, owing to their exem-
plary habits and mode of living), all would unite
in condoling with the bereaved, and in honoring
the memory of the deceased.

During the summer months it was custom-

ary for the young people of both sexes to attend camp-meetings, revivals, geography singing-
schools, and other religious or instructive gather-
ings. In winter the male portion of the population engaged in the exciting pleasures of the
chase, hunting deer, bear and smaller game.

Never since my youth have I been so much
impressed with fond recollections as I now am, in
recalling the happy days spent with these light-
hearted and whole-souled young fellows and
their pretty and unaffected sisters, whose blooming cheeks were suffused with nature's beauteous
glow alone. The refreshing comeliness of these
rural lassies was something that vigorous manhood could not fail to note, surpassing as it did
the artificial charms of many a pampered daughter of wealth and fashion.

When I assumed the responsibility of trying to
instruct the young men, composed of this good
and honest material, in the first rudiments
of military duty, I addressed a few remarks to
them and said, among other things: "The law
of the State governing her militia requires the
members of that body to assemble periodically
for the purpose of instruction and drill. It is,
therefore, right and proper that you should obey
this law and the authorities appointed to enforce
it. Your having to quit your general avocations
in obedience to the provisions of the law would
seem to make it obligatory upon you to occupy

the time thus taken from your ordinary duties to some advantage. The very general practice of talking in the ranks, with arms akimbo, is in violation of orders and both disrespectful and embarrassing to your superior officer; giving, as it does, our drill the appearance of a burlesque on military movements. You may think that these periodical drills are all idle formality, or pastime, having no meaning; but, if I mistake not, the time is not far distant, when whatever instruction you may now receive, will be brought into stern requisition. There is a cloud lowering overhead, already almost surcharged, which will assuredly burst and cause trouble in these parts before you have many general musters; therefore, 'tis best to prepare."

In the month of August, 1862, I enlisted the larger part of my company on the same grounds upon which these remarks were made, and I reminded them of the words I had addressed to them so short a time before. It required no endowment of the prophetic spirit, however, to discern the impending danger; anybody who read with attention could see from the vindictive, cutting and sarcastic tone of both the Southern and Northern press that hostilities were determined upon for the near future.

I did not make the slightest effort to secure advancement in the militia, but the people treated me very kindly, and in a short time, through the suggestion of some of them, I was promoted to the rank of Major in the 192d Regiment Virginia Militia.

In the winter of 1860 there was quite a military stir throughout the State; reviews and general musters were the order of the day. The authorities, John Letcher then being Governor, were using every effort to put the militia of the State on a war footing.

Matters continued in this shape until the following spring. About two months prior to the passage of the ordinance of secession, which occurred April 17, 1861, and which, even months before, was openly discussed, and was seemingly a foregone conclusion, General Mustering Officer Conrad issued an order directing the 125th and the 192d Regiments of State militia to proceed to muster near Weston, Lewis county.

About two weeks previous to the day appointed the officers of the regiments above named held a meeting, at which I was present, to consider the expediency of taking out our regimental flag and the Stars and Stripes at the time of the coming drill and review. The final and almost unanimous decision of this meeting was, that such a course would cause bloodshed. I do not recall a dissenting voice to this arrangement except that of the writer, who was a comparative stranger among them, having been scarcely six years in the United States at the time. The fact of my holding a commission as Major under the seal of Virginia and signature of Governor Letcher made my position an unenviable one; but the die was cast, and, sink or swim, my course was determined on, and I expressed my intentions in the following brief remarks:

"Gentlemen-Officers: We are about to be confronted with a most serious crisis in the affairs of our common country. The time is coming, it appears, that will try every man throughout the length and breadth of this land, 'as by fire.' 'To be, or not to be,' that is the question. Whether to be true in our allegiance to the United States of America, or to a single State, is the issue. I question no man's motives; but for myself, my oath of allegiance to the United States is yet too fresh in my memory to permit me to forget—according to my interpretation of it—that my first duty as a citizen is to the Government of the Union, and that my obligation to the State of Virginia must be, and is, secondary. You propose, on the day appointed, to muster, to drill, and march your regiments in review; but you have no flag, no banner, or other insignia of military display in accordance with long established military law and usage. Has such a spectacle ever before been witnessed? And has it come to this, that the Stars and Stripes, the emblem of liberty, honored by all nations and peoples, on land and on sea, under whose folds the

oppressed of all climes have found an abiding
refuge and protection, shall be abandoned now
by a people who were once, and should still be,
justly proud of its expanding influence and
honor? I will say for myself, I shall be present,
in obedience to orders, at this muster; but if I
move at all, in a military attitude, it shall be under a flag, and that flag shall be no nameless
shadow, but the flag of the Union, and 'long may
she wave.'"

The meeting, after voting as above mentioned,
adjourned.

The action of this meeting soon became known
throughout the surrounding country and was received by the larger portion of the citizens with
approval. I, however, determined to set about to
create, if possible, a counter sentiment, and to this
end I made a trip through the county, making
Unionist speeches, putting up "posters" of the
same purport, which I had written and copied
myself, there being no facilities for printing in the
vicinity at this time, and by stirring up the dor-
mant patriotism of the people generally; so that,
when I had finished, I had secured the pledges of
about fifty Union men, mostly members of my
command, to stand by the flag and myself when
the occasion should require it.

The action of the regimental officers had, of
course, deprived us of our flag, and it became
necessary, therefore, to procure one. In this con-

nection I wish to introduce to the reader a character who gave us valuable assistance in this particular. He is no less a personage than the inimitable and eccentric Gasper Butcher, Jr., a son of one of the most hospitable, obliging and kind-hearted individuals then living in the section of country of which I write. Gasper, or "Gap," as he was invariably called, deserves all the kind things that I can say of him. He was the embodiment of soft-heartedness. He could not possibly refuse anybody a favor. No "frolic" for miles around but languished in his absence. If they lacked whiskey, Gap was away for it instanter. If they wanted music, he would procure it; and when this was not possible, he would rasp away himself. If he could not find funny practical jokes ready-made, to amuse the party, he would make them himself, no matter at whose expense. He was a member of my militia company, and lived near me. I told him of the arrangements for the general muster and described to him the cowardice, or lack of patriotism, that must have actuated the officers in deciding to abandon the old flag, and added that I did not intend to appear at drill or review without one.

"Never mind," said Gap, "we will show them what Leading Creek can do; she has always held her own."

Very few words passed between Gap and my-self before it was resolved to have a United

States flag. He started immediately for Weston,
nine miles distant, and procured the necessary
material; and in coming homeward, at about a
half mile from the town, he stopped at the house
of Mr. John Flesher, a worthy blacksmith and a
staunch Union man, whose family included two
amiable and patriotic daughters, Julia and Cecilia.
All of the family were loyal in spirit and devotion
to the old flag; one, a fine-looking young man
named James, had he been less brave, might be
alive to-day. He died one of the earliest martyrs
to the cause of his country. He was killed by a
party of rebel cavalry at Big Birch river, while
bearing despatches to Colonel Tyler, of the 7th
Ohio Volunteers, who had been sent out as a
pioneer in the direction of Gauley Bridge. I
often saw his grave while superintending the
same dangerous mission, some months later.

On the day of Gap's visit to the Flesher house
this noble boy's two sisters went to work on the
material which he had brought, and in a short
time they had finished in very neat style a complete United States flag. By no persuasion could
they be induced to accept any remuneration for
their trouble. Neither would Gap Butcher allow
any one to share with him in the purchase of the
material; so to him and the two Misses Flesher
belongs the honor of furnishing the flag on the
occasion of this muster.

The day appointed for the review at length

arrived. The militia formed on the farm of Henry Butcher, two miles east of Weston. The weather was very fine, and great numbers of the farmers of the neighborhood, with their wives and daughters, had driven or ridden to the grounds to witness the spectacle, and everything bore an outward appearance of gayety; but there were many present who had silent forebodings of coming trouble. The Stars and Stripes were abandoned; we were virtually in a seceded State; things had, indeed, an ugly look for the little band of Unionists in the assemblage.

I had often been exempted from duty while in the English service for my general cleanliness and proper appearance on parade, and, as on this occasion I was well mounted on a fine black charger, and knew how to sit in a saddle, the reader may infer that I presented a fair military appearance. I avoided coming on the field until the brigade was in its proper position. My place was in the centre of the column, and I rode leisurely forward until I came within a few hundred yards of the command, when I advanced at a full gallop and did not check up when I came on the field, but continued to move to the centre of the column, and, when within about one hundred yards of the alignment, I stopped, and unfurling the Stars and Stripes shook its clean beauty in the gentle breeze and the beaming sun.

This action was noticed by the entire command,

and was greeted by a few with spirited cheers, but by the majority with loud protests and angry mutterings. There was now manifest a very uneasy feeling throughout the whole line. I handed the flag to John Newman, then of my company and also afterwards in the field. The brave fellow had volunteered for the honorable duty beforehand. The colonel, Hansom M. Peterson, a fine young man, who subsequently joined the forces of the other side and died early in the conflict, now rode up and requested me to take down the flag, stating that the feelings of the majority could hardly be controlled, and at the same time ordering, or rather requesting, me to conduct the marching at the head of the column as it passed in review. I respectfully declined the honor, and said: "I wish to stop by the flag, as I think this my proper place." No further remarks passed between us, although he appeared deeply chagrined at what he, no doubt, considered my obstinacy and insubordination. He then rode away, and a few minutes later Colonel Caleb Boggess, a military graduate, was assigned to the position which I had declined.

The review then proceeded, but I fear the impression made upon General Conrad and the spectators was not the most flattering. Several times during the drill I lost my temper at the awkward movements of the men, whose mistakes appeared to be more glaring on this than on any

former occasion.   It was evident that the minds
of these embryo soldiers were not on the matter
in hand, but rather on thoughts of an impending
serious conflict.   Standard-bearer Newman performed his duty well throughout the trying ordeal,
and to the surprise and delight of some, and the
disappointment of others, not a single star was
touched.   I was told afterwards that there were
United States officers *incognito* on the field at the
time, but if such was the case I was not personally
aware of it.

If, as I have remarked, I was comparatively
unknown before, I assure the reader I was no
longer so after this event.

Immediately after the review at the Butcher
farm, the greater part of the militia repaired to
Weston, the county-seat of Lewis county, where
they listened to speeches made by several of the
officers.   I recall two of these speeches—one by
Colonel Peterson, and the other by Captain Boy-
kin—as being especially stirring and strongly
Southern in sentiment.   Colonel Peterson's address was quite lengthy.   He dwelt particularly
on the rights and privileges of a sovereign State,
and the subordinate position occupied by the
general government, in any controversy involving
the claims of each ; pointing out, in fervid language, the duty of all good citizens of the grand
old State of Virginia, the parent of Presidents, in
the approaching crisis in her history.   All this

and very much more in the same tenor was delivered in a florid style and embellished with many gesticulations.

It was evident that the sympathies of the crowd were with these speakers. More or less of subdued but very earnest discussion went on upon the borders of the crowd, but Union sentiments found no open advocates, their staunchest representatives feeling that they had scored their victory in deeds rather than in talk.

After the addresses the assemblage quietly dispersed, and thus ended the last general muster of the militia of Virginia before the War of the Rebellion.

CHAPTER II.

HERE on the border, in the western part of old
Virginia, where Union men were so greatly in
the minority, they frequently had to leave their
homes at night and take to the woods upon the
approach of marauding bands of guerillas, or
bushwhackers, who waged a constant depredatory
war upon them.   There were numerous bloody
encounters and several shocking murders com-
mitted by partisans of both sides during this
period; one fine young man of my acquaintance,
named Mulvey, was taken from his house one
night by a party of guerillas and shot dead,
simply because he was an avowed Union man.

I recall another tragic incident of this fratricidal
strife, which I think worthy of mention.   There
were in Lewis county two brothers named Connelly.   One was a hot and determined secession-
ist and the other was equally devoted to the
Union.   They both were conspicuously brave,

and soon became partisan leaders. At different times their adherents had rough encounters, and with an increasing spirit of hostility at each meeting. At last the two parties met in a sanguinary hand-to-hand combat at or near Sutton, Braxton county, West Virginia. Their forces were about equal in numbers and strength, and, for a time, the result of the conflict looked very uncertain. At length the two captains, the Connelly boys, confronted each other. Both were intrepid and daring, of fine physique, fair and rosy-cheeked young men, the common hope and pride of their fond mother. The struggle was sharp and fierce until, after a final thrust, the rebel leader fell by the hand of his brother, who subsequently became a lieutenant in the 10th West Virginia Infantry. The members of the dead leader's band soon after his fall dispersed. There were several other bands of rebel sympathizers, who were harassing and terrorizing the loyal people of Lewis and adjoining counties about the time of which I write. Ben Haymond and Perry Hays were two of the most notorious leaders of these marauding bandits. Of these, Haymond gained the greater notoriety for his personal valor and daring depredations.

About this time I got my first glimpse at the beauties of American volunteer discipline, as enforced by the newly made officers. Among the troops that arrived earliest at Weston was a detachment of the 1st West Virginia Cavalry; their commander, Captain Shuman, had adopted a rather novel mode of punishment—that of "nose-bagging" his men. On coming into town one day, and while going up Main street, I saw on the porch in front of the Bland Hotel, then occupied by some of the troops, three cavalrymen, soldiers of Captain Shuman's command, standing with their hands behind their backs, tied and securely strapped to the pillars of the porch, each with a horse's large "nose-bag" pulled down over his head and made fast around the lower part of his neck, rendering respiration on his part very difficult. If Lord Norbury in his day had known of the existence of such a ludicrous and disgusting hangman's cap he might have adopted it in Ireland, in order to make hanging completely odious.

Seeing two comrades of the ill-treated men on the street, I inquired of them where their captain might be found, stating that I wished to remonstrate with him on this singular mode of punishment. They told me where he was stopping, but looked at me in some surprise, and one of them added, "You don't know the captain, do you?"

"No," I answered; "but I am desirous of expostulating with him on this humiliating spectacle."

"Well," was the rejoinder, "he is a rough customer to talk to, and those who know him best would not care to approach him on such a subject."

Shortly after this dialogue I encountered the redoubtable captain at his "quarters;" his appearance and manner were in keeping with the opinion of him held by many, that he was a "big, blustering bully." With fear and trembling I approached the burly dignitary. He was attired in a costly and glittering new uniform. I saluted *a la mode*, without arms, of course; but he simply stared, and did not return my salute. Possibly he felt himself too big to do so, or, what is more likely, he probably was ignorant at this time of the common usages of military law.

" Captain," said I, " my object in calling on you is, in a measure, in the interest of the government and the cause which you have espoused. Although but a mere civilian, I beg to offer you a friendly suggestion in relation to the three men of your command who are now pilloried in the most public place in town. Their punishment is extraordinary. I have never seen anything like it; 'tis both humiliating and degrading, giving satisfaction to the enemy, who are quite numerous here, and also discouraging in the extreme to your own men and to the friends of the Union cause—"

" By G—d, sir," interrupted the captain; " I'll have discipline, or know the reason why; these d—d thieves have been pilfering and thieving

3

from the citizens for some time past, and I am determined to make an example of them."

"I am aware of that, sir, having suffered myself from the depredations of some of the troops; yet, were these culprits the men who stole my property, I would plead just as earnestly for their release as I now do for these poor devils, simply on the grounds of proper discipline. I would, however, have them placed in confinement, and then prefer charges against them, and let a regimental court-martial adjudicate their cases; or, in minor cases, when on detached duty as you are, I would impose extra duty, knapsack drill, etc."

The captain's eyes had opened considerably by this time, and in a somewhat modified tone of voice he asked:

"Who are you, sir?"

"My name is Egan," I replied.

"Are you a relative of Tom Egan, the contractor?"

"Yes, sir; he is a brother of mine."

"I know Tom well," said the captain; "he is a number-one fellow, and he and myself have had many pleasant times, socially, at Clarksburg."

I then recollected having heard my brother speak of a Mr. Shuman, whom he appeared to think a good fellow, although somewhat rough in manner.

The captain and myself soon became more friendly, and when I finally left his quarters and walked up town, I had the pleasure and gratification of seeing that the men with the unsightly nose-bags over their heads had been released. They probably never learned the cause of their speedy deliverance.

Soon after this unique experiment at discipline I saw another—that of "bucking and gagging"— practised on an unfortunate infantryman. He had been placed in a vacant house near the West Fork bridge, at Weston, which little town was fast becoming notorious for such displays of newly found and blind authority.

The soldier was lying on the broad of his back, with his hands and feet securely tied, and had a stout stick placed in his mouth and made firmly fast behind his head. The poor creature, who was under the influence of liquor, was suffering severely from his violent and futile efforts to extricate himself from his bonds. He also was charged with theft and drunkenness.

This propensity for pilfering was not confined to the troops alone. Even the unenlisted teamsters in those times entertained the idea that they might plunder and steal with impunity. They did not hesitate to purloin the property of former neighbors, as well as others, along their line of march. A case in point came under my observation that was visited with such speedy punishment that it served to give a salutary check to these depredations in our locality.

Colonel Stanley Matthews, of an Ohio regiment, now an Associate Justice of the Supreme Court of the United States, had just arrived at Weston, with a part of his command, from Glenville, Gilmer county. Some of his teamsters in the supply train, who had been neighbors of ours, when about eight miles from town, on Leading creek, saw a flock of sheep on my brother Tom's farm, grazing near the pike upon which they were marching. Two or three of the teamsters at once commenced firing on the sheep, killing a couple and crippling several others. I was at my home, a mile away, at the time, but soon got word of the outrage. Considering it an act of wanton deviltry, as I learned they had not taken the carcasses of the sheep, I became very much incensed, and, hastily picking up my rifle, I hurried to the woods overlooking the field where the sheep were, fully determined to "bushwhack" the next sheep-killer. But I was too late; the main body of the troops had by this time passed the farm. Going to my brother's house, I found him feeling very much annoyed at the mean action of the teamsters, two of whom he recognized.

I immediately got on a horse and rode into town and up to the headquarters of Colonel Matthews, and laid the case before him. He was quite indignant at the action of the men and assured me that he would at once investigate the matter, and that I should receive ample satisfaction. He did as he promised; the culprits were arrested by his orders, and brought before him and ordered to make full reparation. The prisoners, by this time thoroughly frightened, willingly promised to do so, and the colonel requested me to name the amount of damages that we had suffered. Seeing the men penitent, and having been acquainted with them previously, I relented and placed a merely nominal value upon the sheep, and at the same time interceded with the commander to save the men from further punishment. They were finally permitted to go with a severe reprimand.

I take pleasure in stating that these boys afterwards performed services of such value, both to the Government and myself, that more than overbalanced the offence above related. I would not dream, for a moment, of giving their names for publication, in this connection.

About this time Colonel Lightburn called to see me for the purpose of securing my aid in organizing a regiment. He afterwards proved himself to be a good officer, and I have often regretted my inability at that time to accept his offer. I had, however, a short while before his visit, written to Mr. David T. Hewes, who was then recruiting for the 3d West Virginia Infantry. Hewes was a handsome, usually well-dressed fellow and a good drill-master, and he had made a favorable impression on me. In my letter to him

I expressed a desire to be with him, and volunteered to furnish some good material for his command. I never received an answer from him. He was made Colonel of the regiment (3d West Virginia Infantry) on July 23, 1861, but when called into action he proved an entire failure, and, in consequence, was dismissed the service.

And now, ready to don the uniform and march to the front, I proceed to Clarksburg, intending to become "a high private" in the first congenial command that offers, "for Uncle Sam and during the war" (if I should live so long). But when I arrived at the little town mentioned I met my friend Croghan, who brought me to the quarters of Captain Leib, Assistant Quartermaster, where I was offered, and accepted, the perilous position of a military express courier.

My experiences on this line, during the seven months following, will be found in the succeeding chapters.

CHAPTER III.

ON the 31st of August, 1861, General Rosecrans, with his brigade, moved out of Clarksburg,
W. Va., and took up his line of march in the
direction of Gauley Bridge, 133 miles distant.
He encamped that night near Janelew, fifteen
miles west of Clarksburg.

In consequence of the stoppage of the mails it
became necessary to establish an express courier
line to his headquarters, to convey to the officers
of his column their letters and official documents
from the headquarters of the army at Washington. General Rosecrans therefore ordered Captain Charles Leib, Assistant Quartermaster, at
Clarksburg, to establish a line of couriers in his
rear for this purpose.

Captain Leib had, at this time, a large depot of
supplies at Clarksburg, and consequently a large
number of subordinates; but amongst all his
small army of teamsters and other employés he

failed to find one volunteer to bear despatches to
the general, notwithstanding the fact that Captain Leib tendered them the use of his finest
horses, a complete set of small arms, and wages
to the amount of forty dollars per month, with
rations.

None of his employés were enlisted men, so he
could not enforce his orders in this particular.
Their reasons for refusing were obvious. A
short time before two young men attempted to
convey despatches to Colonel Tyler, of the 7th
Regiment, Ohio Volunteers, in the same direction, but they were rather summarily disposed of
by the bushwhackers; one, a splendid young fellow, James Flesher by name, of whom I have
already made brief mention, was killed outright,
and the other, Mifflin Cutwright, was badly
wounded; they both resided near Weston.

Captain Leib, in his book, "The Chances for
Making a Million," thus describes these marauding bandits:

"The bushwhackers are composed of a class
of men who are noted for their ignorance, indo-
lence, duplicity and dishonesty; whose vices and
passions peculiarly fit them for the warfare in
which they are engaged, and upon which the
civilized world looks with horror. Imagine a
stolid, vicious-looking countenance, an ungainly
figure, and an awkward, if not ungraceful, spinal
curve in the dorsal region, acquired by laziness

and indifference to maintaining an erect posture; a garb of the coarsest texture of home-spun linen, or 'linsey-woolsey,' tattered and torn, and so covered with dirt as not to enable one to guess its original color; a dilapidated, rimless hat, or cap of some wild animal's skin, covering his head, the hair on which had not been combed for months; his feet covered with moccasins, and a rifle by his side, a powder-horn and shot-pouch slung around his neck,. and you have the beau ideal of the West Virginia bushwhacker.

"Thus equipped he sallies forth with the stealth of the panther, and lies in wait for a straggling soldier, courier, or loyal citizen, to whom the only warning given of his presence is the sharp click · of his deadly rifle. He kills for the sake of killing, and plunders for the sake of gain. Parties of these ferocious beasts, under cover of darkness, frequently steal into a neighborhood, burn the residences of loyal citizens, rob stores, tan-yards and farm-houses of everything they can put to use, especially arms, ammunition, leather, clothing, bedding, and salt.

"They do not stop at pillage, for ofttimes is their track marked with blood. The leaders of some of these bands have acquired great notoriety by their cold-blooded brutality and adroitness at theft; one of these is a man who in days gone by enjoyed to a great degree the confidence of the people of West Virginia. He, together with ex-Governor Wise, did much to make bush-whacking respectable in the estimation of the depraved and ignorant. . . . .

"A notorious bushwhacker is Bill Parsons, or 'Devil Bill,' as he is called. Bill is filthy in appearance, and, like the rest of his class, has low instincts, and is as ferocious as a hyena. It is said he has eleven wives, and it is a fact well known that one of them is his own daughter. He resides in Roane county, where he has been guilty of many gross outrages."

The quartermaster's employés had ears for news of this kind, and, naturally enough, none of them were prepared to run the gauntlet. Thomas H. Croghan, a dashing, military-looking fellow, was foragemaster under Captain Leib; he told the captain that there was a man in town who he thought would do the work. Croghan and myself had both received a military training in the same school in Ireland, and were well acquainted and good friends. He introduced me, with considerable eulogism, to Captain Leib, who received me very affably, and said he hoped that I would undertake the duty spoken of.

I was fully conscious of the dangers and responsibilities of the position, but after the flattering introduction of my friend, and the apparent confidence reposed in me by the appointing power, I decided to accept. Having done so, I was soon well armed and mounted, and received my despatches about five o'clock P. M., with orders to deliver them to General Rosecrans, and, if possible, to ride at the rate of eight miles an hour. My horse being a good one I made good time, and arrived in camp, at Janelew, some time before seven o'clock P. M.

It was about dusk as I approached camp, and I was promptly challenged at the outpost with:

"Who comes there?"

"A friend without the countersign. Call a corporal of the guard and have me conducted to the general's headquarters," I answered.

This was complied with immediately and I rode along leisurely with the corporal to the general's tent. The soldier entered and announced his message, and the general soon after came out; I saluted him, announced my name and delivered my despatches. He remarked that my name was not unfamiliar to him, and we had quite a friendly chat of a few minutes' duration; he then directed me to put up for the night at the little village of Janelew, and return with despatches to Clarksburg in the morning.

I was so highly impressed with the general's qualities as a gentleman and a soldier that I was prepared to serve him at all hazards, even had I no higher stimulus.

I returned to Clarksburg as directed and there waited for return despatches until eight o'clock the next evening, when, well mounted on a horse of high mettle, I proceeded at the regular schedule rate of eight miles an hour and arrived at Weston, a distance of twenty-four miles, at eleven o'clock P. M., September 1st.

On approaching the town I slackened up, expecting to find an out-post of our troops reported to be then stationed at Weston, but found none. I then thought I should encounter one at Coal-Stone bridge, the eastern boundary of the town, but did not; and reached the centre of the town without being challenged. I learned from a few stragglers whom I met on my way in that there were two or three regiments encamped on, or near, the State Asylum grounds; the main body of the troops having continued on the march and encamped near Bulltown.

My horse had slipped a shoe, and, although a good animal, showed signs of fatigue. I wished to report to the officer in command and either get a fresh horse or have some proper person proceed with the despatches. I crossed West Fork bridge, on the northern part of the town and in close proximity to the asylum ground, the encampment of the troops, where above all other places there should have been a guard, without being halted by any one; in fact I had entered and passed through the town and up to the head-quarters of Colonel Ewing, who was in command of the troops, the 30th and 47th Ohio Regiments, without once being challenged.

MAJOR-GENERAL WILLIAM S. ROSECRANS.

I reported and showed my despatches to the colonel, who received me very kindly. Understanding my late and fast ride, he asked me to partake of some refreshments. Captain Smith, his gentlemanly quartermaster, handed me a glass of good liquor, of which I drank moderately. I then said that if I had a fresh horse I would proceed to Bulltown with the despatches. Colonel Ewing directed me to report to the post quartermaster, Ransom, who would either relieve me of the despatches or furnish me with the needed animal. Before leaving the colonel asked me how I got into the quarters. This was a ticklish question. A straightforward answer would be a serious charge against all the pickets. I therefore simply told him that when I approached the camp I called for a corporal of the guard to conduct me to his headquarters.

I found Captain Ransom in bed at Bailey's Hotel; he told me he would have the despatches forwarded early next morning.

Upon coming down from the captain's room I was taken into custody by a guard, and placed in close confinement in a Sibley tent. The officer in charge of this guard had been, for some time previously, stationed at Weston, and therefore he must have known me, but being in command, as I suppose, of the pickets on that night, September 1, 1861, and conscious of having been derelict in his duty in allowing them to desert

their posts, he was fearful, no doubt, of this fact
becoming known through me, knowing, as he did,
that such a serious breach of discipline was, according to military law, punishable with death.
He had, therefore, in order to save himself,
helped to trump up false charges against me;
some of which were, I afterwards learned, that I
had been seen prowling about the precincts of
the encampment on that evening; that I had
been a rebel spy at the first battle of Bull Run;
and that I must have killed the regular courier,
or despatch-bearer, etc.

At the time, however, I was kept in total ignorance of all this; they did not even once intimate
to me their reasons for my arrest and the placing over me of an armed guard, which later on
they saw fit to double.   In answer to my inquiries
as to the meaning of it all, the men in whose immediate custody I was either could not or would
not tell me.

Some time after midnight I was aroused from
a deep reverie by the entrance of a gentleman.
That he was a gentleman, brave and intelligent,
became deeply impressed upom my mind, because,
among all the officers of these two regiments,
he was the only one whom I found to possess
these desirable qualities; this was Captain Smith,
brigade or regimental assistant quartermaster.
He was the first and only one to make me aware
of the tragic rôle I was about to play.   He told

me that they were then trying me under "Drum-head" Court Martial, for being a rebel spy. He was quite sympathetic and kind, and seemed, personally, to entertain no doubt of my loyalty. He wanted me to take something to eat, but I declined, with thanks. Captain Smith then left, but returned again an hour or so later, and informed me that I had been found guilty and was to be shot at nine o'clock that morning. This would leave me just five and a half hours to live. The thoughts of my wife, then about twenty years old, who, with our two dear little ones, aged respectively four and two years, was then living nine miles northwest of Weston, and in a delicate state of health, in which a sudden shock or fright might be attended with serious consequences to her, might well have unmanned me during this trying ordeal : but when the dawn of morning came, and after the tap of the martial drum, squad after squad of the troops appeared at my tent, at the entrance of which I stood, and with exulting and taunting remarks called me "d—n rebel spy," their conduct only served to steel me to a bearing of scornful defiance, and I called them cowards and poltroons, whom Russell, of the *London Times*, had published as such, for throwing down their arms at the first battle of Bull Run.

There was one individual, Vixbeck by name, that figured in this little tragedy, who could, I

think, be safely called a counterpart in disposition
of the atrocious Simon Girty, of Indian notoriety.
He was one of the guards placed over me, and he
cruelly overstepped his orders in adopting every
method he could devise to annoy and intimidate
me, or induce me to run from his demonstrative
threats, in order that he might have a slight pretext for appeasing his evident thirst for my life.
With the eye and grimace of a fiend he would
bring his musket to the position of "charge
bayonets" with the cold steel scarcely two feet
from my breast, the hammer at full cock, and all
the time fingering the trigger nervously, urged
by many of his comrades of the same gentle
stripe to "let it go off, accidentally, into the d—n
rebel spy," as they kindly styled me. This creature, if he is alive to peruse this description of
himself, may feel that I have done him an injustice;
but I do not think he is possessed of sufficient
courage to ask me to retract it.

My brother, Thomas Egan, two years my senior,
together with his family, was living at Weston at
the time of my arrest. He was then the proprie-
tor of the Union House, and was himself Union
to the core. He was a most kind and affectionate
brother. He had heard of my dangerous situation early that morning, and, in a state of distraction, hurried over to the officers' quarters to
explain to them their mistake. They did not
allow him to approach me, but from the entrance

of my tent where I stood I could see a squad of
men driving him out of the camp at the point of
the bayonet. This treatment of my brother by
the troops created considerable indignation among
the citizens of the town, where he was very well
and favorably known.

In my behalf Colonel Ewing was also waited
upon by several of the most prominent and influential men of the place. They assured him, in
the strongest terms, of my loyalty, and of the
impossibility of my being guilty of the charges
made against me; and, in conclusion, stated that,
unless I was at once released, a full report of the
proceedings would be forwarded to General
Rosecrans. The colonel, however, remained
obdurate, and, as it was now about nine o'clock,
the detail for my execution was made. I was led
forth, and they loaded in my presence.

At this critical juncture, and after I had given
up all hopes of life, a telegram was handed Colonel Ewing, dated Clarksburg, from Captain
Leib, demanding, in language he well knew how
to employ, my instant release.

The colonel then, for the first time since my
arrest, condescended to see me. He ordered his
men to set me free, and approaching me in the
most affable manner he could assume, said he
hoped I would excuse him for the hasty and harsh
treatment I had received, adding that "the exi-

gencies of the times, and the necessity for strict discipline, justified rigid measures."

I took occasion to remind him that it was the total absence of discipline that had endangered my life; that the enemy possessed of half his force might on this night have annihilated his entire command before it would have been possible to check the onslaught; that he did not have a picket, or outpost, in any direction surrounding his camp, and concluded: "I was, sir, about to pay the penalty of this very strict discipline you talk of, but I shall lay the circumstances, in proper form, before General Rosecrans." When I had finished I turned and walked away.

We will now revert, briefly, to the cause of my deliverance. When arrested I was divested of everything of value, including my memorandum book and pencil. When Captain Smith visited me the second time to inform me that I was to be shot at nine o'clock the next morning, I asked him for paper and pencil, which he cheerfully furnished me. I thereupon indited a telegram to Captain Leib, stating as briefly as possible my critical condition, brought about, I claimed, by the culpability of Colonel Ewing and his command, and requesting that he (Leib) wire Ewing to release me. Captain Smith kindly took this message to the telegraph office, and had it forwarded to Clarksburg. The reader knows the result. To the kindness of Captain Smith therefore, and the efficient working of the telegraph line, which had been in operation only a few days, do I owe my escape from the ignominious death of a spy.

Upon my release my effects were returned to me. On going into town from the camp I took out my diary to make some entries, as was my usual custom, when Dr. T. B. Camden, who was accompanying me, wisely reminded me that I was acting imprudently, as this action on my part might be noticed and taken advantage of by the angry and still doubting troops.

When I appeared before my brother and his family at their home, I found them and my wife, who had come into town early that morning, in a state of great distraction, and lamenting me as dead; but—

> "Soon my presence allayed their fears,
> While reactive joy smiled through their tears."

My wife and brother Tom's family now united in entreating me, in the strongest terms, to discontinue so hazardous and ill-requited a position, the duties of which would now compel me to run the gauntlet of a twofold enemy—that of the rebel bushwhackers on one side and this portion of our troops on the other; the latter being fearful of the results of my threatened report, and being anxious, my friends insisted, "to remove me on a very slight pretext." I loved my family as tenderly as could any husband and father; the salary,

forty dollars per month, was no inducement, as
for that amount alone I would not make one such
trip, and I was under no legal or binding obligation, military or civil, to detain me in the service
if I wished to retire. It may therefore appear
strange when I state that the only motive I had
in remaining was a desire to be of use to the
government in my humble though perilous way,
a way, too, where few volunteers seemed willing
to take a chance. Expert horsemanship also
was essential to a military courier's work, and
many good soldiers were lacking here.

CHAPTER IV.

General Rosecrans was now briskly following
Floyd and Wise towards Gauley Bridge.

Captain Leib, Assistant Quartermaster, appointed Mr. A. F. Newman Superintendent of
the Express Courier line, with instructions to
establish stations eight miles apart, prepare a time-
table, and order the couriers to push forward as
rapidly as possible with the despatches for General
Rosecrans and his command. They were also
directed to watch the military telegraph line, and
to report to the nearest office when the line was
discovered to be out of order.

Newman, on his first trip, when he had penetrated some distance into the enemy's lines, became painfully suspicious of danger; many of the
horses of his line were captured also, and others
were returned to Clarksburg with sore backs, and
lame, and otherwise ill-treated by their riders; the
mails became very irregular; the general grumbled; his staff grumbled, and there was a general

grumbling time at headquarters, so he was discharged.

Mr. Angus M. Reiger, an itinerant preacher from Clarksburg, was next appointed. He made two or three trips and then resigned, nor could he be induced to make another trip. This is not surprising when it is known that the wild bushwhackers along the line were so unchristianlike as to fire, with deadly intent, upon his reverence.

About this time two stout, intelligent men, named, respectively, Peter Bryson, who served with credit afterwards, and J. L. Merryman, were captured by Captain Imboden, and a squad of rebel infantry, at the house of Mr. James Boggs, a loyal man, on the top of Powell mountain. The prisoners were taken as far as Meadow Bluffs, where Merryman begged off. He had been a school-teacher, and was gifted with an easy flow of language and a good address. He was a widower, having several young children dependent on him for support. He dwelt with pathetic earnestness upon this latter circumstance before Captain Imboden, and said that he sympathized with the Southern cause as much as anybody, but that the necessity of providing for his motherless children found him in the position of courier, which was but a civil one at most. He was successful in his pleadings and was allowed to return home, while Bryson was taken to Libby prison.

Soon after this, Merryman reported to Captain

Leib, at Clarksburg, and recounted to him, in thrilling words, his marvellous exploits in effecting his escape from the "rebs." He stated to the captain, with many additions, that shortly after his capture by the rebels he was escorted by one of their number to a spring to procure water; arrived there, he knocked down the guard and effected his escape, and by the exercise of great bravery and shrewdness he finally got through, after suffering many privations. His plausible story was believed, and, as a reward for his brilliant achievements, he was immediately promoted to the superintendency of the line. I never could understand, except on one hypothesis, how Merryman could be induced to undertake such a perilous position, which he so cheerfully did immediately after being paroled by Captain Imboden. He now set about picking up several of his friends for the purpose of giving them the fancy places on the line, discharging or transferring old and good men to do so. He made a requisition on Clarksburg for fresh horses and other supplies; and in his personal outfit the inner man was not forgotten.

Being the first courier on the line, my station was eight miles from Clarksburg, but this was a place that he had his eye on for one of his favorites. He showed considerable pomposity when he came out where I was stationed, and soon gave me to understand that he purposed making a number of changes on the line, and that he

would have to place me about thirty or forty miles
farther out.   I was aware that I stood well at headquarters ; that I could have superintended the line
from the start if I had wished to, and that I might
disregard with impunity the orders of the new
superintendent; but I told him that I was ready
to go immediately on any part of the line that he
wished, but at the same time suggesting that it
might be better to permit me to remain where I
was.

He paid little attention to my remonstrance but
ordered me to get ready to start.   Fully equipped,
Merryman and myself proceeded to Janelew, our
next station, a good Union village, notwithstanding the chief residents were relatives of "Stone-
wall" Jackson.   It had always been a hospitable
town for the weary stranger to put up at, and
being acquainted there I introduced Mr. Merryman as our new superintendent, and he was received with great cordiality and respect.

Here at Janelew was stationed Robert Carruthers, an intelligent Englishman.   He was well
adapted to the business, being a light weight and
a good horseman.   He too had to leave in order
to make room for another pet.

I wish to remark just here, that the appointment
of competent citizens on a courier line through an
enemy's country was a wise idea, as they were
subject to less danger and interruption than a
uniformed soldier would have been.

The change of stations proved a bad one for Carruthers. Merryman placed him in about the worst place on the line, in consequence of which he had several narrow escapes, and lost considerable Government property. We now pushed on for Weston, where we made a short stay; next to Crowell's, thence to Jacksonville, where Merryman left me. On my second trip after arriving at Jacksonville I rode to Weston, fifteen miles distant, and reported by wire to Captain Leib, at Clarksburg, the circumstances of my transfer. He telegraphed Merryman and myself to return to headquarters immediately. I noticed on our return, that the new superintendent was not quite so merry as when he first started out to make wholesale changes on the line; he was now very affable in his manner toward me and appeared to suspect that he may have made a mistake in ignoring the respectful suggestions I had made to him.

Captain Leib had the reputation of being a man of ability and good judgment; he was also a man of few words, and these were generally sharp and to the point. Mr. Merryman and myself soon stood before him in his office. He addressed himself to Merryman, and, in his characteristic style, said:

"Sir, I do not require your services any longer; render up whatever government property you may have in your charge."

During this scene the large, intelligent eyes of the dashing foragemaster of the post, Tom Croghan, were fixed on the short-lived superintendent; there was a short but funny history in the peculiarity of the broad, quizzical grin of the inimitable Irishman as he surveyed the now crestfallen ex-superintendent.

Captain Leib now turned to me. "Mr. Egan," said he, "if you had so intimated you might have been in charge of the express line from the start; and now, I wish you to take charge of it, and if you do so I am satisfied it will be efficiently worked."

I thanked him for his confidence in me, and said that I should strive to not disappoint him in his favorable impression of me. It is apparent from the following paragraph taken from his book, "The Chances for Making a Million," that he did not change his first opinion of me:

"Michael Egan," says he, "was the only superintendent of the express line who was really efficient. He was the first courier sent forward, and in the discharge of duty stopped at nothing: swam streams swollen by the heavy rains of that country, crossed the mountains when he knew the bushwhacking bloodhounds were on his track, and when warned not to attempt their passage would quietly reply: 'Captain Leib ordered me not to stop until I had reached headquarters, and I must obey.' He is an Irishman by birth, had received a liberal education, and in his younger days was in the British service. He knew not fear, and finding him competent and meritorious we promoted him."

I now proceeded to make an inventory of all the government property on the line, which occupied some time. Being aware of the existence of many defects in the system, I at once went to work in earnest applying remedies. I made no sudden or ill-advised changes, however, but carefully examined the condition of affairs at each station, particularly the treatment given the horses. As a result of my first trip out I became very angry at the manner in which a large number of the poor animals had been treated. I am fond of horses, and am always painstaking in my care of them, but on this inspection I found the majority of them lame, or afflicted with sore backs, or both, and otherwise neglected. I could not understand how a horse used only two hours in the twenty-four could by any reasonably fair treatment be used up in such a brutal manner.

I soon shaped things differently at every station, and, as a result, thenceforward there were no complaints, nor causes for complaint, from headquarters.

CHAPTER V.

In addition to the express mail-route General Rosecrans established a military telegraph-line between Clarksburg and Gauley Bridge. This line had suffered from more or less interruption for some time before I was made superintendent. I used it quite often afterwards to transmit to headquarters any information that I thought of benefit to the service. I have frequently, while travelling over the line, dismounted and repaired the wire where broken, having a slight knowledge of " splicing," acquired previously.

I was now almost incessantly in the saddle, not remaining a single day in one place. Swollen rivers and streams sometimes checked general travel, but I was never balked by such impediments, invariably plunging my horse into the streams and swimming them, generally without mishap.

On one of my trips over the mountains, when approaching Summerville, Nicholas county, West

Virginia, I was confronted for the first time with something like military order. I was halted and challenged, in accordance with strict military rules, by a soldier well put up, orderly, and clean. I at once thought there must be an officer in command who knew his business. That officer was General George Crook, then colonel of the 36th Ohio Infantry. In winter, when other troops were languishing in idleness, his were healthfully employed in cleaning their accoutrements and in drilling under large sheds, which he had erected for the purpose.

In 1861–62 a number of government horses and a large supply of forage, including hundreds of bales of hay, were kept at Clarksburg as a depot of supplies for our troops, then pushing out into the wilds of West Virginia after Floyd and Wise. Thomas H. Croghan, whom I have several times mentioned, rode a very fine horse, selected by himself from among the choicest in the corral. As superintendent of the express line I was also provided with a good animal, and when in Clarksburg, Croghan and myself almost daily practised jumping our horses over the bales of hay which were piled up in an apple-orchard near the quartermaster's headquarters. A great many of the men who were unacquainted with this style of horsemanship looked upon these feats as foolhardy, and anticipated the breaking of our necks sooner or later. But we were used to this sort of equestrian exercise, having acquired, while boys together in Ireland, a considerable profi- ciency in hurdle and ditch jumping.

The necessities of the express line made the securing of extraordinarily good horses for the couriers very essential, and in my capacity of superintendent I was always on the alert to ob- tain for them such needed animals. I secured possession of one, by chance, in November, 1861, that served me nobly as my individual saddle- horse on many occasions afterwards, and he once undoubtedly saved my life.

One day about noon, on arriving at Clarks- burg after a continuous ride of 133 miles from Gauley Bridge, I saw, when opposite Dent's ho- tel, a dashing and fiery gray horse and his rider both furiously contending for the mastery. The horse, I learned, was government property, and was known as "Hannibal;" the animal was in the habit of going when and where he pleased, and had conquered, since his purchase by the quartermaster, three or four of the clerks who had undertaken to master him. Jimmy Runyon was now astride of him. Jimmy was a son of the master of transportation, and was a plucky lad who seldom failed in doing anything he undertook.

There was quite a crowd collected around the horse, attracted by his rearing and plunging; he had quite a hard mouth, and the boy's tugging at

GEORGE CROOK, Major-General U. S. A.

the bridle-reins seemed to have little effect upon him. Rushing to the side walls of adjacent houses, and to the sign-posts on either side of the street, the vicious animal sought to scratch and bruise his rider's legs. In one of these collisions with a sign-post the saddle-girth broke, and Jimmy received a hard fall and some severe injuries in consequence. Once again the horse was victorious and confirmed in his sulks. It was, as I said, about noon, and the horse, after throwing his rider, was led over to the corral to be fed. I had my eye on the horse and followed, determined to have him, if possible.

Colonel Runyon was a ruddy and robust man, about five feet ten inches high and weighing about 200 pounds. He had a long, flowing, silvery beard, and was quite stern and imperious in his commands, but withal possessed of great kindness of heart beneath his rough exterior. He had learned of the accident to his boy and was at the stables when the gray was led in. He was in a towering rage and angry enough to shoot the offending horse. He opened on Dominick Tierney, the stable-boss, and gave him a severe overhauling for permitting his idolized son to have the dangerous horse, knowing him to be such. He then sternly forbade Tierney to let the vicious brute out again. Now was my time. As the colonel started to leave the stable I spoke up and said:

"Colonel, let me have the horse, please; I need a good one in my courier express business."

He looked at me as if doubting my sanity, and replied: "I do not wish to have a hand in your death, sir. Samuel Selby, 'Chap' Wheeler and others, as well as my son, Jimmy, have tried him, and each trial has been a failure and attended with increasing danger."

I still persisted in my entreaties for the horse. "Egan, you may have him," said the colonel finally; "but he will most certainly kill you."

"I'll try him right now," I rejoined; "and if he does kill me, the bushwhackers will be saved the trouble of doing it."

I went into the horse's stall and proceeded to bridle and saddle the steed. While doing so, Tierney, with whom I was well acquainted, whispered to me to let him finish eating before attempting to take him out, as to do so would, he thought, be very dangerous. I disregarded this friendly advice, however, and after securing a good riding-whip, with a heavy butt, I took out and mounted the gray.

As was to be expected, there were a number of employés and hangers-on waiting to see the exhibition, when they learned that I had asked for and received the horse.

I had a very unfavorable place—an apple-orchard with trees, bales of hay, wagons and other obstructions—in which to make the trial of subjugating the beast. The trees, being numerous, were the most dangerous. The animal, failing in his efforts to unseat me by high kicking, plunging, buck-jumping, etc., made a direct drive for the trees before mentioned, seeming to have, in doing so, no more regard for his own safety than he had for mine. But, by one who can use the bridle and roller-spurs properly, a horse going at a good rate of speed may be easily turned from an obstruction in his path. In this case I saved the horse and myself from injury, although his mouth and sides showed evident signs of punishment endured from the bit and spurs. He now became quite obedient and passive in my hands, and I rode out of the gate and up and down the pike several times without any further trouble.

This rough riding reminded me of a feat of horsemanship, and about the finest that I ever witnessed, which occurred in June, 1845, on the grand parade grounds at Phœnix Park depot, in the city of Dublin, Ireland.

It was just after morning parade, and several squads of constabulary were yet drilling in the park, when an orderly, who was an expert rough rider, mounted on a splendid dark bay horse, which was then being broken for the cavalry, came out of the depot yard and started to the "castle" for orders. When at the entrance to the

5

barracks the horse refused to go out. Then ensued a long and exciting struggle between horse
and rider for supremacy, resulting, finally, in the
horse coming out victorious.

There now approached from the direction of
the stables a gentleman who walked rapidly to
the centre of the square, where the excitement
was. This officer, for such he proved to be, was
about twenty-five years old, and about six feet
high; in general build he was a perfect model of
physical manhood; he was fair as a lily, with
large, intelligent blue eyes, somewhat piercing in
their glance; a healthful, blooming tint suffused
his cheeks, and his fine yellow hair was parted
behind, in the then prevailing fashion, and kept,
like all his person, in the neatest military style.
In his right hand he carried a small but cutting
riding-whip, and on his heels were two highly
burnished roller-spurs. This was Head Constable
Pilkington, Chief Drill-Master of the Cavalry.
The horse had just succeeded in throwing and
severely bruising his rider as Pilkington approached. Grasping the reins firmly, he made
one bound and was in the saddle; and no sooner
was he safely seated than he pressed the cruel
"rollers" into the wild steed's sides. The animal
reared straight up on his hind legs, poising there
for a second, and then pitched forward a great
distance, tearing up the fine gravel in all directions in his frenzied efforts to throw his rider.

Now the officer reversed his whip, bringing the handle, or butt, down with a crashing blow on the brute's head whenever the latter would rear up, at the same time applying, with all the strength of his legs, the "rollers" to the sides of the devilish horse, now stained red with gore.

Among all the numerous spectators to this thrilling scene, the head constable was the most cool. The horse now ceased his plunging and dashed ahead towards the adjutant's office, where his rider turned him, and flew up the square and down in the direction of the city at full speed, and then back again, repassing the main entrance, where the horse made another feeble attempt to go in, but he was no longer his own master. The horse was now broken, but might relapse into vicious ways again if allowed to fall into incapable hands.

The occurrence here narrated was as vivid in my mind that day, after the lapse of seventeen years, as upon the day when it took place, and it struck me as being not dissimilar to my experience, except, of course, the wide difference in the appearance of the two riders and their surroundings.

" The grand old Phœnix Park that Nature, more than art, adorns;
Perfumed so richly by the giant old hawthorns,
Whose majestic limbs expand to meet their neighboring row,
Filled with blossoms, thick as hops, and fair as falling snow;
Or like soft showers, descending on the emerald sward below.

"There, too, in classic, sculptured art, you'll find on observation,
    That rare bird whence the Park derives its appellation;
    Methinks the Eagle, emblem of Liberty, would improve the breed
    Of this mystic fowl, whose unproductive seed
    Has lain too long dormant in a land unfreed.

"Here, also, the aristocratic child, with attendant maid,
    Daily from Dublin City came to sport and promenade,
    And breathe the gentle breeze, so bracing, fair and mild,
    Imparting rosy-tinted cheeks alike to maid and child.
    On a fairer, lovelier spot Dame Nature never smiled."

It may not be amiss here to introduce to the reader a few other of the gray horse's peculiarities. The one I found the most difficulty in breaking him of was a propensity for rushing headlong into rivers, creeks, etc., whenever he met with them; and the deeper they were, the better he seemed to enjoy it. He was a pacer, 'loper, and a fair trotter. While galloping he moved so smoothly that a good marksman could do some fair shooting from his back. I believe he was a brave animal also, as shooting did not annoy him, or cause him to swerve in the least from his course. As I have before stated, I am very fond of horses, and, in this case, there seemed to be a growing mutual attachment between the horse and his rider. I had him about four weeks when he showed one of his best and most reliable qualities.

On the night of the 15th of November, 1861, I put up at the house of Mr. Benjamin Skidmore, in the town of Sutton, Braxton county. The night proved very stormy; a heavy rain accompanied by high winds prevailed for several hours. Next morning on repairing to the stable where our relay horses were kept, I was agreeably surprised to find the gray there and in seeming good condition. I had several horses at my disposal, but I preferred to hold Hannibal in reserve for the most dangerous part of my route.

As I advanced in the direction of Gauley Bridge I noticed considerable havoc done by the late storm. It was about noon when I forded the Little Birch river. This stream is one of the clearest in the State, and is bordered for a long distance on both its banks with spruce-pine and evergreen. On approaching the river from the east, the roadway had quite a steep descent to the bed of the stream, and when on the other side, it wound around the hill in a zig-zag fashion for about half a mile until a level plain on the summit was reached. This strip of road was known as the "hog-back," because of its narrow surface and precipitous sides. It was not at any part more than thirty feet wide, but was level and in fair condition for travel. At its very narrowest part, I discovered a large oak tree lying squarely across the road, one of the results of the previous night's storm. The tree completely blocked the road, its huge limbs and roots holding it about three feet from the ground.

I came to a halt, staggered by the obstruction;

how should I proceed? The interlacing of the smaller limbs with the roots of the tree made it impossible to lead the horse under the fallen oak.

The almost perpendicular sides of the "hog-back" made any attempt to go around it impracticable and dangerous. The only thing remaining to be done was to jump it. I had not up to this time been checked by the elements, and I did not feel disposed to give up now. The gray had some practice in jumping over the hay bales at Clarksburg for our amusement, but never met anything like that which now confronted him. I walked him up to the tree, which was fully five feet high, and the animal could barely look over it. Turning, I rode back some twenty or twenty-five yards, and, wheeling him right about, faced the tree. The road was level, as I have said, with a fine white sandy surface. Pressing the rollers to the faithful animal's sides, he made a straight shoot for the obstruction, and, when within two yards of it, he rose gallantly in the air and cleared it like a bird.

The scene from this mountain road is very fair to look upon. In front one can see for miles away a beautiful and richly cultivated valley, but not the vestige of a house or enclosure; while on both sides of the road rise high and majestic huge rocky, circular-shaped ranges, surmounted by a wide expanse of primeval forest; the whole reminding one of what we read of the Great Wall

of China. So we move along, amidst the friendly
solitude, more engrossed in the contemplation of
the beauties of nature than on the belligerent
spirit of man.

When a half mile from the fallen tree my
pleasant meditations were suddenly interrupted
by the appearance, as I turned a bend in the
road, of a small party of Confederate cavalry. I
did not take long in deciding on my line of action, but fell back instantly. As I did so, the
"Johnnies" raised a yell and dashed towards me
at full speed. Several shots were fired at me
without effect, and I returned the salute by
emptying the chambers of one of my "navies."
They then ceased firing, and it became an exciting race, narrowed down to a question of the
speed and endurance of our horses. On we go
in this way for some time, when, in a hurried,
backward glance, I see them coming pell-mell and
apparently gaining on me. One of their number
was far in advance of his comrades, and was
mounted on an exceptionally fleet steed. Things
were looking "blue" for me when I again approached the fallen tree. I braced up as I neared
it, and, checking my noble animal slightly, I raised
him at the right moment, and he cleared the obstruction beautifully, coming down firmly on his
legs on the other side. I then descended the
mountain leisurely, feeling satisfied that my pursuers' game was blocked. The literal interpreta-

tion of the old adage, "It's an ill wind that blows nobody good," struck me very forcibly. What was now to be done? Should I proceed, or turn back and once more run the risk of encountering the enemy, who would, no doubt, keep a sharp lookout for me. If it were simply a question of profit, or remuneration for the risk incurred, I would not hesitate a moment to continue on my backward way. Mr. Peter Duffey, an old resident, and one of the best posted men as regarded its dangers on the whole line, told me he would not make the trip over it, in my capacity, for one thousand dollars. Had I been killed, or crippled in this service, neither my family nor myself would have received a cent in compensation for my loss or injury, as I was not at this time an enlisted man.

Determined to finish my journey, I rode down to the Little Birch river, about a half mile from where my pursuers were baulked by the tree, and, turning down the stream to the left, followed its meanderings for some distance, until I came to a favorable place for ascending the mountain. Leading my horse, I scrambled up its steep and rocky sides. At last I found myself upon the road again, after making a toilsome circuit of about three miles, and from there to Big Birch river, five miles away, I kept a sharp watch out for the enemy.

On arriving in the afternoon at the home of

Mr. Frame, I found his wife, an estimable lady, in quite a nervous state of mind. She was aware that the rebels were on my trail, and was fearful of my having fallen into their hands, or of my possibly having received injuries. I did not tarry long, but, after a hasty dinner from the good lady, I sped away over Powell mountain, and landed all right in the dusk of that evening at Peter Duffey's, where myself and horse were well cared for.

CHAPTER VI.

During the seven months that I was in charge of the express line very little government property in that service was lost. Personally, I did not lose a dollar's worth, although there was a sharper lookout kept for me than for any of the couriers. Of these latter, a few who sustained repeated losses were plainly given to understand that their continuance in the government's service would depend, in a great measure, upon the care taken of the property submitted to their charge.

On my second inspection trip I took with me two couriers and two horses required for the western end of the line. The horses were to be exchanged for such as were used up from sore backs and ill treatment, and their riders were to replace the men who so abused and neglected the other animals. The couriers, two young Irishmen, were named, respectively, Patrick Power and Patrick McManus. They were heavier than I should have wished for the purpose, but being brave and

(80)

reliable, they proved more serviceable than would lighter weights not possessing these qualities.

Although, as yet, I had no proper test of it, I did not doubt my judgment in selecting these men for their pluck and intelligence. Before they reached their appointed stations, however, one of them underwent a satisfactory trial.

When nearing the eastern base of Powell mountain, the dusk of evening was closing in on us and a soft, fleecy snow had commenced falling thick and fast, increasing the intensity of the gathering darkness. Travelling over this dreary and solitary mountain, never pleasant, was now doubly lonesome, because of the blinding snow-storm, which made our effort to keep the trail extremely difficult, and further, on account of the uncomfortable knowledge of the immediate presence of besetting perils in the shape of murderous guerillas.

Power had occasion to stop and dismount, while McManus and myself rode leisurely ahead. Soon after Power came cantering up, but missing his belt, containing his navy revolvers, he returned to find them. While he was gone we came in sight of a small log-house standing close to the road. It was the only one for miles around, and was owned by a loyal man named Boggs, who had to leave both house and farm, because of the constant warfare made upon him by the guerillas, who thickly infested this section. I told my companion to keep about eight or ten paces in my rear, and to move as fast as I did until we had safely passed the house, which, although deserted by its owner, was known as a rendezvous for small parties of bushwhackers.

At the very time that we were hurrying past the place, these robbers and murderers, whose eyes were as sharp as the nocturnal prowlers of the mountain forest, had drawn bead on us, and were only prevented from shooting us by one of their number, Clinton Duffel, who, as we subsequently learned, told them that they might safely secure our horses and other property that night at our intended stopping-place, a short distance ahead, without the trouble of killing us. To do Duffel justice, it is but fair to state that he preferred to secure his share of Uncle Sam's property without killing anybody.

Arrived at the base of the opposite side of the mountain, we turned to the left and entered a valley of some extent, at the entrance of which was a scattered settlement known as Hookerville. Here "Mac" and myself halted and awaited the approach of Power, who had not yet rejoined us. Owing to the lateness of the night and the heavy falling snow, we could see only a few feet in our front. So we waited a short distance from the path, determined to surprise and possibly frighten the new courier. Shortly the portly Power came unhurriedly down the hill, and when he was directly opposite to where we stood concealed, in a counterfeit voice I cried out sternly, "Halt!" Without drawing rein for a moment, the brave fellow answered in a clear, strong voice, "All right," and at the same moment his revolver came on a line with our heads and we gladly called a truce.

This incident, together with the nerve he displayed on other occasions while on the line, had no small influence in securing his promotion in my company afterwards.

The night was growing darker and travelling was every moment becoming more difficult, as we were compelled to ride slowly in order to avoid pitching into the numerous holes and pitfalls lying concealed beneath the freshly fallen snow. In about an hour after leaving the mountain we arrived at the house of Mr. Craig, which was our next station. The local courier, Carruthers, met us at the gate. He requested me to remove his station a half mile farther west, to the house of Mr. Peter Duffey, where he said he could obtain better accommodations. He had already talked with the Duffeys on the subject and they were satisfied. I agreed to do as he requested and decided to make the change at once. Mrs. Duffey, a kindly and much esteemed middle-aged lady, English by birth and education, and Courier Carruthers, a thorough "John Bull," were delighted at my conceding to the latter's wishes so readily.

It turned out to be a very lucky move for all concerned. On this very night we had four valuable horses, including my gray, at Mr. Duffey's— a prize not likely to be overlooked by the hungry bushwhackers. Carruthers, while stationed at Craig's, had been robbed twice previously to this time, his station being in about the worst place on the whole line for that sort of thing. Bearing these latter facts in mind, I determined to keep watch upon our animals, a precaution I had often taken before, and often took afterwards, when I chanced to be in a questionable locality.

The stable was situated about one hundred yards from the dwelling-house and at the foot of a small hill, whither we repaired, after having done justice to a hearty supper, and gave the horses a thorough cleaning and rubbing down; after which I examined the stable and its surroundings carefully and found it fairly satisfactory as a defensive position in case of attack. The building was a barn and stable combined, of goodly dimensions, constructed of large, hewn logs, the interstices of which would serve admirably for port holes. We returned to the house and passed a pleasant evening until about eleven o'clock, when we again went to the barn and, disposing of ourselves under the hay and corn-fodder, awaited the arrival of thieves.

We were so placed that we could all command a range of the entrance to the barn. I cautioned the men to remain about ten or twelve feet apart, so as to divert the fire of the bushwhackers, and to waste no ammunition, but to make every shot tell. Our weapons were Colt's navy revolvers, with ten rounds of cartridges to each man. We kept to our posts until morning, but were happily not disturbed. By mere chance we missed an encounter with horse-thieves that night, as we learned afterwards. A party of ten or twelve men had broken into Mr. Craig's stable in the expectation of finding our horses there; but the change effected by Carruthers' request had averted the trouble, and no doubt saved to Uncle Sam the four animals they sought.

Some time later, in November of the same year, I found on reaching Sutton, going west, a part of Captain Rowand's command, Company C, 1st West Virginia Cavalry, quartered in the town. This squad had just succeeded in bringing into camp four prisoners: John Cole, his wife and son, and Samuel W. Windom, all of whom were charged with murder. The wife and mother, a hardened old wretch, and her son subsequently escaped with very light punishment, by giving evidence against the two others that resulted in their execution.

Cole appeared to be about fifty, and Windom about forty years of age. The older man was well known in the locality as a grafter of fruit trees. In appearance he would pass for anything but an Adonis. Windom was a heavy-set man, with a large head, heavy eyebrows and coarse, bushy whiskers that almost completely covered his face. The pair looked fully capable of committing the awful crime with which they were charged, and of which they were afterwards clearly proven to be guilty.

Their crime was the murdering in cold blood of a private soldier of the 36th Ohio Infantry Volunteers. He was a young lad, not over nineteen years old, who had foolishly straggled from his command, alone and without arms. In this way he had visited Cole's house, a few miles from town. He talked to Mrs. Cole and her son for a while, and got a drink of milk from the former; he then went to the meadow and stopped for some time, boy-like, looking at the two men, who were mowing.

In the meantime Mrs. Cole called to her husband, who laid down his scythe and went to her. She said to him: "What are you going to do with that Yankee spy?" On his not appearing to understand her meaning, she told him plainly that he ought to kill the soldier. Cole thereupon returned to where his partner was and held a private conversation with him, divulging his fiendish intentions towards the innocent lad, to all of which Windom readily agreed. All of this time the poor "boy in blue" had not the remotest idea that final judgment had been passed upon him; but he was soon awakened to a realization of his danger by Cole approaching and coolly telling him that they were going to kill him, and asking him what he had to say. To this heartless announcement the frightened lad made no response, but ran away as fast as his legs could carry him. Windom, being a powerful and active man, pursued and shortly overtook and brought back the scared and dejected captive to where old man Cole was awaiting them. Windom held the boy in a firm grip, while his companion deliberately unfastened his scythe-blade from the snead, and with one mighty cut of that sharp instrument severed the head from the body of the unfortunate soldier. They then covered the headless trunk with a pile of brush and stones.

Next morning, after seeing the prisoners, I resumed my journey towards Gauley Bridge.

On my return a couple of days later, when about eight miles east of Gauley, I came to a creek that crossed the road and emptied into Gauley river, which at this point flowed parallel with the pike for some distance. The creek was near the farm of Mr. M. F. Morris, and was then much swollen, very turbulent and overflowing its banks from the recent heavy rains.

About the time I reached this stream General Crook, then Colonel of the 36th Ohio, appeared on the other bank, accompanied by a mounted escort. It looked foolhardy to attempt to swim the horses across the rapid current, especially so when, as now appeared to be the case, the animals were not adequate to the undertaking. The colonel, after surveying the situation for a few minutes, wisely took up the left bank of the stream for some distance, until he found a more favorable place for making the effort.

It would certainly be the height of arrogance in me to lay claim to anything like the intrepidity of the noble Crook, but on this occasion I had a long-legged horse, whose qualities as a swimmer I had previously tested, so we took the stream, heading up the current for about ten yards, and after a severe struggle luckily made the riffle; but we had such a narrow escape from being swept into the river, that I would have been very loath to try it again.

Crook was, at this time, on his way to Charleston, on the Big Kanawha, where, as president of the general court martial which later convened at that place, he tried—among other cases—that of the murderers referred to in the preceding paragraph. I chanced to be at Sutton on the day that Cole and Windom were executed. They showed considerable nerve during the trying ordeal. Both confessed to the commission of the crime substantially as I have told the reader, and their act of cruelty illustrated the antipathy many residents of that section then felt to all representatives of the government, and the utter lack of conscientiousness among these evil-doers.

CHAPTER VII.

TEN days after this unpleasant occurrence at
Sutton, when going east on a tour of inspection,
I rested at Sommerville, then the headquarters
of General Crook. I called at the telegraph
office, as was my usual custom, and the operator,
a young, smart and brave little fellow, named
Smith, told me that all connection east by wire
was cut off; that the line was broken and destroyed
in several places; that he was going to get a team
and a detail of men from the commanding officer
and start the following day to rebuild the destroyed
portion; and concluded by requesting that, as I
was going in that direction, I should remain and
accompany his party.

I replied that if I could be of any use I would
willingly do so. Early next morning the team,
with coils of wire, tools, rations, etc., was in readiness. The detail, consisting of six men and a
sergeant, together with the operator, lineman and

teamster, eleven in all, made a quite harmonious, though somewhat heterogeneous, crowd of Americans, Dutch and Irish.

It was night when we reached William Frame's house at Big Birch river, after passing over fourteen miles of the line and doing a surprising amount of work. The wire had been most injured near where we halted for the night; in fact, it was one of the worst places for the enemy's cavalry raids on the whole route. For such a small party we had considerable government property with us, enough at least to make it worth an effort on the part of one of these hungry bands to raid us during the night. Sure enough, we received information from a friendly source that we were to be swooped down upon that night by a party of rebel guerillas and our property carried off.

We held a consultation to devise means to protect ourselves and avert the threatened loss. Entirely unsolicited, I was requested by the boys to assume command of the little party during the night. I modestly accepted the responsibility, and when the time came I disposed of the members of our party as, in my opinion, best suited our purposes. I placed a man at each of the three most important approaches to our camp, and arranged for their relief two hours later by three fresh pickets, and so on until nine of our party should have performed guard duty, by this method giving each of them two hours on and four hours off duty.

The sergeant's duty was to relieve the guards at the proper time; the operator we held in reserve. The sergeant and myself did not sleep any during the night, but continued to visit the pickets occasionally during the long hours until morning. Once or twice the dogs raised a howl, alarmed at some unusual noises not far distant, but we were not disturbed. Our intended visitors may have received word that we were reasonably well prepared for them, and decided, no doubt, to defer their contemplated attack for a more favorable opportunity.

After breakfast next morning I took leave of my late comrades-in-arms, and about noon arrived at Sutton, the central station on the line. This place was a small village before the war, but at the time of which I write it had grown still smaller by reason of the frequent raids its inhabitants were subjected to. A result of one of these depredatory visits was the burning of about half of the houses in the town.

When I arrived I found about one-half of Company C, 1st West Virginia Cavalry, quartered in the village. The officer in command had just received information that a force of rebels, more than twice his number, were going to assault him that very night. The result of this announcement was considerable excitement among the troops, a majority of whom were in favor of falling back to their regimental headquarters at Weston. I was made aware of the situation, and was asked what I thought of it. By this time I had become pretty well accustomed to the numerous raids that were always about to, but rarely did, occur; and so I replied that I intended to go to Weston in the morning, and would have to see, or feel, the enemy before starting the other way.

The troops finally concluded to adopt my course, and remain where they were. A guard was kept up during the entire night, however, and I volunteered to assist in the duty. In addition to my two "Navies," I was provided with an old sabre, but of course had no occasion to use it. In the morning I laid down my bloodless sword and hied me away to Weston.

There were sixteen stations on the line, as follows:

	Miles Distance from Clarksburg.
Basil's	7
Janelew	15
Weston	22.5
Crowell's	30
Jacksonville	38
Bulltown	46
McNemer's	55
Sutton	63
Little Birch	71
Big Birch	80
Duffey's	90
Sommerville	98
Brown's	106
Gross'	114
Morris'	123
Gauley Bridge	133

The farmers along this route were in the best
of times poor in circumstances; but at this time
they were badly stripped by both armies. Notwithstanding this fact, they cheerfully made the
greatest efforts to feed and house our men and
horses. Neither the commissary nor quartermaster's supplies could be furnished at most of
these places, even at a cost three or four times
greater than these people charged; their usual
price being only twelve and a half cents per meal.

For seven months these farmers bore the bur-
den of the maintenance of this line, receiving
therefor during all this time but two months' pay.
I told these people at the time that the United
States Government would surely pay them. They
seemed to repose confidence in me, but probably
had more in the government whose humble servant I was. I am sorry to state that, after the
lapse of nearly twenty-seven years, our Government has not yet paid this debt.

I have always thought that there rested on me
a moral obligation to try to have these poor and
honest people paid a debt of such evident just-
ness. With this end in view, immediately upon
the discontinuance of the line, which was at my
suggestion, I went over the route and secured
from the farmers itemized statements of their
claims for board and forage, and returning to
Clarksburg presented them to Captain Hunting-
ton, a newly appointed assistant-quartermaster.

This gentleman was a great stickler for "red tape." He was very pompous in his manner, and evidently had a full appreciation of his own importance. He ignored the claims, and refused, in addition, to pay me two weeks' salary then due. Being now anxious to get into active service in the field, I dropped all consideration of these claims, and proceeded to organize a company of infantry, which I did in eight days.

After the war I removed with my family from the locality of the line, and later from the State, and for a long time I did not have the means or the encouragement to make another effort in this direction; but in March, 1877, I became troubled with the idea that these people generally might be impressed with the belief that I had made personal use of their claims. The possibility of such an imputation so weighed upon me that I started from Allegheny City, Pa., a distance of over four hundred miles, went over the old line, and made a personal visit to all of the claimants. or their heirs, and found that my suspicions had a basis in fact, at least with a majority of them.

From these claimants I procured a new set of claims duly signed and sealed by the clerks of the different county courts, with certificates attached. These I took to Washington, D. C., and placed in the hands of a claim agent, to whom I agreed to give ten per cent. of the amounts for his assistance in adjusting and securing their payment.

After sending out three sets of papers, at three different periods, each time causing the claimants the trouble and expense of preparing revised claims, paying clerk fees, etc., and expending quite a sum personally, I have secured as a result the munificent sum of thirty dollars as a partial payment of these claims.

CHAPTER VIII.

AFTER trying without success to adjust the business of the express line, I returned home, and soon after received from Governor Pierpont a lieutenant's commission in the volunteer service of the State. I made no application for this honor, and up to the present time I am unaware of how it was procured. The commission empowered me to enlist men for the volunteer service for three years, or during the war.

Within eight days after the receipt of this document I had enlisted a first-class company, seventeen of whom were six feet high or upwards; six were six feet two inches, and one, Daniel Arbogast, was six feet five and one-half inches in height. This was not such a bad showing, considering the previous drain of volunteers from our sparsely settled border county.

During the months that I was engaged on the express line efforts had been made at forming two other companies in Lewis county, but the recruits finally had to join forces in order to make one company, and even then they fell one short of the minimum number of men required. A week after we had been mustered in we gave them a man to enable them to complete their organization. His name was Benton Flesher, and the poor fellow, I am sorry to say, was afterwards killed in action at Berryville, Va.

We arrived at Wheeling Island in September, 1862, and were mustered in as Company B, 15th Regiment West Virginia Volunteers, and I was commissioned captain in command. During the time we were stationed at Wheeling learning to be soldiers, there were besides our own two other good regiments, the 12th and 14th, drilling on the island.

The officers in command of these two regiments at the first were soon lost sight of. One was a lawyer, who afterwards became a judge, but he could not learn soldiery, and had to return home, where he resumed the practice of his more congenial and less hazardous profession.

The weather was fine during our stay at Wheeling, and we had a pleasant time drilling and otherwise preparing for active service. Our boys seemed proud of their new uniforms, especially those fortunate enough to sport straps on their shoulders, or the official " V " upon their sleeves. Patriotic ladies visited us frequently

and cheered the boys by words and smiles, and
ofttimes with more substantial presents of inviting delicacies for their mess.   Thus were we
urged forward on our path of duty by many kind
acts and endearing expressions.

On October 18th, 1862, our regiment (Companies G and K not yet having been mustered
in) left Wheeling Island under orders to go to
New Creek, Va., on the Baltimore and Ohio
Railroad, where we arrived safely the following
day. We found, on reaching that point, the
beautiful valley of New Creek dotted for a great
distance on both sides of the railroad track with
handsome new white tents, erected and occupied
by the twenty-seven thousand troops under the
command of Generals Milroy and Kelley, then
stationed there to protect the railroad and guard
the highway running east and west throughout
the length of the valley.

One of the most important and easily accessi-
ble approaches to this encampment was a road
crossing the valley at right angles, and extending
to the southwest and far into the Confederacy.
This road skirted " Knobbley Mountain," one of
the Allegheny range, but standing out from its
companions solitary and alone, and lying about
three miles south of our camp. From this point
a vidette could command for a great distance
a good view of the meanderings of the pike, as
it wound around the base of the eminence. To

guard this approach was a post of considerable danger, and one requiring the exercise of constant vigilance to prevent a surprise from rebel raiders who frequently came up from the south over this route on predatory excursions.

When our company had been at New Creek for probably a week, we were sent on detached duty to this mountain. The singling out of our company for this important outpost was looked upon by all as an especial honor, and one which we, as raw recruits, fully appreciated. There was, in addition to Company B, a section of Colonel Mulligan's Battery already stationed at "Knobbley," and I was placed in temporary command of both companies. We pitched our tents and formed a camp upon the farm of Mrs. Trush, a widow lady who had two of her three sons in the Confederate service.

Shortly after our arrival the boys proceeded to gather fuel for their camp-fires, and instead of going into the adjacent woods for this purpose, they commenced demolishing the rail fences running along both sides of the road, and belonging to the widow just mentioned. As this was being done, I returned from a cursory observation of our surroundings, and discovering the wanton destruction in progress, I immediately ordered it stopped.

The remarks I made to the men on this occasion were, as near as I can recollect, about as follows: "This is the first time I have had occasion to reprove you since your enlistment, and no one, I assure you, would feel happier at the absence of cause for so doing than myself. It is true that the offence appears trivial in itself; but experience has shown that small infractions of discipline, if allowed to go unpunished, may, and generally do, lead to more serious ones.

"Knowing the sterling material of which this company is composed, I anticipate but little difficulty in securing your hearty co-operation in my efforts to inculcate and pursue an honest, honorable and soldier-like course in my command during our term of service, be it long or short. By such a line of conduct we are not only complying with the rules and regulations of the army but also of a higher power, from whom all other powers derive their existence. In this connection I venture to suggest, that it behooves a soldier in active service, more than any one else, to be prepared at any moment to render an account of his stewardship to the Supreme Commander.

"I know that you did not reflect that in destroying these fences you were committing a depredation upon a helpless widow. She is, I learn, very nervous and much excited at the arrival of fresh troops upon her land, fearing from them more trouble than she experienced from their predecessors.

"You may have heard that one or two of her

sons have gone to the rebel army, but this fact does not, in my opinion, mitigate our offence. It is nobler to forbear through mercy than to desist from fear of certain punishment. You have an abundant supply of firewood about as near your camp as is the fence. You have axes and you know how to use them, so you can have good fires without destroying anybody's property for fuel.

"In conclusion I would suggest that if the old lady has milk or fruit to sell, and you want either, pay for it like men. If it were my last cent, I would much rather contribute it to this purpose than that we should bear the stigma of thieves."

Never after this had I any occasion to reprove any of the men for trespass. They cheerfully replaced the rails they had displaced, and soon had the fence in good shape again. Mrs. Trush secured a good and ready market for her milk, butter, and fruit; and was more sorry at our departure, I am glad to say, than she was at our arrival.

Some time later in the day, as I was making a more careful inspection of our encampment, I noticed six very fat artillery horses belonging to the section of battery of which I was, for the time being, in command, standing in a field of growing corn. The horses were loose and at a consider-able distance from the camp, where of course

they should have been kept.   This latter fact is
what concerned me most, and I ordered the
lieutenant to have the animals taken at once to
their sheds, which were close to their riders'
"quarters."

After this had been done I learned that the
standing corn in the field where the animals were
surfeiting themselves had not been husked.   The
owner of the grain was a son of Mrs. Trush, the
widow just mentioned.   He was at this time confined to his bed. suffering from a white swelling, and
was unable to husk and crib his corn.   The following morning, after parade, I took occasion to
somewhat severely censure this portion of my
command for permitting their horses to wander
about, and especially for allowing them to consume and destroy a sick man's property.   I
reminded them, in the course of my remarks, that
if Colonel Mulligan was made aware of the circumstances there was no one in the entire army
who would feel more indignant at such conduct,
but that I hoped it would not be necessary to
trouble him with any such news.

I was pleased to see soon after substantial evidence of the good effect my words had upon the
boys.   This appeared in their voluntarily turning
out and going into the field of growing corn,
infantry and artillerymen together, and indulging
in an old-time husking frolic.   They not only
husked the corn, but took it to the cribs and stored

it safely away.   This action on the men's part
gave me more satisfaction than I had experienced
from any cause of a military sort for a long
time.

After a stay of twenty-six days—until November 19th—at Knobbley Mountain, we returned to
New Creek, where we remained until December
22d.   During our stay of over a month at New
Creek we got the first real taste of the severity
of camp life, owing to the rigorous inclemency of
the weather.   It was about this time, when at the
commissariat department at New Creek station,
that I received an irreparable injury while leaving
the freight depot one evening.

I had just purchased some things from the
assistant commissary, Mr. Peter Bryson.   The
night was dark, and, when leaving, I started to
step from the platform to the track, which was
some three feet lower, but my feet went through
a "cattle-stop" in the road-bed and, falling forward, my breast came violently in contact with one
of the rails.   The force of the blow threw me
heavily back against the other rail and I fainted
away.   I was picked up, borne into the office of
the commissary, and placed in a chair.   For two
weeks following I was under the treatment of Dr.
Oliver, a United States army surgeon : a rupture
resulting from this accident, from which I have
never recovered.

7

CHAPTER IX.

AFTER leaving New Creek we went to Sir John's Run, where our regiment established headquarters, and from which place we were detached to Back Creek Bridge, on the line of the Baltimore and Ohio Railroad, where we arrived December 23d. Five or six of the companies were stationed at the most important points along the line of this road; companies C, H, I, and B were located in the order named. As may be seen, Company B was the farthest east. Our company's orders were to go to Back Creek bridge and protect it from destruction by the enemy, who had on two previous occasions burned it to the water's edge.

The bridge was only a mile from North Mountain, and spanned a creek that emptied into the Potomac river, which at this point flowed parallel with the railroad for a considerable distance. The troops placed here prior to our arrival for the specific duty of protecting this property, had on both occasions of its destruction ingloriously run

(104)

away. I was therefore resolved that, so far as I
was concerned, my company should not avail itself of the cowardly precedent to shirk or evade
so plain a duty as was set before us here.

After pitching our tents I made an inspection
of the surroundings, and, as a result, felt satisfied
that we occupied a good defensive position. Our
camp was located in a skirt of woods lying between
the river and the railroad, the river on our left
and the creek in our front, making the position
one of great natural superiority in any skirmish
with the enemy. The approach from the south
side was the only one of which we were at all
apprehensive in case of attack, but this we took
special pains to fortify.

I now availed myself of an opportunity to address my little command on the subject of the
cowardly conduct of the raw troops that had pre-
ceded us at this point, dwelling at considerable
length on their contemptible and unpatriotic
action in running away from their post of duty,
simply on the report of country folks that the
enemy's forces were coming. In thus imbuing
the boys with a proper detestation of unsoldierlike
poltroonery, I was gratified to see that it had the
desired effect in causing them to appreciate and
practise in their daily exercises the opposite virtues. Although not yet subjected to a trial, I was
impressed with the belief that we had some good
material in our little command, composed as it

was of Americans, Germans, Irishmen, and one Englishman, Joseph Hall by name. Hall was one of the quietest and most inoffensive citizens of Lewis county, but when in action he well sustained the prestige of his country for courage. Though doubtless the equal, yet he was in no wise superior to many of his comrades of other nationalities, as was indubitably attested before the close of the war.

We soon had things in fair shape at Back Creek. Owing to the continued severity of the weather we could do but little drilling, as the getting of fuel, doing of picket duty, and strict adherence to a daily routine of cleanliness in person and accoutrements, occupied our time and attention pretty fully. In addition to the above duties I conceived an idea, born of a paternal interest in the welfare of the boys, which I carried into effect. I found that when the paymaster presented his pay-roll to my men, many of them made an "X," requiring in such cases a witness to their marks. I took the occasion to address them in a manner which my innate feelings dictated, avoiding anything likely to wound their pride, and deprecating the circumstances that deprived them of education. I told them that I would furnish paper, pens and ink, and devote all the spare time I had to their improvement. This I did with a feeling of satisfaction that no pay could give. The result was that in a surprisingly short time after their first lessons many of the men signed their names legibly to all documents submitted to them; and they continued to improve until they delighted their folks at home by sending them autograph letters, containing the pleasing intelligence that ever afterwards they would be relieved of the humiliation of having to intrust their family secrets to an unsympathetic amanuensis. That more of the boys did not profit by my humble endeavors in this direction was no fault of mine.

I also devoted a good deal of time to the instruction of the men in the best methods of cleaning their arms and accoutrements, and in properly folding and rolling their kits and greatcoats. I was well assisted in this duty by one of my men, Private Lawrence May, of whom more anon. I introduced another feature, not then practiced in the volunteer service, the utility of which my men did not understand until near the close of the war, when they came in contact with the soldiers of the regular army. In making a detail for picket or guard duty there were always selected two more than the needed number for such service. The officer whose duty it was to inspect these guards was each day required to carefully pick out two of the cleanliest men in the ranks to complete the quota of men called for under this rule, and then to exempt them from duty until it again became their time, in regular turn, to perform the unpleasant service.

When quartered near a town, or regimental headquarters, they were also permitted to visit these places on a leave of absence for pleasure or business of their own. It was a privilege worth contending for, and had the desired good effect on the conduct and habits of the men. Later on, when we were with the Army of the James, where this practice prevailed, the boys began to realize that there was something in it; especially after they had succeeded in carrying off the honors for soldier-like neatness and cleanliness from over one hundred picked men of the command.

I was absent from my command from March 9th to May 3d, 1863, sitting on general court-martial at Cumberland, Md. Colonel M. McCaslin, of our regiment, was President of the court, and John F. Hoy, Lieutenant-Colonel of the 6th West Virginia Infantry, was Judge Advocate. Both were men of marked ability and experience. At this court I made the acquaintance of Colonel E. D. Yutzy, then a Major in the 54th Pennsylvania Volunteers, and afterwards State Senator from his district. Colonel Yutzy was well educated and embodied the most ennobling and desirable qualities of chivalry, vivacity, and geniality. When in action he fully bore out the high opinion I had conceived of him. Although our duties were important and were conducted with somewhat of a judicial solemnity, yet we found opportunities to enjoy many jovial times together.

The particular case which occupied most of our attention was that of a cold-blooded murder. A man named John Martin, of the 23d Illinois, came in from New Creek to Cumberland, and while at the latter place was set upon by three or four armed men of the 3d Maryland Brigade, without any just provocation, and was cruelly murdered. The surgeon who held the post-mortem examination on the body of the dead soldier testified before the court, among other things, that Private Martin was the finest specimen of physical manhood that had ever come under his professional observation.

When the finding of the court, to which I had stoutly dissented, went before President Lincoln for his approval, he returned the papers with the indorsement that he did not understand how the court could arrive at such a conclusion, in view of the incriminating character of the evidence submitted during the trial. The finding inflicted a slight punishment only.

CHAPTER X.

I RETURNED to my command at Back Creek after
an absence of fifty-two days and the boys seemed
glad to see me, but it was a false and sickly attempt with the majority of them, who had shown
their true colors in the shape of a petition drawn
up, and numerously signed in my absence, and
presented to me on my return, asking me, in effect,
to resign my commission as captain, and by so
doing oblige the petitioners. On one so con-
scientiously devoted to the best interests of the
company as I felt myself to be, this act of base
ingratitude fell with crushing weight. Acting on
the impulse of the indignity, I instantly repaired
to headquarters and tendered my resignation to
the colonel, who as promptly refused to accept it.
He sat down, however, and gave me a kindly
lecture in his own pleasant and forcible manner.
He said that he was highly pleased with my conduct personally, and with the discipline I had in-

stituted in my command. My resignation, he added, would please my enemies only, and hurt my friends, among whom, he was pleased to tell me, where the best soldiers in my company.

On leaving for headquarters I had not apprised the petitioners of my intentions in the premises, and when I returned I said nothing of what had transpired. When I reflected on the influence, which, as I subsequently learned, had prompted the men to this act, I was enabled to bear the stigma with more equanimity. Among the motives actuating many of the signers to this petition was a petty ambition,—as my resignation, if accepted, would create about fifteen opportunities for promotion in the company.

The parties most zealous in circulating the paper for signatures enlarged considerably on this fact. Another reason, and the one probably that had the greatest weight with the boys, was an inducement held forth by the lieutenants, that in case of their succeeding to the command of the company the men would be permitted to enjoy greater liberty of action in camp, and be granted leave of absence with more frequency than they were able to obtain under my system of discipline.

As an evidence of their good intentions in this particular I found, upon my return from Cumberland, that there was not a good-looking young lady within a circle of three miles surrounding the camp, that the boys were not more or less intimately acquainted with. Some of the friendships thus formed by the soldiers left visibly marked and lasting impressions; notably so in the case of private Daniel Arbogast, for whom the government had no pantaloons long enough, he being six feet five and one-half inches in height.

There were three men in the company whom we had considerable trouble in inducing to practice ordinary habits of cleanliness. Dan was one of them. He was by no means a bad-looking fellow when he had made his toilet, but this latter hygienic exercise was of such rare occurrence that one's memory failed to retain the impression of his real appearance, in the long intervals which stretched between his ablutions. Notwithstanding this seemingly insuperable barrier to the good opinion of the fair sex, Dan succeeded in making an impression, and in his turn was impressed for life by the small-pox.

This misfortune befell him in the following manner.

About a mile from our encampment was a snug farm house, the sole occupants of which, during the time we were stationed at Back Creek, were three sisters, all good looking and grown to womanhood. The male portion of the household it was rumored were in the Confederate service.

The proximity of this abode to the camp did not, as may well be supposed, long remain a secret to the young fellows of the company, but, strange though it may appear, of all the visitors at their house Arbogast appeared to be the most favored by the girls. He was known to be one of the best rail-splitters and wood-choppers in the section of country whence he came. He was also a fair house carpenter. These acquirements, coupled with a willingness to perform other little services around the place, proved decided helps to his rapid advancement in the good estimation of the lonely females.

Dan was quite a character in his way; of a slow phlegmatic temperament, almost impossible to make angry, yet an absolute stranger to fear. Whether receiving punishment by the boxing-gloves on the hands of smaller but better scienced boys of the company, or confronting the enemy in the hardest contested engagement, he invariably wore the same imperturbable, good-humored smile, apparently as indifferent to pain or danger as he was careless of his personal appearance.

He possessed another natural gift, not the least of his attractions from a feminine point of view. He was a ventriloquist to the extent of producing musical sounds from his lungs without any visible movement of his lips. This last accomplishment completely charmed the maidens, and Dan became a doubly welcome visitor in consequence. But all earthly pleasures are transitory, and in this case the end came suddenly, and from an unexpected source. The news reached camp one day that the home of the three girls had been visited by that loathsome and much-dreaded pest, the small-pox. The sisters were each stricken down, in turn, with the disease, and so rapidly did they follow one another that the last to fall sick was unable in the short interval prior to her own illness to properly attend or nurse the others. Arbogast, however, did not desert them in this their trying hour of need; or, rather, I did not permit him to do so, for it was at this critical period that I returned to my command. After learning the situation of affairs at the farm-house, I refused to allow him to come near our quarters; so he remained like a brother with the girls until they were up and convalescent, when he fell a victim to the disgusting disease himself. On the humane rule that "one good turn deserves another," the girls were now assiduous in their care of Dan until he was entirely well.

Notwithstanding the close and intimate relation. ship subsisting between the soldier and these foolish girls I incline to the belief that their intercourse was purely of a friendly sort. In fact I may say while on this subject that there was not an instance that came to my knowledge during the war in which any member of my company was charged with paying unwelcome or ungentlemanly attentions to the fair sex.

While Arbogast was lying sick at the house of the three sisters one of our men, who had a couple of years previously been afflicted with small-pox, was permitted to take a daily supply of rations to within hailing distance of the premises and leave it there for the use of the beleagured inmates, one of whom would shortly appear and take the food into the house. By this means, and the adoption of other precautionary measures, the disease was happily confined to its source, and all of the boys, except Arbogast, escaped the dreadful scourge.

This then was the lax system of discipline I found prevailing upon my return; and for these, and kindred reasons, the boys wished to be relieved of my restraining influence.

Seeing that their request for my resignation did not have the anticipated effect, they resorted to other methods known to have been successful in removing obnoxious commanders in our regiment, the case of the captain of Company C being then quite recent. This was to resort to general insubordination and intimidation. To this end about half a dozen of the most unruly members of the company asked permission to attend a dance to be held some distance from the camp, with the avowed intention, in the event of my refusal, to test the question of mastery between us. With a knowledge of the facts I accepted the gauntlet thus thrown down, and promptly refused my assent to their going to the dance or elsewhere, and issued an order that no one should leave his quarters after the last "tattoo" without permission. I also instructed the non-commissioned officers in charge of squads to report to me any infractions of the above order. The following morning nine men were reported to me as having been absent from their quarters without leave during the whole of the previous night.

I sent word to the first lieutenant to prepare for duty, but the orderly returned with the reply that that officer was sick. The second lieutenant was next called on to report for service, but he also was indisposed; and so on down the limited list. In fact I never found, before or after, so many of my company ill as on this occasion.

They all appeared to be *enjoying* poor health. In short, the officers and a majority of the men were aware that the culprits intended to resist arrest, and they did not, therefore, care to respond to the disagreeable call, for the double reason that they were in secret sympathy with the offenders, and that the latter were known to have in addition to their muskets a good supply of "six-shooters," thereby making an attempt to place them under arrest extra hazardous.

In this emergency I took hold of matters myself. I promptly wrote out charges and specifications against the men, and addressed the document to the colonel of the regiment. After this was done I dressed in full uniform, with sword and side-arms, called an orderly-sergeant, took him with me to the men's quarters, had him call out a detail of eight privates and a sergeant, armed and equipped for duty, marched to the quarters of the malcontents, and in double-file opened order. Leaving them in this position, and without telling them what the exact nature of their duty was to be, I walked into the Sibley tent and over to where Thomas Hynes, one of the bravest of the culprits stood, revolver in hand. I did not lay hands on any of my weapons, but walked directly over to where he stood, and with a quick movement wrenched the revolver from his hand. I then took him by the shoulder, and he went out into the ranks ready to receive him about as quickly as had the revolver disappeared from his hand.

There was no trouble with the remaining offenders.

While this little scene was being enacted the sick lieutenants were outside of their tents taking particular notice of what was transpiring. The (to them) unexpected result worked a wondrous change in their physical conditions, and they recovered their health as suddenly as they had lost it.

When all the prisoners were secured the word to "forward march" was given, and I delivered them a short time later, together with the papers addressed to the colonel, into the charge of Captain Newman, of Company I, with the request that he escort them to Captain Luken, of Company H, and thence to the captain of Company C, at Alpine, with instructions that they be forwarded to headquarters of the regiment at Sir John's Run. By this time the boys began to realize that I not only had some idea of the prerogatives of my position, but was not particularly backward about exercising them.

After reaching headquarters the prisoners were sent to Cumberland, there to languish for two or three months in dark and noisome cells, awaiting the next sitting of a general court-martial. When they had endured this sort of thing for a couple of weeks they began writing humbly worded letters to the colonel, begging his intercession in their behalf. The latter was, if possible, more tender-hearted than the immortal Lincoln himself. By repeated entreaties, they so worked upon his feelings that he corresponded with me on the subject of their release. Before doing so, however, he gave the prisoners to understand that he could do nothing unless I consented to withdraw the charges I had preferred against them. They thereupon turned their attention to me, writing in a very submissive spirit, and promising to be good soldiers in the future if permitted to return to their company.

My only object—the enforcement of a proper respect for discipline—having been attained, I readily consented to their release, and we soon

had them back with us.   It gives me pleasure to
state that after their return they all made first-
rate records, and were, during the war, among the
most subordinate of my command.

About this time we were busy erecting at a
short distance south of the railroad track a block-
house for better defensive purposes.   It was to
be a good structure, though comparatively small,
being intended to comfortably accommodate one
company only, but in case of an attack two companies might be disposed within its walls.   While
still working on it, and just before the roof was
placed in position, we received reliable information that the enemy was approaching in the direction of our camp.   Corporal Monypenney and
myself made a reconnoissance, and found the report to be correct.   Just as we returned a cavalryman, named Peiffer, came dashing into camp
badly scared, and his horse covered with foam,
carrying the intelligence that Longstreet's division of the enemy was only a short distance in
his rear.

The long-looked-for issue, I thought, was now
at hand that would test the kind of material of
which we were composed.   The men had been
schooled so well in their duties that I do not recall
a single instance of any of them suggesting ignominious retreat.   We hurriedly detailed half a
dozen men to go with a handcar and water-vessels
to a spring bordering the track in the direction

8

of North Mountain, and quite close to its base, for a supply of drinking-water for our use in case of a siege.

By this time we were reinforced by Company I, Captain Newman in command, who had been stationed a few miles westward from our camp. The captain, on learning of the critical situation, had wisely decided to join us at the block-house. In view of the reported large force of the enemy approaching, he objected to going with his company into the fort, preferring, he said, to take to the little skirt of woods bounded by the river and the railroad.

Being senior officer I vetoed this suggestion, pointing out the fact that in such a position he would be sure to be captured, as retreat would be impossible; and finally, that he could not hope to do much effective damage to the enemy before the latter would be upon him. Both companies were then instructed to retire within the block-house, and prepare for the stern duty apparently before them. This they complied with, and in a short time all the men were safely inside.

While a squad of four or five, under my immediate charge, were bringing in the last remnants of our camp traps, I heard the shrill whistle of a locomotive shrieking away around the bend in our rear, the train coming eastward. I knew in a moment what it meant, and, although not to my credit to say so, I pronounced a hearty malediction on this, the instrument of our deliverance; for such, indeed, it was, and with its arrival were blasted all hopes of our having an opportunity to give a good account of ourselves in the expected engagement.

Looking back at the situation now, with a calmer and more experienced mind, I am free to confess that it is altogether likely the timely arrival of this train saved many, if not all, of the lives of our small body. The engine, tender and four or five flat-cars came to a standstill at a point near where I was standing, and Captain S. F. Shaw, of Company G, jumped from the train, and approaching me hurriedly said, in his concise and off-hand manner:

"Captain, it is the colonel's orders that you at once get your command aboard this train, and not to wait even for your knapsacks."

Deeply chagrined, I replied that I should obey orders, but that I would have to await the return of the men sent down the track for water, before complying. Glancing towards the engine, I took a mental survey of the individual who presided at the throttle. His appearance indicated seemingly that he was the right man for an emergency. Approaching, I asked him if he would run down the road a short distance and pick up the water squad. He assented readily, and with the air of a man who could be relied upon to do his full duty. I have always been sorry that I did not learn the brave fellow's name. I sent five or six privates armed with muskets with him, and they cut loose from the train, taking but one car with them. While they were gone we loaded our camp and garrison equipage on the remaining cars.

The rebel skirmishers were now in plain sight. That they did not open fire on the boys who had gone for the water, or their rescuers on the loco-motive, has always been a mystery to me. Per-haps, seeing the train loaded with soldiers, it impressed them with the belief that if they opened the ball first, they might awaken an unwelcome response of grape and canister from us. How-ever this may be, the engine soon returned unmo-lested, bearing back all of the men but three who had become separated from their comrades, and who, on seeing their retreat cut off by the enemy, procured horses and succeeded in crossing the Potomac and escaping. To our agreeable sur-prise, they rejoined their company at New Creek, a few days later. We not only took our knap-sacks, but every other article of property we had charge of at this station.

When moving off, I could not help feeling, as I took a last look at that unfortunate bridge— doomed for a third time to destruction—that our running away without making an effort to save it, while it might evidence good generalship, savored considerably of cowardice. On our ignominious retreat to headquarters we picked up two other companies, I and H, at short intervals apart. They each had their equipments in readiness to load as we came up. No incident worthy of mention occurred during the ride, and we arrived unharmed at Sir John's Run in due time.

Thus did we add our names to the long list of those who "run away," but who thereby "live to fight some other day."

CHAPTER XI.

WE remained at headquarters until June 16th,
when we received orders to proceed, for the second time, to New Creek. After a stay of about
twenty days at the latter place, and about the
time of the great battle at Gettysburg, our brigade, under command of General B. F. Kelley,
received hurried marching orders to proceed in
the direction of that historic field.

We marched direct from New Creek to Cumberland, Md., thence northeasterly on the pike to
Hancock. We tramped all day and night in an
incessant and drenching rain that had not abated
when we arrived the following morning at Hancock, amidst a terrific downpour, tired, soaked
and miserably wretched.

Of the entire brigade there were only ten or
twelve men on the ground when morning broke.
Only two of these, Sergeant May and Corporal
Hitt, in addition to myself, were of Company B.

"We tramped all day and night in an incessant and drenching rain."—Page 124.

The poor fellows composing this advance squad were in a pitiable state from fatigue and loss of sleep.

The rear guard, finding a great portion of the command lying on the roadside asleep, would awaken and drive them in their front. It was a sad sight to see the tired soldiers staggering and falling like drunken men, urged onward at the point of the bayonet in the hands of their comrades in their rear.

Having arrived at Hancock, I lay down in a fence corner, with a rail for a pillow, and was soon sound asleep. When I awoke, a couple of hours later, a rippling current was playing through my long hair, and my body was, if possible, more thoroughly water-soaked than when I first laid down. It is strange, but true, that at the time I felt no ill effects from this wretched exposure.

We rested at Hancock until July 11th, when we continued our march to Fairview, one of the most elevated points in Maryland, and commanding a fine view of some of the grandest scenery in the State. We are reinforced by General Averill's brigade, consisting of cavalry and artillery, making our total force about seven thousand strong, all in prime condition, and—if judged by their appearance and actions—spoiling for a fight.

From the indications then observable it looked strongly as though their desires in this particular were to be fully gratified within a very short time.

General Lee was known to be retreating south-
ward, after his disastrous meeting with Meade.
He was moving over the route leading through
the section in which we then were, and the prob-
abilities of our meeting him were strong. During
the night of July 11th I slept but little. Although
not assigned to duty, my mind was busy with
thoughts of the battle likely to be fought on the
following day.

It may seem, and doubtless it was, quite absurd
in an obscure captain, commanding but a handful
of men, to be revolving in his mind, as was I,
plans upon which to conduct the expected engagement; but I could not help it. I believed firmly
that the auspicious time for ending the bloody
strife had arrived. The fall of Vicksburg on July
4th, the day following that on which the long-
contested and famous battle of Gettysburg was
ended and won for the Union, had discouraged
the whipped and retreating enemy now approaching us; and I felt that, aided by the natural advantages of our position, we might safely engage
Lee at a time when his army was divided by the
booming waters of the then swollen Potomac,
with the undoubted assurance of harassing him
greatly, and possibly winning a partial victory
from him after first making the division of his
forces complete by smashing his pontoons.

I learned during the night from two deserters
that Lee was about to cross the river at Williams-

port, Md., a small town a few miles below us. The knowledge of his intentions thus acquired suggested the idea above mentioned, of dividing his army. I submitted my views, as soon as possible, to General Kelley, to the effect that I had a good local knowledge of the topography of this section, acquired while stationed at Back Creek, and was aware that there were a great number of large trees overhanging the banks of the then turbulent stream for a considerable distance on both its sides, which, if cut down and allowed to fall into the rapid current after a portion of the enemy had crossed, would undoubtedly crush and sweep away his pontoon bridges, and effectually separate his army. This accomplished we could safely engage the first portion of his command with at least equal chances of success.

I tendered the general the services of my company for this work, which could have been easily and quickly accomplished by them, the majority of them being practical wood-choppers, had they received orders to do so; but the order never came. Every man of Lee's army who wanted to do so got safely across the river without molestation or interruption from us, while we were calmly squinting at their progress through field-glasses at a high elevation and a civil distance. In my humble opinion there never was a grander opportunity for a brilliant *coup de grace* than was lost to the Union cause on this occasion.

At eight o'clock the next morning, July 12th, we could hear some splendid cannonading east of Fairview. A little later we located it east of Williamsport. It soon died out, however, and we could only surmise its cause.

We lay inactive, or nearly so, at Fairview for the next two days, or until July 14th, when we received marching orders and started at dawn on double-quick time. Major E. D. Yutzy, of the 54th Pennsylvania (afterwards Colonel, and later State Senator), was with me a good deal on this march. I greatly enjoyed, when it was possible to indulge in it, the companionship of Yutzy, who combined the very essence of intellectual perspicacity with high military chivalry.

From later information received from fresh deserters we learned that the last of Lee's army was safely across the Potomac river before we got our eleventh hour orders to move quickly. This news made our hurried efforts now appear so ridiculous and unnecessary that it was more than Yutzy and the writer could quietly stand. The former loudly and severely criticised the stupid dilatoriness of our commanders on this occasion, to all of which I cordially agreed in terms equally emphatic. Our uncomplimentary and insubordinate remarks were made in the hearing of the generals, as we marched along, and might easily have been made by them the basis of a trial by court-martial with my friend and self as defendants; but our indignation made us for the time being, indifferent to any risks we might be running in this particular.

On arriving at Williamsport, after our hurried march, we found, as we had all along anticipated, the game safely gone. Everybody felt disgruntled at this farcical outcome of our long and arduous tramp from New Creek; and considerable grumbling was indulged in by the men at the expense of our commanders.

It is possible, and may be probable, that the latter were acting under orders, and carrying out instructions received from a higher authority; or that their object was simply to keep the enemy from foraging on the loyal people living along the route he was then following. If the latter, our trip was fairly successful. Whatever may have been the reason, the fact remains that, judging from apparent results, we had not accomplished much. What made our disappointment complete was the common expectation of great things from Generals Averell and Kelley, both gentlemen of unquestioned bravery.

In following the retreating enemy we returned on the 15th as far as Cherry Run, after enduring considerable hardships owing to the rough condition of the roads over which we marched. On the day following our arrival General Kelley became anxious to cross to the south bank of the Potomac. The river was still high and rapid and the only available means of crossing consisted of three or four small and poorly constructed flat-bottom barges, scarcely large enough to hold more than one company on each trip, and one large barge, capable of answering the needed purpose, but which could not be utilized until a cable was first stretched from bank to bank to guide the craft.

For a suitable rope we did not know how long we might have to wait, there not being one long enough, or strong enough, in our wagon train, so it was found to be necessary to send back several miles to secure what was needed. There seemed to be great impatience among the men to get across the stream ; and a number of them cast about for a means for doing so other than the cable. But nobody seemed to think of using the small flats for that purpose, as they appeared useless, being without oars to propel them.

Struck with an idea that I thought might be of service, I went to General Kelley, and asked him if he desired some of the troops put over at once. He replied that he did, but could not see how it could well be done until the arrival of the large rope mentioned.

"General," said I, "if you order me to do so, I will put my company over in a short time."

He was somewhat doubtful of the success of such an attempt; but upon my reaffirming my ability to perform the feat, he directed his adjutant-

general, Captain Thayer Melvin, to issue orders
to our regiment to cross the river.

Expecting to be the first called upon, I anticipated my colonel's orders to the extent of sending a few of my men into the woods to cut down
saplings for poles long enough and stout enough
for our intended purpose.   While they were
gone we secured one of the small flats to be used
by us in making the trial.   We then awaited the
return of the men from the woods, and orders
to make the effort from our regimental commander.
These latter did not reach us, however, until two
other companies had first made the attempt, and
were swept down with the current for fully a mile
from their starting-point.

At last our company got the looked-for orders
and immediately we were in the swift and angry
waters.   Stripping to our shirts, we cast wide
our poles and bent to the work with a will ; each
man straining every nerve to accomplish the feat,
his pride aroused to the utmost in the effort.
We poled the boat in a diagonal course to a point
some distance above, and after great exertions
made the landing safely, before the others, who
had almost an hour's start, had touched the shore.
After making one or two more trips without
mishaps, the large rope arrived and the remainder of the troops made the passage easily
and expeditiously.

On the 17th we marched to within a mile of

Hedgersville, near where we could see the enemy's videttes in a skirt of woods lying between the village and our main body. Back Creek, now overflowing its banks, lay between them and us. Volunteers were now called for to cross the creek, move in the direction of the town, and flank the rebel pickets. One hundred and ten men, a captain and two lieutenants, volunteered for the duty; but on reaching the stream at the point intended for the passage they found that the bridge spanning it had been swept away. All halted, undecided what to do. Plunging in, I offered to lead the party across, and we all started to ford the creek. The water took us breast-high, and was running very strong, causing us no little trouble to keep our feet. By holding their guns high above their heads, the men succeeded in keeping them dry.

Once over, we started in hot pursuit of the "Johnnies;" finding them well mounted, however, we had to abandon the chase, but not before our places were taken by a squad of General Averell's cavalry, who pursued the enemy so successfully that they returned in a short time with twenty prisoners. The gaunt and hungry appearance of these captives and their animals was ample evidence that General Lee's army, horse and foot, had been on decidedly short rations for some time previous to this date.

It was after nightfall when we returned, well

tired, to camp, after having driven the enemy's foragers from Hedgersville. From trustworthy information received at the above place we learned that Lee, aware of our pursuit of him, was preparing to turn the tables on us and entrap our entire command; and that his apparently hurried flight was only a ruse to this end. Acting in good faith on this news, we at once fell back towards Cherry Run; and, as it proved, not a moment too soon, for only by keeping it up far into the night did we escape capture.

On July 20th four companies, including Company B, in charge of Major Yutzy, were detailed to act as skirmishers on our second advance in the direction of the enemy. Shortly after starting, we espied a squad of rebels. We pursued them for an hour and a half, keeping them on the backward move all of that time. A company of the 14th Pennsylvania Cavalry joined us later in the chase, and two of their men were badly wounded in a sharp engagement that followed.

The Confederates continued to retreat very rapidly until they were in the immediate vicinity of their main body, when we in turn were ordered to fall back. When night shut out our view, it was learned that Lee was again closing in on us. I was placed in charge of the most advanced pickets, with instructions to keep a sharp lookout for the enemy. Nothing transpired until about midnight, when all of our command except the

ever faithful Yutzy and my company stole quietly
away in the darkness, leaving us where we were
to act as a blind; thereby making the approach
of the enemy more slow and cautious, under the
impression that the remainder of our troops were
in our front.   The trick succeeded and no doubt
saved the entire command, as when morning broke
the last of our troops were scarcely five minutes
on the other side of the river when an overwhelm-
ing force, under General Lee in person, came hurriedly down upon us.

That the rebels were suffering severely from
hunger was evident from the avidity displayed by
the poor fellows in picking up and eagerly de-
vouring the crumbs and scraps left by us in our
late camp.   When we reached the north side of
the Potomac river our artillery was placed in a
commanding position and trained on the enemy;
and so we rested until the 24th, when, General
Lee having withdrawn, we recrossed the Potomac
to the Virginia side, and in a short time were once
more encamped on the old grounds at Back Creek,
where we remained until July 31st.

Little of interest occurred during our second
stay at this place, except that deserters continued
to come in regularly every day.   Owing to the
absence of proper police regulations, the sanitary
condition of our camp became miserable, and the
place becoming very unhealthy we were all glad
to get away.

On the 31st we followed in the wake of a part of Lee's forces, retreating southwestward, keeping between them and the Baltimore and Ohio Railroad. On this march we went through Rocky Springs, Birchtown, Big Cacapon, and Blue Gap, in Virginia, and on August 4th we encamped ten miles east of Romney, the county-seat of Hampshire county, West Virginia.

9

CHAPTER XII.

On August 5th we marched ten miles before dinner, and in the afternoon encamped at Mechanicsburg Gap, two miles west of Romney. Our camp here proved an agreeable change from that of Back Creek, the air being pure and the surroundings mountainous. The valley of the south branch of the Potomac was very level and fertile, showing evident signs of a prosperous people in this section before the war. Here the pursuit of Lee, so far as our brigade was concerned, ended, and we remained encamped at Romney for several months.

Many incidents transpired during our stay here which I should like to mention, but space will hardly permit of my doing so. I shall, however, venture to make one exception. One of the many pastimes in which the boys of the brigade in their leisure moments indulged, was the practice of the manly art of self-defence. A majority of the younger element of the rank and file were

(136)

enthusiastic "boxers," were fairly well scienced and frequently participated in lively "slugging" matches. As was to be expected, quite a rivalry soon sprang up regarding the question of supremacy in the fistic art, between the men of the different companies. At the time of which I write, it appears that the boys of Company B had been declared winners in several friendly set-tos, and, as a result, were permitted to wear the "belt" as champions. This fact had, of course, somewhat nettled the other members of the brigade, and as a means of equalizing honors, they taunted the winners with the claim that they had an officer (a captain of a company from one of the chief cities of our State) who, if he could be induced to put on the gloves, would easily get away with anything that Company B might bring up.

I afterwards learned that private Malia, one of our best boxers, and no less an intrepid soldier, spoke up in answer to this defiance, saying: "By ——, our 'Gray Eagle' (a term not infrequently applied to me in those days, by reason of my being prematurely gray) can do the business for him, if we can only arrange to get them to the scratch."

Well, this bantering by both sides was kept up until at length they did succeed in bringing the captain and myself to the mark in the following manner: among all the officers of our command, the captain in question was my especial friend and favorite, and we were a great deal together in consequence. It so chanced that on the 20th of August, he and myself were at headquarters receiving orders from the colonel, and as we started to leave we noticed, about ten yards distant, a number of the soldiers amusing themselves with the gloves. Curious to know who they were and how they were getting along, we strolled together leisurely in that direction. As we approached, the contestants ceased sparring, and they, together with the on-lookers, came smilingly towards us and, with a bow, presented us with the "mits," at the same time requesting us, in the most persuasive manner possible, to show them a "little fun."

We were both diffident in accepting the proffered gloves, but the boys were persistent in their importunities until, at last, we reluctantly consented to gratify their curiosity for a few minutes. When we were in our shirt sleeves, I found that I had in the captain a finely-built young man to encounter. He was in the prime of life, about twenty-seven years old, and about my own height (five feet eleven inches), but was considerably heavier than I then was.

I soon found that the captain, as a boxer, merited the good opinion in which he was held by his men, who were themselves well up in the science. We continued sparring longer than I first intended we should, owing to a mutual dislike to inflict injury. Finally, after satisfying myself from the

manner in which my opponent handled himself,
that I was master of the situation, I said: "Captain, let us take them off; we've shown the boys
enough of fun now."

My proposition looked so much like throwing
up the sponge that the boys of Company B were
greatly crestfallen, and none more so than the
spunky Malia, at my seeming unwillingness to test
the question to a conclusion. Notwithstanding
this fact, it was my intention to submit gracefully
to the humiliation attaching to my offer to cease
boxing, but the captain appeared to look upon
my request in the same light as did the men, and
persuasively invited me to continue. His over-
confident air decided me, and I agreed, remarking
that I construed his invitation to mean "business."

The sparring after this was sharp and effective,
terminating rather suddenly when the glove on
my right hand came into too forcible contact with
my opponent's nose, staggering him badly and
causing the claret to flow freely. This ended it
by mutual consent, for in truth I felt more disgusted than elated at my performance; however,
I presume our boys felt differently, owing to the
before-mentioned rivalry.

On November 5, 1863, our command broke
camp at Mechanicsburg Gap and departed under
marching orders for Springfield, Virginia. On the
25th of the same month Companies B and C, with

the writer in command, received orders to report
for detached duty at Alpine, Virginia, a small station on the Baltimore and Ohio Railroad, opposite
Hancock, Maryland, and divided from that place
by the Potomac river.

We arrived at Alpine on the following day, and
found that, owing to its situation, the war had
made it a most important post, and one devolving
upon its commandant, in the discharge of his
duties, a heavy responsibility.   Company C of
our regiment had at one time been on duty here,
but for some time previous to our arrival a company of cavalry had occupied the post.

Colonel McCaslin (15th West Virginia) had
been for some time before our assignment to
Alpine the recipient of many complaints from the
citizens of the place and the officers of the railroad company, whose line ran through it, charging that a serious lack of discipline existed among
the soldiers detailed to guard the post, and he
had now decided to make a complete change of
commandants and men at Alpine.   Companies B
and C were, as I have stated, placed under my
command, and we were soon ordered to our new
quarters ; the latter company would, the colonel
feared, be likely to cause me considerable trouble,
as they had, he said, contracted some loose and
vicious habits while on duty at this station before.
I assured the colonel that I would do the very
best I could to enforce a proper discipline among
the men of both companies.

In this connection, it gives me pleasure to be able to state that my conduct of affairs at Alpine met with not only the entire approbation of my immediate superior, but later also with that of the Secretary of War, with whom I had the honor of a personal correspondence relative to the attempted passage of goods contraband of war across the river at this point, and who, in recognition of the honesty and zeal displayed in putting a stop to this illegal traffic, and as a further means of its prevention, increased my powers by appointing me a provost-marshal during the time of my stay at Alpine.

CHAPTER XIII.

ON arriving at our new post we found the
weather very inclement, and as army tents would
afford poor shelter for the troops during the coming winter—for which length of time we expected
to remain—a rough plan of our encampment was
made out, with a parade-ground running through
its centre, on both sides of which, for a good distance, were erected by the men a number of log-
huts, well plastered with mud, and provided with
large fire-places, except in a few instances in
which old stoves were utilized. By such means
the men were made comfortable during the
months of intensely cold weather that followed.

The thriving little city of Hancock, just across
the river, with its many stores and licensed
saloons, together with the close proximity of the
railroad to our camp, afforded the soldiers unusual
opportunities for stealing away unknown to their
officers, and indulging in many wild orgies. The
post was also a transfer-point on the "underground
railway" between Maryland and Virginia, where,

before my arrival, large amounts of goods contraband of war were permitted to pass with a
superficial examination, or without any inspection.

The necessity of constant vigilance on my part
to prevent breaches of discipline on the one hand
and smuggling on the other made the position of
commandant and provost-marshal by no means a
sinecure. This was especially true in the first
respect, as in this work I lacked the active co-
operation of a majority of my subordinate officers,
who, though sober, moral, and passively obedient,
yet connived at many infractions of the rules of
camp discipline.

Another source of annoyance and indignation
to me was the attempted continuance by some of
the men of the policy of my predecessor in charge
here, who had permitted his troops to rob, harass,
and terrorize the citizens of Hancock, a majority
of whom were supposed to entertain Southern
proclivities. Of the truth or falsity of this suppo-
sition I had no direct evidence. But without the
commission of some overt act on their part,
showing that their hearts were really in sympathy
with the now "lost cause," I did not feel justified,
nor could any true soldier, in permitting the
further pillaging of their homes, and therefore I
put a peremptory and final stop to it.

As an evidence of the extremes to which this
wantonness was allowed to extend during the

period prior to our arrival, I learned from an old gentleman named Murray, who had at that time been for seven years successively mayor of Hancock, and who was a man of undoubted veracity, that during the time mentioned he was powerless to protect the lives and property of his people, and that he remained in constant dread of the taking of his own life by our drunken soldiers.

While determined to prevent any further unlicensed liberty on the part of the soldiers, I still wished to allow them all the privileges compatible with good order and discipline to which they were at all entitled. In order to avoid the suspicion of favoritism in dispensing such privileges, I had prepared a blank book, with alternate pages for each company, wherein should be entered the number and kind of permits, or "leaves," granted, such favors to be equally divided.

Notwithstanding this and other means adopted by me to treat all fairly, I early began to notice signs of a sullen determination among the men of Company C to resist my authority. The captain of this demoralized command (which, by the way, afterwards became a good and efficient body of troops) was named James Devore. He was a good-natured, good-looking young man, a fair amateur musician, very fond of the society of ladies, and an accomplished dancer. He visited Hancock almost nightly, as did a majority of his men, in pursuit of these pleasures.

On one occasion this officer and a squad of his men, all bound for Hancock, met at the river bank, and a spirited scuffle ensued for the possession of the one boat available, resulting, greatly to his discomfiture, in the undignified captain being left behind. Long indulgence in these and similar habits of soldiering, caused the men to look upon my methods in no very favorable light. Having, however, in Company B a body of men who were beginning to take a pride in the practice of true military decorum, I was enabled, after one or two conflicts with insubordinates, to establish the standard of discipline I had determined to enforce.

After the failure of sundry attempts at intimidation, the malcontents set about to trump up false-charges against me, with a view to securing my removal in that way. In this they were ably seconded by interested civilians, who had been making fortunes by handling the contraband goods that were formerly allowed to cross the river at this point. Together they formulated a number of charges, general and specific, which were elaborated by a Colonel Strother, of Berkley Springs, a scholarly gentleman, who was then a contributor to some of the leading magazines of the country. The report was quite voluminous, and well calculated to make a strong impression at general headquarters, whither they forwarded it without delay.

These charges were, as was customary in such cases, "respectfully referred" by the officials at headquarters to the brigade commander, thence to our regimental headquarters, and by our colonel to me. I lost no time in replying, and my answer to the charges, specifically and as a whole, was deemed so satisfactory and complete that my action in the premises, and my conduct generally, instead of being questioned or rebuked was highly approved, and the scope of my authority was greatly enlarged.

A few years after the close of the war, when at Cincinnati, Ohio, whither I had taken my youngest son for medical treatment, I put up at the house of a Lieutenant Pratt, who, upon hearing my name, remarked that he had read in a magazine an article from the pen of a Colonel Strother, wherein that gentleman stated incidentally, that on one occasion during the war he had engaged in an epistolary controversy with an Irishman, Captain Egan, in which the latter, with genuine Irish pugnacity, had returned his assault with compound interest.

The colonel doubtless had reference to the Alpine charges.

CHAPTER XIV.

A FEW days after this latest attempt by the boys to remove their obnoxious commander, I happened to be some distance from our quarters visiting a picket post on the Potomac. It was about noon-time, and as I started to return I saw a two-horse carriage coming hurriedly down the river bank in the direction of the ferry-landing, evidently bent upon crossing to the Maryland side. The team and conveyance were very much mud-bespattered, showing unmistakable signs of a long and hard drive. I approached and halted the driver, a smart-looking young fellow, and seemingly an expert with the "ribbons."

I was beside the head of one of the horses when the carriage, which was closely covered, came to an abrupt stop, and the face of its sole occupant peered cautiously from behind one of the curtains. A glance at the face proved it one that could scarcely fail in making a strong impression upon the beholder; beauty of a high type, intellectuality in a marked degree, and undoubted refinement were seemingly stamped on every feature, while handsome dark eyes flashed indignantly from beneath a crown of raven-black hair, artistically curled and arranged in the fashion then prevailing. That this was a lady, and evidently a highly accomplished one, that I now confronted would have been apparent to the most obtuse.

I was attired in a loose-fitting blouse, without shoulder-straps or insignia of rank, and as the lady surveyed me with a look in which hauteur and entreaty were equally blended, I could not help doubting for a moment the propriety of subjecting such a beautiful and aristocratic looking female to the degrading humiliation of an inquisitorial and personal examination.

Failing to overawe me by her imperious gaze, and seeing that I did not relinquish my hold of the horse's head, the fair one changed her manner, and with a most bewitching smile and a superb air of patronage said:

"Please do not detain me, sir; I have had a long and rough ride this morning, and am very tired and hungry, and in a hurry to reach Hancock in time for dinner, of which I stand much in need."

"Madame," I politely replied, "it is my duty (an unpleasant one, I assure you, in this instance) to carefully examine all goods and persons that attempt to cross the river at this point; if all is right in your case I shall not detain you long."

"Why, sir," said the lady, with rising indignation, "we have just been forced to submit to the
closest possible scrutiny by the intelligent officers
at the last post we passed, and their examination—most carefully made—resulted in our being
allowed to continue our journey." She paused a
moment for a reply.

"Your persistency in detaining me now, in the
face of what I have just told you," continued the
angry woman, "is wholly unnecessary and extremely annoying. Your superior, when your
action in my case reaches his ears, will not feel,
I assure you, very highly pleased at the over-
zealous stupidity of his subordinate at Alpine. I
tell you this, sir, because you may discover, in
the near future, that it would have been to your
best interest to have foregone your present intention of subjecting me to this indignity."

My reply was that I had no wish to embarrass
her in the slightest; but that my duty was quite
plain in such cases as the present one, and that
she would have to come back to our camp
with me.

As a last attempt to escape this ordeal, and in
a tone of mingled menace and reproach, the lady
concluded: "I have kind and influential friends
in the Union service who will hold you to a strict
accountability for my ill-treatment to-day. Every
intelligent soldier," asserted the irate female
scornfully, "either knows or has heard of the

famous 'Fighting Parson' Moody, of Ohio; that gentleman and patriot is my brother-in-law."

The names of a number of other gentlemen, prominent in State and army circles, were furnished me in quick succession by the excited lady, whose volubility proved her an adept in the use of the English language, and explained, to my mind, how she had succeeded so admirably in escaping detention and discovery earlier on her journey.

I ordered the driver to wheel about his team and drive to the post, which he reluctantly did.

The lady's nervousness was now quite apparent, and as we approached the camp she several times tried to engage the driver's attention and tell him something; but I kept so near the window of her carriage and such a close watch upon their movements that she failed to do so. I conducted them direct to my own quarters, a large roomy brick-house in about the centre of the village. Arrived at the house, I turned over the man and his team to a guard, and then proceeded, without ceremony, to make an inspection of the lady's baggage. I soon found a number of letters, accompanied by several watches and other trinkets, from rebel officers in the field to their friends in Maryland, and also a diary containing mention of dates of interviews with no less personages than Jefferson Davis, Generals Lee, Braxton Bragg, and others of similar rank.

Finding so much, I was now convinced that
Mrs. Moody must have concealed upon her person, where shrewd female spies know best to
conceal them, documents far more important
than any that had yet come to light. I thereupon intrusted the delicate duty of searching the
spy to my wife and two other ladies, wives of two
of my men, who were then upon a visit to their
husbands. I instructed these ladies to make a
careful search of the person of the spy, who,
notwithstanding all her tact and coolness, was
béginning to show, in her nervous excitement,
conclusive signs of the importance of this contemplated personal scrutiny. She kept restlessly
pacing up and down the large room to which she
had been taken. It contained in one end a
heating-stove wherein a glowing fire was burning. It was noticed that her walk was always in
the direction of this stove. When the ladies were
all ready to begin I walked out of the room, at
the same time telling them to proceed with their
search.

When I was gone they attempted to do their
assigned duty, but the resolute Mrs. Moody was
too sharp for our timid ladies, who, if the truth
must be told, by no means liked the task. I had
hardly left the room before I heard a startled
scream from within. Hastily returning, I found
that the spy had just taken from her bosom a
large packet of letters, and walking deliberately to

the stove and throwing open the door, had, while the soldiers' wives looked helplessly on, consigned the incriminating bundle to the flames, leaving nothing to tell the tale of that which might have compromised her life, and thrown much light on the mysteries of the rebel secret service.

The beautiful spy was now a changed woman. Satisfied that the evidence of her guilt could no longer be obtained, she looked at us with a calm air of serene defiance, and made not the slightest effort to conceal the pleasure my palpable discomfiture gave her.

As may be judged, I was anything but pleased at this unexpected and annoying ending of what I felt satisfied was an important capture. Had I been less observant of the duty which all men owe to the gentler sex, I should not have been thus outgeneraled by this lady, whose calling rightly exposed her to the imposition of indignities at once degrading to herself and her sex.

I made a statement of the case, which I enclosed, together with the papers found in her baggage, to General Schenck, department commander. These, with the lady, I sent by an armed escort to the general's headquarters.

This was the last I ever heard of Mrs. Moody. Whether this name was real or assumed I never learned.

CHAPTER XV.

A DAY or two after the incident just narrated
a well-dressed elderly gentleman, of fine appearance and aristocratic bearing, presented himself
at our quarters and applied for a permit to pass
two large trunks containing a quantity of rich dry-
goods and fine dress suitings. He stated that he
was a resident of Richmond, Va.; that he had
relations living in the city of New York, where
he had just been to purchase the several hundred
dollars worth of goods contained in the trunks.
These goods, he said, were intended solely for
his own and his family use. He claimed to be
as neutral on the issue of the war as it was
possible for any one to be and live in Richmond.

His manner throughout was straightforward,
and his story to my mind bore the impress of
truth; but I told him that while I entertained no
reasonable doubt of the correctness of his statements I could not, consistently with my duty,
permit goods of such a character and value to
pass. I gave him to understand, however, that

(153)

if he would procure an order from my colonel, or a higher authority, I would not offer any further objection to the desired privilege. The gentleman accordingly went to the headquarters of our regiment, at Sir John's Run, and had a long talk with our colonel; but that officer refused to interfere, as he stated, in a duty he thought me so competent to discharge.

Upon his return, the old gentleman reported what the colonel had said, and seeing the discretionary power I was permitted to exercise, renewed his request that he and his goods be allowed to pass; but I was obdurate, and so he left. Some days later he again appeared bearing a letter from Secretary of War E. M. Stanton, addressed to me, as provost-marshal, instructing me to permit the bearer of the communication, with his trunks, to pass over to Maryland. This letter I have mislaid, and the gentleman's name has escaped my memory.

On December 8, 1863, I was ordered to headquarters to assume temporary command of the regiment, during the absence of the colonel, who had been called to the command of the brigade. On the day following my arrival, acting on information received, I ordered fifty men to Bath, Va., to prevent a threatened interruption by the rebels of the proceedings of the United States Circuit Court, then in session at that place. I accompanied and took personal charge of the little force, and had them quietly secreted in proper position, in a strip of woods adjacent to, and commanding a complete range of the buildings in which the business of the court was conducted. My information, from an apparently reliable source, was to the effect that the enemy, with a larger force than ours, under a Major Farrell, was less than two miles distant from us at the time.

What may have restrained him from his threatened project I cannot say, but he did not interrupt the court during its sitting. We remained at Bath (or Berkeley Springs) until the 12th, without anything of note transpiring; then the court and the troops departed for their respective stations.

On the 13th, when back at Alpine, we were startled about 11.30 o'clock P. M. by a report that the enemy was approaching rapidly from the direction of Bath, for the purpose of making a night attack on us. Soon our little encampment was in commotion. As a first step, I at once ordered out a squad of skirmishers in the direction of the enemy's expected approach. By this time all were under arms and ready for orders. Finding them thus prepared, I called the officers together, and we held a miniature council of war. Every one present either suggested or strongly counselled an immediate retreat across the river to Hancock. This could have been quickly and safely accomplished by means of the ferry-boat then moored to the Virginia shore and lying at our feet.

I ordered the two companies into line immediately; but, instead of turning our backs to the expected enemy, we faced them. Then I briefly explained my intentions, which were to march out the Bath road, the only practicable approach to our camp for the attacking party, to deploy ourselves in a small woods bordering the road, and there prepare to give the expected comers a warm reception in a night surprise, when they should come within easy range of our muskets. Leaving an officer in charge of a small squad of men to guard the quarters, I gave the word to "forward march," and we silently departed to meet the foe at least half way. Arrived at the point intended, the men were noiselessly disposed of as stated, and remained on watch until morning, when we fell back quietly to Alpine.

This is the manner, dear reader, in which we retreated to "Maryland, my Maryland."

CHAPTER XVI.

IN April, 1864, our regiment received orders to prepare for active service, and we were shortly ordered to the Kanawha Valley, and assigned to the command of General George Crook.

About this time our worthy and respected colonel, M. McCaslin, who was not less than sixty-five years old; and who was by no means fit for the privations of a hard campaign, was taken sick, and compelled in consequence to remain behind. Four or five months later he resigned the command of the regiment, which then devolved upon the gallant Colonel Thomas N. Morris, the pride and beloved of his regiment, who was afterwards killed in action at Snicker's Ferry, Virginia, July 18, 1864, while bravely leading his regiment.

After remaining a short time at Camp Piatt, Kanawha Valley, we moved from there under orders for Gauley Bridge on the 30th of April, and on that date marched seventeen miles, encamping in the evening on the southeast side of Painter's creek, amidst a drenching rain. The prospect of lying down on the thoroughly water-soaked earth was not the most pleasant of contemplation, but it could not be avoided. Near to our encampment that night was a field of about ten acres, very nicely inclosed by a high board fence. In about five minutes after our arrival the whole of this fence disappeared in one loud crash. Almost the entire command assisted in its demolition. Soon there were many pleasant fires, and over their cheerful blaze coffee-pots, tin-cups, and frying-pans were doing good service. Although these fires were an undoubted actual necessity I did not enjoy their warmth very much; it was too painfully expensive to the poor farmer.

On May 2 we arrived at Fayettesville, Fayette county, West Virginia, where the three brigades of this division were united. The entire force then marched on the now celebrated "Dublin raid." Our encampments after marches for the five days preceding the engagement at Cloyd mountain (one of the most destructive battles of the war, for the time and number of troops engaged, and which occurred on May 9) were as follows:

May 4......Camp at Loup's Creek, Fayette county, W. Va.
" 5...... " " Mercer, Mercer county, W. Va.
" 6...... " " Princeton, Mercer county, W. Va.

May 7...... Camp at south of Rocky Gap, Bland county, W. Va.
"   8......   "   " Shannon, Giles county, W. Va.

At the last-named place, and when in near
proximity to the enemy, I was detailed as officer
of the guard to post and visit the night pickets.
It is needless to say that I got no sleep that night.
Early next morning, when I had drawn off my
pickets and was following in the rear of the entire
command, we heard the music of the contending
forces in our front. We thereupon quickened
our pace and soon came up with the main body,
which was now halted at the foot of Cloyd mountain, where it remained for some time, finding it
very difficult to advance farther, owing to the
sharpshooting of the enemy's skirmishers, who
lined the woods for a good distance at the base
of the mountain, and kept up a galling fire upon
our forces.

Several companies of our command had already
been sent forward to dislodge and drive back the
rebel skirmishers, but they offered a dogged resistance, and for quite a long time we remained
halted awaiting the result of the conflict between
the sharpshooters of both armies.

Becoming impatient at the delay, General Sick-
les, of the 3d Brigade, asked Colonel Morris for
a good company to do more effective work. The
intrepid Morris called on Company B. In answer
to this call, the column opened and we marched
from the rear to the extreme front, and while pass-

ing the 15th Regiment, our comrades of that command had many warm greetings and words of encouragement for us. "Bully for Company B; bully for Company B," was often repeated as we pressed forward.

When some distance in advance of the main body we were halted by the colonel, who placed me in charge of the entire skirmish line, and instructed me in what he wanted us to do. We then filed to the right of the road and into the woods, facing the enemy's skirmishers, who were occupying a high ground in our front. While engaged in deploying my men in a somewhat open space at the edge of the woods, the officer in command of Company E of our regiment, who had been sent forward earlier and who was now about one hundred yards in advance, lying down protected by a ledge of rocks, called out warningly to me that we were in a bad place. We soon discovered the correctness of his statement, in the whizzing of cold lead about our heads; one of which swift messengers passed through the whiskers of Corporal John Laurell, cutting a wide swath of hair therefrom and grazing his jaw, whereupon the little fellow coolly remarked: "I did not intend to shave until the war was over, but these pesky 'Johnnies' appear determined to do it for me sooner."

I now ordered, "Company, by the right to four yards, extend intervals." When the required

distance was effected, I commanded: "Skirmishers, halt;" and a second later: "To the front,
march."

And that line never halted until we brought on
a general engagement, by forcing back the enemy's
skirmishers, with increasing rapidity as we advanced.

The heroic conduct of Corporal James F. Ellis
on this occasion, as well as in every engagement
in which he participated until he was captured by
the enemy—and from which captivity I am sorry
to say he never returned—was, for cool, unostentatious, silent bravery, equal to anything done in
all our great army.

It is hardly fair, perhaps, to mention two or
three names in particular, belonging to a company in which there were so many of conspicuous
merit, but I cannot refrain from volunteering my
humble testimony to the sterling worth and
bravery of Sergeant Lawrence May, a German;
Corporal James F. Ellis, an American, and Corporal Thomas Brown, an Irish " Kerry game-bird,"
whose respective qualities and attainments—I say
it advisedly—would reflect no discredit on the two
stars of a major-general, although each was content to do his full duty in the humble position he
occupied. May was especially useful to me; he
had fought "mit Sigel" in the old country, and
was the best assistant I had in the company.

After the enemy's skirmishers were all driven

in on his main body, we rejoined our regiment, now supporting a battery of light artillery, which had just been brought into position within about two hundred yards of the enemy and right in his front. Had the gallant 9th West Virginia, under the lead of the intrepid Duval, delayed charging the enemy a few minutes longer, or until this magnificent little battery could have been trained on him, he would have had to get from behind his *cheval-de-frise* in short order; and the 9th would have been saved many noble lives in consequence.

The battle that ensued was one of the most destructive of the war, considering the time occupied and the numbers of the forces engaged. The general engagement did not last over forty minutes, and only about eight thousand men on both sides participated, but our losses included about 600 killed and wounded, and the enemy lost, perhaps, about 400. It has ever since been a wonder to me that the proportion of fallen combatants did not exceed one in eight of the whole number engaged.

The rebels had an advantage in the fight, being protected by breastworks constructed of logs and fence rails. The fight was continued at a most destructive range, as the space dividing the contending forces did not at any time exceed a distance of two hundred yards. This sort of desperate fighting could not last long, and so, when

"We had only a small detachment of cavalry, but they dashed after the rapidly retreating enemy."—Page 163.

the gallant 9th West Virginia charged the enemy, who fought with admirable bravery, they had to yield, and that, too, in a hurry, before the impetuous charge and wild yells of the " boys in blue."

We had only a small detachment of cavalry, but they dashed after the rapidly retreating enemy and pursued them vigorously until stopped by some of Morgan's men, who reinforced and covered the rebels' retreat to Dublin Depot. By the time our forces got into proper shape and moved forward in a solid line of battle, the enemy had made good his escape. When we reached Dublin Depot, we found very little of value there. It now being near night, we fell back from the railroad a short distance and encamped in close quarters on a large farm.

The following is the published report of State Adjutant-General E. P. Pierpont, upon the subject of the 9th's action in this engagement:

"The 9th Regiment from this point marched with General Crook's command to the Virginia and Tennessee Railroad, striking the road at Dublin, May 9th, meeting a strong rebel force under command of General Jenkins, at Cloyd Mountain, four miles from the railroad, and after a desperate battle defeated him; marched and took possession of the railroad at Dublin depot, same evening. This regiment, in this battle, carried the rebel breastworks with bayonets, killing and wounding about 600 rebels and capturing over

200 prisoners, and two pieces of artillery, losing 189 men, 45 of whom were killed instantly. The color-bearer, guard, and Colonel Duval, eleven in all, mounted the works a short distance in advance of the line, every one of whom was killed or wounded, except Colonel Duval. Twenty-one men were killed under and around the colors of this regiment, nine of the regiment and twelve rebels, the enemy having made a desperate effort to capture them.

"In this battle the rebel General Jenkins received his death wounds, and that too from the same men he had captured and so cruelly treated at Guyandotte, W. Va. *On the next day they marched to, and engaged the enemy at New River bridge, routing him and destroying the bridge.*"

The italics in the last paragraph are mine and are used because the claim made therein for this regiment by the adjutant is a misstatement which I think, in common justice, should be corrected. The truth regarding the burning of that bridge is as follows:

Early on the morning of the 10th, the day after the Cloyd Mountain battle, while encamped opposite to, and near Dublin depot, I was ordered with my company to march towards New River bridge. We moved out to Dublin depot, thence to the left, down the railroad, and in the direction of New River.

On our way down we noticed a farm-house some

seventy or eighty yards from the road. The house and its surroundings showed its owner to be in good circumstances. Having had no breakfast that morning, our boys could not resist throwing anxious and longing side glances at the comfortable dwelling. Presently a badly scared negro was noticed making a "shoot" from the direction of the house, and running for dear life away from us. I called to him to halt, and ordered him to come over to where we were. The poor fellow came as if going to the gallows, so reluctant and apparently fearful was he. I asked him a few hurried questions as we leisurely walked along, as to the whereabouts of the rebel army:

"Da'ar done gone to de bridge, sah," was his reply.

"Where is your master?"

"He done gone, too, sah, an' he tole me to stop an' mine de place, but I got scared, sah, an' I thought I'd go too," answered the darkey.

Some of the boys who had been "all ears" during this brief dialogue, and who were decidedly more interested in discovering a square meal than the whereabouts of the enemy, now spoke up, and question followed question in rapid succession until they had ascertained from the darkey that the house contained "Ham, flour, an' tings to eat an' a ten-gallon keg of apple brandy in de cella'."

We had three corporals to whom I would not wish to refuse anything in reason, and so, when

they waited upon me and united their importunities to be allowed to go to the house in question,
I consented after securing their promise to be expeditious.   They were so, and returned in good
condition to participate prominently in the good
work we had on hand later.

We were now joined by Captain James W.
Myers and his Company B, of the 11th West
Virginia; all the remainder of the troops being
out of sight and fully a mile in our rear.

Soon General Crook and staff were noticed
coming up behind us at a rapid canter.   We filed
to the right on high ground overlooking New
River bridge, the destruction of which was the
chief object of the expedition.   When within
plain view and near range of the two forts with
their frowning heavy artillery, erected by the
rebels to defend the bridge, the general called a
halt.   Riding up to where the skirmishing companies were, he gave me precise instructions regarding our next move.   He ordered me, in sub-
stance, to assume command of the two companies
and file to the right and left from the summit of
the hill.

The fact of the general's giving me command
of a senior officer showed a mark of confidence
that was highly gratifying, although I confess to
feeling somewhat diffident in exercising the power
granted me.   However, the results of our efforts
appeared to please the general very much.

While in the act of deploying skirmishers the enemy's batteries opened on us at a distance of about one thousand yards. The concentrated fire of the enemy seemed now to be chiefly directed to the general and his staff, who were occupying the most conspicuous spot on the battle-ground. The concussion of a cannon-ball very near the general had such a sickening effect upon him that he was forced to dismount for a moment from sheer weakness. As he did so, his horse, which had become frightened, broke away and dashed back to the rear, slamming the saddle-skirts and stirrup-straps in his rapid flight. At the sight of the riderless steed the rebels raised an exultant yell, believing that they had accomplished the death of our gallant leader; but we thank God they were mistaken, as was indubitably proven by that noble officer in many a hard-contested struggle afterwards.

In passing, I wish to say that in my opinion George Crook as a general, in all that that title implies, had few, if any, superiors.

Word was now sent to me to try to procure a canteen of fresh water for the general. I sent twice, in quick succession, for the water, but it was running the gauntlet of the enemy's sharpshooters to get it, and the two messengers returned empty-handed. Being an admitted good runner, especially when under the potent stimulus of fear, I took the canteen myself, and soon returned with some pure, clear, cold water for the general, and now our commander could be seen bold and erect in the extreme front of his entire command, a place not very generally occupied by com·manders.

About this time there opened the nicest piece of artillery practice I ever saw. I have seen, it is true, greater precision and more rapid movements in the exercises of the English Flying Artillery on such occasions as the anniversary of the battle of Waterloo, but the nature of the ground and the attendant circumstances made such a vast differ-ence that it would not be fair to draw comparisons. Here Captain McMullin, 1st Ohio Artillery, in immediate charge of four pieces, brought them into quick and effective action at a time when the enemy's artillery was directed towards him in a determined effort to spoil his movements.

The attention of our command was attracted by the execution of a splendid evolution by Mc-Mullin. On came the spirited horses at top speed, under the spur of their gallant riders, rattling and dashing right to the front, and while at this rapid pace they described a circle to the right, and on a declivity so steep and rough that we thought it marvellous that there were no upsettings or collisions. In a moment they unlimbered, and then commenced what we termed the artillery duel—there being none of our infantry engaged, except the two companies, B 11th and B 15th, in my charge, lying directly in front of our guns, and consequently between two fires, the enemy's and our own. Fortunately we occupied low ground, which fact no doubt was the cause of so many of our number getting out safely. A cannon-ball during the engagement struck deep in the ground right in front of me, stunning me severely for a few minutes, but causing no other injury. There was some of the most accurate and effective artillery practice now by Captain McMullin that occurred at any time or in any engagement during the late war. From where we lay we could see the execution done by our boys quite plainly, and almost every shot had a telling effect. McMullin silenced two of the enemy's guns in quick succession while we were driving back the gray skirmishers.

An aide of General Crook's now rode up to me, and said that whoever would burn the bridge should be remembered. I got some matches from one of Captain Myers' men, and moved for the bridge immediately. From where I approached the bridge it was necessary to climb some ten or twelve feet up one of the abutment piers to reach the bed of the bridge and get upon it. The structure was a long wooden one, covered with a tin roof. Once up, I broke off some dry pine from the side-works, and ignited the bundle in the west end of the bridge. The weather was dry and warm, with a fresh breeze blowing, and the fire caught quickly and spread rapidly, and soon the whole structure came down with a loud crash in almost as short a time as it has taken me to describe it.

The destruction of this bridge over New river, on the Virginia and Tennessee railroad, was now (May 10, 1864) an accomplished fact. It being a chief artery of supplies for the rebels, its destruction was important. It would take them some time to repair it were it not for the piers, which were still standing in almost perfect condition, affording rather too great facilities for reconstruction. Appreciating this latter fact, I went to the general, and asked if he had any material for blasting the piers. He replied that it was the intention to have taken some explosives for this purpose, but somehow they had been overlooked. He then tried some solid shot on the piers without effect. All of the troops were then ordered forward, and marched in the direction of Union, except my two companies, which, having had nothing to eat that day, were kindly permitted by the general to remain behind, after admonishing us to be careful and to make as little delay as possible.

In the "History of the War" I find that General Averell is accredited with the burning of this bridge, whereas, in truth, he was several miles behind at the time of its destruction. Averell has plenty of well-earned laurels, and does not, I am

sure, want those which belong to others. Errors
will occur, and some omissions in ostensibly
authentic reports that are hard to account for,
even on the assumption of ignorance of the facts.

From time to time since the close of the war I
have been told of several who claimed to have
burned this particular bridge. On one occasion
some years after the war, I heard a gallant major
entertain a party of friends with a graphic description of the achievement as performed by himself
and command. I was on friendly terms with the
major, and so sparing of his feelings that I remained silent on the subject. He did not know,
nor could he be expected to know, that I was the
only one in the entire command that put a foot on
that structure that day, for he was too far in the
rear to witness the manner or the instrument of
its destruction. Furthermore, the bridge could
not well be injured without first getting upon it,
as it was twelve or fourteen feet from the ground
upon which our forces approached.

In the adjutant-general's report of the 15th
West Virginia there is no mention made nor
notice taken of this and other matters of far more
importance with which that regiment was connected.

CHAPTER XVII.

The weather on this 10th of May was beautiful,
the air warm and pleasant, with a refreshing
breeze blowing steadily from the west. Our two
companies, although very hungry, felt compari-
tively happy; they had done their work well and
received therefor the hearty approbation of their
noble general with the unusual privilege of being
allowed to remain behind the entire command, in
order to enjoy one of the most sumptuous repasts
of all their experience in the war, and perhaps,
in some cases, out of it.

Our first move after the departure of the main
body was to secure some of the domestic fowl,
hams, flour, coffee and various other articles of
like nature, which the enemy had considerately
neglected to remove from his block-house, before
his hurried flight. Such rations as we now
chanced upon were, I must say from subsequent
experience, very scarce in the Confederacy, and it
required more than a gentle reproof, on my part,

to induce our poor fellows to leave anything eatable behind.

This was the first time, since the date of our enlistment, that I had allowed the boys to appropriate any of the "spoils of war," but in this case I told them to "go in" with a right good will; which advice they were not slow to act upon. Three of them at once proceeded to an enclosure surrounding the enemy's late quarters, in which there were a good many domestic fowl running about. At the sight of these the boys raised a shout and started after them; but were suddenly confronted by two officers of the 23d Ohio (ex-President Hayes' regiment), who had just emerged from the block-house and now with drawn revolvers proceeded to drive my men from the enclosure.

I was engaged elsewhere at this time, and did not witness their action, but was soon made aware of the trouble by my three boys, who came direct to me with their grievance. Immediately I took the same men back again to where the two brave heroes stood, revolvers in hand, ready to hold possession of the plunder within the enclosure, apparently at all hazards.

This dog-in-the-manger spirit on the part of the two officers created in me a curious impulse, hard to restrain. I therefore ordered our boys, in a sharp tone, to go and take anything and everything in and around the quarters.

Up to this time I had paid no attention to the

two strange men further than to observe what they proposed to do, until now, when they again threatened to shoot our men if they dare attempt to obey my recent order. Walking directly over to where they stood, I told them to put up their revolvers and reserve their ammunition for the enemy, who, I feared, had not received much of it.

The ranking officer demanded my name and authority for interfering with him in the discharge of his duty; saying that he had been ordered by General Crook to guard the place and that he would report my conduct to him.

"All right," said I, and I gave him my name and added: "Notwithstanding your assertion that you are here by the general's orders, I will now relieve you on my own responsibility, and abide by the result."

"I would be among the last," I concluded, "to disobey my superior's orders, but I am sorry to have to doubt your word, sir, in this case. An officer and a gentleman should be synonymous terms, but your action to-day would seem to prove you an exception to this general rule."

While this disagreeable interview was being held the boys were securing, with commendable expedition, all the good things obtainable. Calling Captain Myers, who participated with us in the late action, we insisted upon him and his men sharing with us in the coming feast, as there was plenty of food for both companies.

And now the lately belligerent gentlemen
from Ohio came meekly forward and asked to be
allowed to join us at our mess, but our boys unan-
imously decided that they had, by their selfish
action in the start, forfeited all rights to our consideration; and so the unfortunate fellows were
forced to content themselves with the thoughts
of what they had had for breakfast.

After several fires had been started to prepare
our much needed meal, we had time to look at
our surroundings. The ensemble might truly
be called picturesque. Nature had not withheld
her prolific hand in this beautiful garden spot in
Virginia. Her fairy touch had bedecked with
verdure the scene in every direction. The winding, limpid river flowed sparklingly in our front,
dividing the fertile plateau, where we were now
encamped, from the more level though less
elevated meadow land upon which the enemy
had made his first stand after crossing the river.
A little mill lay snugly ensconced beneath the
bridge; its wheel driven by water clear as crystal
and pure as snow. Into this cool, clear stream
our boys plunged and took a refreshing bath,
after which, when all was ready, we sat down on
the green sward and partook of a repast not
often found, nor ever more relished in army life.

We now also enjoyed with peculiar pleasure the
tangible results of the darky's information to us
early that morning, regarding the whereabouts

and contents of that ten-gallon keg. There soon were half a dozen canteens filled with "apple-jack," circulating eagerly among the men; the corporals before alluded to having secured a quantity of the liquor. The unselfish impulse of a soldier is generally to divide, so every boy in the two companies who wished to do so took a little of the brandy; but the majority of them were, I believe, strictly temperate. I was with the minority, however, and secured a small canteen-ful, which proved of agreeable service to more than myself afterwards.

What a blessing it is that we know not the day of our fall! Nineteen of the brave fellows, who were among the gayest of this gay party, lay dead within a year following to add to the vast pyramid of patriotic slain; but no gloomy thoughts marred their buoyant spirits now, whilst the "apple-jack" was sparkling in their wit and humor and making fun enough to enliven a regiment.

After a hearty meal we made haste to depart, and by double-quick marches soon caught up with the main body of our troops. A raw, drizzling rain now set in, adding much to the discomfort of our tramp.

On the 12th, after a trying and laborious march through mud and rain, we reached and commenced the ascent of Salt Pond mountain, in Giles county, Va. This was a dreary and painful operation for both men and horses, to be ploughing through that yellow mud, tough enough for brick-making. Many a noble animal, in going up this mountain, laid down, and his carcass soon became a prey for the carnivorous birds of the forest. Whosoever participated in this raid, unless he fared many times better than I did, can never forget the biting pangs of hunger he suffered. In the strict observance of the orders of the general prohibiting foraging, or straggling from the main column, I suffered keenly from want of something to eat, and if not for the timely kindness of Captain S. Porter, of Company K, our regiment, I could not possibly have continued the march. Whatever may have been the amount of rations issued occasionally to the enlisted men, there were none issued the officers.

Arrived at the summit of the mountain, just as night was falling, we halted on the borders of a small salt lake, a remarkable body of water several hundred feet above the level of the sea. When the teams came up, urged by the pinching necessity of my situation, I made an inspection of one of the wagons, and found a box containing "hard tack" snugly stowed away in one corner by the driver, who had appropriated them to his own use. He whined piteously when I confiscated his "few crackers." I divided the contents of the box impartially among the men of my company, all of whom were well-nigh famished.

Next morning, when the strong attractive force of the sun had lifted the hazy mist from the soggy earth, we beheld a magnificent scene. The lake, although small, as I have stated, was of vast depth. Its bosom was blue and placid, and its source, as far as I could learn, was unknown. Far away on the borders of Peter's creek, in Giles county, and Indian creek, in Monroe county, could be seen green and fertile valleys, dotted here and there with farm-houses and out-buildings, while grazing in the meadows numerous herds of cattle could be discerned, the whole bright picture being softened and enriched by a dark background of umbrageous forests and craggy mountains.

On the 13th we marched to and encamped at Peter's creek, Giles county. On the 14th we rested at Indian creek, Monroe county, and on the 15th we reached and encamped at the small village of Union, Monroe county, a place situated within easy distance of the famous White Sulphur Springs, of Greenbrier county. The surroundings here were very beautiful, the land fertile and the air pure and healthful.

Apprised of our approach, the people, who were generally well-to-do, had run their stock away into the woods, far from the track of the invader; but a few stray sheep remained, and these were run down by our hungry troops to furnish meat for themselves and comrades.

Owing to the shameful incapacity of Craig, the assistant quartermaster, who it was charged was full of whiskey most of the time, and who was eventually dismissed the service, the troops had very little else to accompany their mutton. A portion of the men were detailed to forage for flour, bread, etc. I was one among the officers sent out in charge of squads for this purpose. About the first place my party went to was the house of a Mrs. Heard, who kept a young ladies' seminary. The building was quite a respectable-looking one and showed outward signs of plenty. I did not know the nature of the establishment, however, until we had made an inspection of the premises.

Finding none but ladies within, and those of a type calculated to command the sympathy and protection of gentlemen, I felt deeply humiliated at our intrusive presence there on such unwelcome business. They gave us the keys to their provision stores, which were found to contain a scanty supply of hams, flour, potatoes, etc., scarcely more than sufficient for their immediate wants. Our hearts failed us at the sight of their helplessness and evident poverty, and we returned to camp without a pound of forage, notwithstanding the fact that we were all the time ravenously hungry.

It is needless to add that I was not sent to forage again.

About this time a long-legged, cadaverous-looking negro boy, named "Gabe," attached himself to me as a body-servant, without any solicitation on my part, and in fact against my expressed wishes. He begged to be allowed to remain with us in the hope that he might reach the "land of promise." My small allowance of rations was made still smaller by the division with ungainly "Gabe."

Leaving Union, our entire command, suffering severely from hunger, took up its line of march for Meadow Bluffs. The roads were badly cut up, making teaming extremely slow and difficult. The mules and horses hauling our supplies, of which we got but little, were fast playing out; in fact our line of march was well defined by many of their carcasses.

On the 16th we marched to and encamped at Alderson's Ferry, where we remained during the whole of the 17th.

On the 18th we marched to and encamped at Palestine, Greenbrier county, W. Va. The weather from the evening of the 10th to this date continued wet and raw, and when on the 19th we reached Meadow Bluffs we were in a pitiful plight and in a state of semi-starvation.

While resting here, waiting for rations, I suppose, but with no immediate likelihood of getting them, some of the officers of our regiment, with a few of the enlisted men, started out in quest of something to eat. Having some greenbacks, I thought I would go too, and try to procure, by purchase, something to keep the "wolf from the door." I selected one of the bravest and most active men of my company, Henry H. Bush, to accompany me.

We intended to form two of the party mentioned, but were delayed for some time in procuring "mounts" (a wretched old horse and a mule), so that when we finally got ready our comrades were quite a long distance in advance of us. We spurred up, however, and followed, but had not yet sighted them when we came to a watering trough on the side of the road about three-quarters of a mile from camp; here we let the animals drink. The road, at this point, was straight and level for a good distance, but closely bordered on both sides by dense woods.

We had scarcely gotten well under way after our short stop when nine fierce-looking guerillas, headed by two lieutenants, jumped out from the protecting trees and into the middle of the road, within four or five yards of our animals' heads.

"Halt," shouted the leader, sternly, and nine "Mississippi" rifles were leveled at the heads of Bush and myself.

We had not the ghost of a chance to escape; yet I instantly slid from the back of the mule I rode on the side opposite to the band, and using the mule's body as a temporary shield drew my revolver. Simultaneously with the click of my "six-shooter" five of the guerillas were beside me with their guns cocked and leveled. It was plainly death or surrender. We submitted to the latter alternative with poor grace, and, were the rôle to be played over again, we might prefer to accept even death itself than to undergo the terrible trials in store for us; that is, if the loathesome grave at Andersonville could render up my noble and youthful companion.

In March, 1877, twelve years and nine months after my capture, I was at Summerville, Nicholas county, West Virginia, on business already referred to in connection with the courier line. On the day of my arrival, while at dinner at the hotel of Mr. Fitzwater, where about twenty-five men sat down at table (court being then in session), a gentleman who sat at the head of the table politely helped me to the limb of a chicken. I thanked him for his kindness, remarking that we were not so regardful of the social amenities on the 19th of May, 1864.

"I do not recall your face, nor the happenings of the date you mention, sir," replied the gentleman.

"You are the Lieutenant Halstead," said I, "who, with your party, captured and made prisoners at Meadow Bluffs one of my men and myself on the date in question."

"Oh, yes, I recollect now. Well, gentlemen,

[addressing the party at dinner], in all my experience I have never met with such fool-hardy bravery as was shown by this man [nodding in my direction] at the time of his capture. He drew his revolver when entirely surrounded, to offer fight to nine men when they were not more than three or four yards from him,"—and in the same eulogistic strain he added much more than I can, with modesty, reproduce here.

Mr. Halstead was an ex-sheriff and was very popular in the county, and I thought it might have been to some extent his object to restrain me by eulogy from making any public remarks connected with the incidents of my capture that would seem to be derogatory to his reputation as a man, or affect his standing, politically, in the community.

But I was not to be flattered on one of the most humiliating episodes of my life; so I told the ex-guerilla, in the presence of the large company at dinner, that his action in taking from me on that occasion everything I had upon my person, including money, watch, chain, diary, revolver, and several trinkets—even including the tassle on my hat—was more befitting the character of a highwayman than that of an honorable enemy in a time of war.

"After reading it, you might have," I concluded, "at least restored to me my diary, which contained, as you must have known, nothing of interest or of value to your cause."

Mr. Peter Duffey, who had often in times gone by entertained me at his home, was now my guest at the dinner and sat on my right. He pinched me several times during the course of my remarks, as a warning to be less free in expressing my opinion of his friend and neighbor, Halstead.

CHAPTER XVIII.

WE were at once hurried to the inner depths
of the dense woods, where we found two other
prisoners, a Captain Tibbles and a sergeant, both
from an Ohio regiment, who were being guarded
by another squad of guerillas. These latter, with
the party accompanying us, now formed a circle,
and placed us on the inside. When darkness
fell they lighted a small fire, and by the aid of its
blaze kept a close watch upon us throughout the
night.

My mind was actively employed all night long
with thoughts of escape. By the light of the fire
I endeavored several times to catch the eye and
attention of my hapless fellow-captives, so as to
convey to them some sign for a simultaneous
dash for liberty. We could, I thought, by running in different directions, avoid the concentration of their fire, and some of our number might
succeed in escaping. This, at least, was my idea;
but all my efforts failed to elicit a response. The

poor fellows seemed to resign themselves to their fate, and were soon sound asleep. Could I get even one of our number to make a diversion with me I would run the gauntlet of their fire; and, with this determination, I pinched my man Bush, who lay beside me, so hard that I wonder to this day how it was that I did not arouse him.

Early next morning (May 20) we were marched to a farm-house several miles distant, and in a direction quite opposite to the camp of our troops. Here we were presented to a smart-looking, active young man, who was to all appearances chief of the band. He was heard to issue instructions to the others; and, I believe, he received all the captured booty for distribution among his men.

Captain Emick was, I learned, the commander of all the forces of this kind that were scattered around this wild and sparsely settled portion of the State. They called themselves "Independent Scouts." Whether or not this personage was Emick I cannot say. There were two good-looking young ladies, inmates of the house to which we were brought, who were apparently more rampant and hard-hearted than their male friends. They were very intimate with the young leader, who was, as I learned, an expert marks-man, and who carried a dangerous-looking long-range rifle. He told me he had drawn a bead with it on General Crook on the day previous, but that the latter's staff and a squad of men coming up immediately behind him caused the young man to forbear.

While resting a short time at this house I was permitted to write two notes, of only a few lines each—one to my wife and the other to General Crook, apprising them of my mishap. After reading the notes, my captors said they would drop them where our men could find them. They did so, and this concession on their part I attributed to the honorable and humane record found by them in perusing my diary, which, however, was never intended for their inspection.

From this farm-house we were marched hurriedly to the narrows of New river, over the same route lately taken by our army on their raid. The forces at this place were under the command of Lieutenant-Colonel Tavenner, a tall, gentlemanly young man, who was born and raised in Weston, Lewis county, West Virginia, and who, like many other brave young men of promise, gave up his life to a cause and theory which, though false and destructive, was yet sacred to him. This young man, as were also a portion of his men, was acquainted with me. He treated me with every courtesy consistent with his duty, and allowed me, on formal parole, the unrestrained freedom of his encampment. He even promised to try to procure my watch, and if possible have it sent to my wife at Weston: but he did not succeed and I never saw him afterwards, he being killed in action.

I was much impressed by the proffered kindness of one of his subordinate officers, a nephew of that estimable lady, Mrs. Minter Bailey, of Weston. He wanted me to accept one-half of the few bills the Confederacy had given him for money, and when I declined with thanks, his willing tears of generous impulse were visible. He told me his brother had been killed in the Confederate service a short time previously, and that he himself did not expect to live to return home. Another sad commentary on that unnatural war.

My treatment here was like an oasis in the desert of my many hard trials and keen sufferings afterwards, and was a potent cause of my entire forgiveness for the awful hardships endured, and to which feelings I gave a willing expression at the final surrender.

On the 22d we were marched back, now prisoners of war, through the village of Union, where, a week previously, we had triumphantly entered and encamped. As we passed the villagers ran out to see the Yankee prisoners, and were, as may be supposed, well pleased to see even so small a number of the hated enemy made captive. Among the many smiling and wondering spectators who were eagerly scrutinizing the unfortunate Yankees we noticed two or three ladies who did not appear to share in the general joy of our humiliation. These were the ladies to whom we had paid a domiciliary visit a week before, but had left untouched their scanty store of provisions. They now had kind words to say in our behalf, which soon caused a marked change in our favor by the people, who seemed to respect greatly these deserving ladies; consequently, we received better treatment than we had anticipated.

Some of the more prominent men of the town who were present engaged us in conversation, and among them Captain Tibbles, especially, found friends. It appears that signs of fraternal recognition passed between the latter and these gentlemen, after which we were conducted to a two-story building, an apartment in the rear of which I judged to be used as a Masonic lodge-room. While detained here the gentlemen in whose charge, we were engaged the captain in close conversation, with the result that our friend Tibbles never accompanied us to prison. As a matter of fact, this fortunate outcome of their consultation was simply an act of justice to the captain, who was in reality a non-combatant when taken prisoner, being unarmed and having no insignia of rank, his term having expired, and he was merely waiting for an opportunity to return to his home in Ohio. Nevertheless, he might have suffered a long imprisonment, as did his comrades, had he not luckily chanced to meet with "brothers," who reposed confidence in his straightforward statements.

Leaving Tibbles behind, who it is reasonable to suppose was well cared for, we were marched from Union to Christianburg. At Christianburg we found a man named Tapp in command of the rebel forces. He was an acting quartermaster also. We had known him at Weston, and did some favors for him before being aware of his proclivities, but he returned our past kindness with brutal cruelty now. He packed us into a dirty cell in the town jail without anything to eat, and on the next day we were put on the cars for Lynchburg, and right glad we were to get out of this tippling painter's clutches.

We remained at Lynchburg but a short time, when we were sent to Danville, thence to Macon, Georgia, where we arrived June 2, 1864. By the time we reached Macon our clothing was entirely divested of buttons, which, from time to time during our journey, we sold to our escort, who appeared to prize them highly. Had our supply of buttons held out we should not have suffered the pinchings of hunger so often.

CHAPTER XIX.

While side-tracked at Macon, we were jeered
and sneered at by the white population. The
white ladies, if indeed in this case they deserved
the title, were especially spiteful. It was the only
time that I ever saw the "black flag" shaken in
the face of a helpless enemy, and this too by fair
Southern belles who seemed to glory in taunting
the hungry and dejected "Yanks." The unworthy
action of these ladies was a great surprise to us,
and for the first time lessened the fair sex in our
estimation.

In marked contrast to the conduct of their
white sisters were the generous actions of the
poor colored women, who braved the displeasure
of their masters and mistresses, and perhaps
punishment, by rushing over to the stock-cars in
which we were confined, and giving us bread and
other food with many pitying and sympathetic
glances. At this place I took an affecting leave
of my dear boy, Henry H. Bush, never more to
see him in life. He was taken to that plague-

spot, that hell-hole of Southern infamy, Andersonville, where the deaths were 12,926, out of a total
of 49,485 prisoners. Poor Bush, soon after his
arrival, was dumped into a pit with the thousands
of other braves, without coffin or shroud. Together with a batch of other officers, I was marched
into the prison pen at Camp Oglethorpe.

When the gates of this prison opened for our
reception, we were met at the entrance, not by a
refined sympathy for suffering companionship
from brothers in misfortune, but by a motley, demoralized mob, who acted more like bedlamites
than sane men in rushing up to us and shrieking
in our astonished ears: "Fresh fish! fresh fish!"

The routine and hardships of prison life in the
South have been graphically described so often,
and are so generally known that I shall avoid a
detailed entrance upon so unpleasant a recital.
The fact of there being sixteen hundred officers
confined at one time in this prison was ample
evidence of the persistent and determined struggle of the Confederacy for the success of their
cause. Our prison was enclosed on all sides by
a high board fence, supported from the outside
of which was a platform that came nearly to the
top of the fence, and extended its entire length.
On this platform at regular intervals were posted
the rebel sentries, ready to shoot down any luckless "Yank" who chanced to put his foot beyond
the *dead-line*.

"We were met at the entrance by a motley demoralized mob."—Page 192.

At one end of the enclosure was a clear, running stream, wherein we used to wash ourselves and occasionally our garments, whenever we were fortunate enough to secure a little soap. These ablutions, however, were attended with great danger, as the dead-line, an imaginary one, lay very close to the bank of the stream. One day in June, as I was taking a bath in this brook, I heard the sharp report of a gun to my right. Looking up quickly, I saw a comrade officer fall mortally wounded by a heartless rebel sentry who was perched over and opposite to where the poor fellow lay. What rendered this wanton act the most cruel I ever witnessed, was that while our brother officer lay groaning in the excruciating agonies of his death wounds, his slayer kept mocking sardonically the words of the dying prisoner. It was positively asserted at the time, by several officers nearest the occurrence, that the stricken man had not approached within several feet of the dead-line. It was currently reported and generally believed by the imprisoned that deeds like this were usually rewarded by a furlough to the perpetrator.

Of kindred atrocities practised at Andersonville, comrade John W. Urban, in his book, "Battle Field and Prison Pen," tells the following terrible story, and my blood curdles when I think of poor Bush, and thousands as noble as he, who witnessed and suffered these barbarities. Mr. Urban says:

"The prisoners, who were seeking for water to quench their thirst, would crowd to the upper side of the prison, and as close to the dead-line as possible, so as to get the water a little more palatable. On one occasion I went to this place for water, when, finding a crowd at the upper end of the stream, which had gathered for the same purpose, I kept back for a few moments to let it thin out, when my attention was drawn to the nearest guard, who, with rifle in hand, was watching the men getting water. His countenance displayed about as much eagerness and expectation as that of the hunter when he discovers his game, and expects to have a good shot. I was watching the demon, and wondering whether it was really possible that he contemplated firing at the men who had gathered there for no other purpose than to get water, when I was horrified to see him deliberately raise his gun and fire into the crowd. I turned in the direction of the crowd, and screamed, 'Look out!' but too late, as the ball had sped on its deadly mission, and the soul of one more poor unfortunate had left its earthly abode, and one more murder was added to the already long list in Andersonville.

"One of the prisoners, in his eagerness to get clean water, had dipped through under the dead-line, when the guard, who had been watching and waiting for just such a chance to give him some kind of an excuse for his inhumanity, and an opportunity to display his bravery and chivalry, fired at him. The ball missed the mark it was intended for, but unfortunately hit one of the others who was in the act of stooping for water in the rear of the one shot at. The ball passed through his head, and the poor unfortunate soldier fell dead alongside of the stream. After the cruel shot was fired, the comrades of the dead prisoner fled, leaving his dead body lying where he fell. Almost riveted to the spot with horror and indignation, I could not run, but, turning around, I took a long look at the monster who could murder a fellow-being for so slight an offense, if an offense it could be called at all. He coolly proceeded to load his gun, turning himself, however, so that he could not see the dead body of his victim. A few prisoners gathered around me, and we commenced to express indignation at the cowardly act. One prisoner exclaimed, 'I want just one good look at him, and then one chance to meet him in this world, and I think I will know him if ever I do meet him.'

"After the guard had finished loading his gun, he noticed that we were watching him and expressing indignation; he raised his gun to his shoulder, and yelled out, 'Scatter thar, or I will blow some more of you over.' I do not think I ever in all my life felt quite as I did when I walked from that spot. I felt as if I would have to cry out, My God, how long must we endure this? I really believe that I would have been willing to give my life for one chance at him.

"A few of the friends of the dead soldier had gathered around his body, and I went up to see if he was really dead. Some of them were shedding tears, and all expressing the deepest horror at his sad taking off. His blood had formed a small rivulet that flowed into the foul stream, which of itself had been a terrible rebel executioner to a large number of our brave soldiers. We had become accustomed to seeing the sight of death in all of its horrible aspects; we saw men dying almost every hour: but this terrible death moved me more than anything I had yet witnessed. It appeared to me so sad that he had to suffer death for trying to get a drink of water. 'Vengeance is mine; I will repay, saith the Lord.' And who can doubt that the blood of the thousands of slain soldiers who were murdered in Southern prisons, has cried aloud to high Heaven—not unheard, but God has or will yet inflict punishment on these murderous oppressors.

"It was said, and never denied by the rebels, that a guard on post who shot a prisoner when trying to escape, or in the act of crossing the dead-line, got a thirty-day furlough as his reward. As the miscreant did not again appear on post, I suppose he was thus rewarded for his courageous act. It was a rule of the prison that no prisoners were allowed to cross the dead-line; but in the case of

"In his eagerness to get clean water, he had dipped through under the dead-line."—Page 196.

this poor soldier it could not have been taken for any violation of this order, as the prisoner had made no attempt to escape or cross it.

" It is but fair to state that not all of our guards were that kind of characters. Almost all of them were either boys or old men, who were unfit to be sent to the front. In justice to the old men, I will say that all the shooting was done by the boys, and at least a few of those old men denounced the shooting as an outrage. I remember hearing one who was on guard, and was speaking to some prisoners on the inside, say that 'God would not prosper a nation or people who used human beings as we were being treated.'"

The *menu*, or daily bill of fare, at the Hotel de Oglethorpe, for each guest, usually was made up as follows :

One pint of cornmeal (cobs or no cobs).

One gill of sorghum molasses.

Three ounces (or enough to grease a pan) of fat bacon, melting with the heat of the sun and alive with maggots.

There were few, if any, who fared worse than did the writer at Macon. A majority of the prisoners were provided with blankets, overcoats, or some other protection from the hot sun during the day and the chill dampness at night, but I was personally quite destitute of such comforts.

About the centre of the enclosure was a large frame building, which sheltered several hundred

of the more lucky prisoners.   Beneath this structure, which was raised about eighteen or twenty
inches from the ground, there might be seen during the heat of the day and the chill of the night,
three woe-begone, forlorn-looking creatures bur-
rowed like moles in a shallow hole scooped out
by their hands and finger nails.   These hapless
individuals were Lieutenants James P. Perley and
John McAdams and the writer.

Lieutenant Perley belonged to the Army of the
Cumberland, and although small in stature, he
was large in every gentlemanly attribute.   Every
feature of his intellectual face was stamped with
candor and truthfulness.   He was a printer in
New York when the call came for defenders of
the Union, to which summons he responded
promptly and like a man.   He appeared to be
the most philosophical of our squad in prison.
Calm, unexcitable and pleasantly patient under
many severe trials and keen sufferings, he was a
constant source of comfort to his companions in
misery.   He was an ardent admirer of General
W. S. Rosecrans, and on this point, as well as
many others, we were entirely agreed.

John McAdams, a Lieutenant of the 10th West
Virginia Volunteers, was a smart, shrewd little
officer, with a weather eye constantly on the lookout for number one.   He had two covers, one to
spread over himself and the other for a pillow;
while Perley and myself had nothing over us, and

contented ourselves with the soft side of a brick
apiece for pillows. In another particular I was
more unfortunate than most of my companions.
I had no vessel of any kind in which to put my
daily issue of molasses, nor any way to cook the
small amount of raw stuff we received in lieu of
food. A few days after entering the prison I hit
upon a plan for receiving my sorghum. I succeeded, after much patient effort with the poor
clay at my disposal, in shaping a little circular
mud-cup which I exposed to the heat of the sun,
and in this half dried daub I deposited my molasses.

After reveling for the first two weeks in this
Southern luxuriousness we received a welcome
visit from a Father Hamilton, one of the truest
and most sympathetic friends that ever showed
his face in Macon prison. He was untiring in his
unselfish efforts towards alleviating the sufferings
of the Union prisoners at Andersonville and
Macon. He told me of his several visits to Andersonville, and how he had begged and pleaded
with General Winder in behalf of the unfortunate
prisoners under his brutal and unfeeling charge,
and of his poor success, as " little impression could
be made," he said, " on the humane susceptibilities
of this Southern Nero."

Father Hamilton, seeing that I had no vessel
for food or drink, gave me ten dollars, with which
I bought a tin cup and a tin plate. The same

13

utensils would not cost over ten cents at the North. This noble young cleric, whom I would like to see again, deserves a much longer and more eulogistic mention for his many acts of goodness than I have space to give. He will, however, receive the full reward of Him who visits those in prison and clothed those who were destitute.

CHAPTER XX.

IN a crowd of large numbers there will always be found some notable characters. Among the sixteen hundred prisoners confined at Macon, Captain Hayes was no obscure one. He was a man of powerful build, with black curly hair, heavy black eyebrows and dark eyes. He was, in short, a fine-looking man, notwithstanding the unpleasant fact that his massive features had been disfigured by the small-pox. This man, who was as brave as he looked, had been prior to his capture a terror to the border guerillas who infested his State—Tennessee.

To relieve the dreary monotony of prison life the boys must have some fun, even at the expense of Chesterfieldian politeness; so, whenever a fresh batch of luckless prisoners were ushered in, it was the invariable custom to greet them with derisive shouts of, "fresh fish!" etc.; or when animated groups of prisoners were discovered, as was often the case, excitedly discussing the proba-bilities of exchange or some other interesting

(205)

topic, some irrepressible joker on the extreme
edge of the crowd, who, debarred from the pleasure of participating in the discussion or unable to
hear the speaker's words, would shout discord-
antly and repeatedly: "Louder, puddin' head!
louder, puddin' head!" much to the annoyance
of the embarrassed orator and to the intense
amusement of the crowd.

Now whenever Captain Hayes chanced to be
engaged in discussions of this sort, and the opprobrious epitaph "puddin' head" was shouted,
the cap invariably seemed to fit him, he having a
head which from its capacious dimensions was
supposed to approach nearest in size and shape
to the toothsome "rolly-polly" of our grand-
mothers. He would instantly retort with great
vehemence and clenched fist: "Who dares to call
me puddin' head? I'll rake the ground with him."

No immediate response would be made to this
irate challenge, but after a pause, "puddin' head"
would again be heard, first from the rear, then to
the right and to the left of him, to which points
the indignant captain would turn his head in
quick succession, at the same time rolling up his
sleeves, exposing his brawny arms, and wildly
challenging any man to apply that obnoxious term
to him; but of course no one within his reach was
foolhardy enough to do so. Still, from time to
time the objectionable phrase would be repeated,
and no matter to whom applied the captain per-

sistently took it to himself, much to the poor fellow's disgust and annoyance.   He denounced the practice as vulgar and demoralizing, and no doubt it would ordinarily be so considered ; but it appears that prison life as a rule had a tendency to blunt the finer qualities of our natures ; at least this was the case in Macon.

There was another character among our number whom we often heard at early dawn, when none but he and his zealous pupils were yet stirring from their still repose.   This individual was a Prussian, with the rank of captain in our army. As a swordsman, I presume it would have been difficult at that time to find his superior, he being a finished adept in that noble science.   He had provided his pupils with wooden swords, and in putting them through the manual exercises, he would name the different parts of the lesson to be practiced, as, "high tierce, high quart," etc.   His English was very imperfect in pronunciation, and there were very few besides his pupils who understood the big, burly Prussian's word of command, shouted in stentorian tones on the still air of morning, and mingled with the loud and vigorous clashing of his wooden weapons: "hiera thiers," hiera kart," etc.

Among those under his tuition there was none more painstaking than Captain John Rourke, of Mulligan's famous battery.   Rourke was gentle and good, calm and easy-spoken, a fine, portly style of officer, whose unostentatious bravery no one ever questioned. He was himself a swordsman of considerable proficiency, but he wanted to mount the ladder high in everything he undertook and he generally succeeded.

His education, too, had been by no means neglected, and his companionship in this dreary prison proved highly edifying. We were very much in each other's company, especially in the latter period of our term of imprisonment, when we were devising plans of escape together. He got away a day or so before I did, but was captured and recaptured several times before effecting his final escape. Rourke was one among the many of my companions in misery whom I had hoped to see once again, but from information received only a few days previous to this writing, I am sorry to say that pleasure in his case is forever denied me.

Another event transpired while at Macon, never to be forgotten by the captives participating while memory and patriotism co-exist. The celebration of the 4th of July, 1864, was one of the most spirited and enthusiastic that I ever witnessed. When the glorious morn was ushered in, reminding every true American of the patriotic duty to the cause of liberty that the day signalized, numerous groups of the boys in ragged blue could be seen with smiles of holiday happiness discussing the programme of the day. It was decided to hold a meeting in the large plank building, about one hundred feet long, and extending through the centre of our enclosure.

When all was ready the large doors at each end were thrown open, so that the assembled prisoners could see and hear the proceedings. Major Thorp was the chief orator of the day, and right well did he acquit himself. As the oration proceeded, Lieutenant Smith, a naval officer, could be seen near the speaker's platform climbing to a cross-beam, about ten or twelve feet from the floor, and which reached from side to side of the building. When up he got astride of the beam, performing the feat in a manner peculiar to the agile jolly tar. This happy-looking son of Neptune now became the centre of attraction. He was youthful, healthy, and ruddy, an unusual combination for a caged bird, and he wore, in marked contrast to his ragged comrades, a brand-new uniform, buttons and all complete. In each of those buttons, with true Yankee ingenuity, were snugly deposited several gold-dollar pieces. This had been done by removing with the help of a knife-blade the outward shell of the rounded button, and, after inserting the money, carefully replacing it again.

Now when the speaker to the great edification of his appreciative audience was swelling with his inspiriting subject, Lieutenant Smith, upon his perch on the cross-beam, slipped his hand into his patriot-pulsing bosom, and drew forth from its hiding-place a bright new flag, the talismanic "Star-Spangled Banner." The applause, as the flag was unfurled to the gaze of its admirers was deafening, and reached far and near, lending animation to all witnessing the unexpected event. When these ringing shouts reached the ears of the Confederates they came cautiously in, but did not then prohibit the proceedings as all expected, contenting themselves with requesting that there should be less noise made.

The noise, however, continued, and soon there could be noticed a commotion among the guards surrounding the stockade. Again the captain of the prison came in, and this time ordered the speaking to cease, threatening to open fire upon us with his battery, which was even then being placed in a menacing position, if we did not comply. So we had to submit, but Tom Lee, a lieutenant-colonel of a New York regiment, who was speaking at the time of the interruption, kept up a dumb speech, embellishing it with many funny gesticulations, which caused great merriment.

A remarkable and pleasing feature of the celebration was the singing of "The Star-Spangled Banner" by a Captain Camerhorn. I have never been so much impressed with the sublimity of a song as on this occasion, and I question if that beautiful production of Francis Scott Key was ever more effectively rendered.

It was known that General Sherman was in Atlanta, Georgia, at this time, and the rebels were fearful that we might possibly make a break for liberty, or that Sherman might attempt a sudden dash for our relief.   In consequence of these contingencies the Confederates began preparing to send 600 of the prisoners to Charleston, South Carolina.   When this intention on their part became known in prison a secret organization sprang up among the officers likely to be transferred, of which number I was one.

The object of this organization was to arrange for a simultaneous and general break for freedom at Pocotaligo Bridge, South Carolina, on the road to Charleston, by first capturing the guards escorting us and taking their arms, and then exchanging uniforms with them.   By these means we proposed to deceive by appearances and surprise by our strength a company of rebels who were the only obstacles then in our path to the United States fleet at Hilton Head.

The officers selected by us to give the signal at the proper time for this hazardous move were a Lieutenant-Colonel Sherman and a Captain Kiblehan.   The signal was to be made in the forward end of the train by displaying a white handkerchief.   When the time came for it to be given there was a stern and intense anxiety pervading the whole crowd of determined men, as, in breathless suspense, they strained their eyes towards the front cars for the wished-for signal. But it never came. And now complete disgust and unutterable contempt for the officers who failed in the duty delegated to them was the general feeling among the much-disappointed prisoners, who ever afterwards satirically designated their cowardly leaders " The Heroes of Pocotaligo."

Their excuse was that the lieutenant in charge of our escort was too smart for them, and had placed a few of his men on the tender of the engine, prepared to fire on the men who should give the signal which, either from information received or natural foresight, he anticipated might be given.

A few of the officers, seeing that the time for giving the signal had passed, attempted to try it " on their own hooks," and at opportune moments quietly dropped off the train, every one of whom, however, was returned to prison within a week or so following the escape, looking a hundred per cent. more miserable than when the experimental jump was made. Among the brave but unsuccessful gentlemen who made this attempt was Colonel Henry M. Hoyt, afterwards governor of Pennsylvania.

CHAPTER XXI.

WE arrived at Charleston, S. C., on July 28,
1864, and were put into a small jail-yard where
we were densely crowded, and exposed to the
scorching heat of the sun, without shelter of
any kind. After about three weeks of this trying
experience, all the officers then imprisoned, six
hundred in number, accepted a parole offered them
in order to secure shelter and better quarters, but
for paroled men our privileges were very limited
indeed.

One sweltering day in August, when sheer
despondency was asserting itself in spite of all
my efforts to shake it off, I noticed three or four
stalwart-looking fellows, in citizen's gray, somewhat the worse for wear, coming down the steps
of the jail, to take their usual daily airing, or
promenade, in the yard where the Union officers
were promiscuously scattered about.

With unprejudiced smiles on their broad, good-
natured faces, they came right over to where I

(213)

stood. The largest of them, glancing down at my feet, asked inquiringly if I would sell my boot-legs. These latter were very long, coming away above the knees, and were quite the thing on a muddy march, but were now, in my weakened and debilitated condition, a positive encumbrance. I thought at first that the fellow was cracking a joke on the boots because of their length, but he soon assured me that he was in earnest, and would give me anything in reason for them. Seeing this, I told him that if he really wanted them he might have them for nothing; and suiting the action to the word, I took a knife and severed the legs from the foot at the ankle and handed them to him.

This act of generosity seemed to surprise him very greatly and he respectfully inquired my name. When I had told him, he said:

"When I was quite a little chap, living in Mannington, W. Va., I drove a team of horses for a railroad contractor, whose kindness to me I shall never forget. His name was Tom Egan."

"What is your name?" I asked.

"Foley," was his answer.

"The man you speak of," said I, "is my brother; and he has several times spoken to me of you."

With considerable emotion and expressions full of pleasure and gratitude the big fellow grasped me by the hand with as much cordiality and feeling as though he had met a near and

dear relative. After a few minutes' further conversation he and his friends bade me good-day
and bore away their prize to their tolerably comfortable quarters in the jail. In about three-
quarters of an hour after leaving me Foley came
back and invited me to accompany him up to his
cell, which I did.

There he introduced me to his friends, six in
number, each of whom tried to excel his comrade
in kind attentions to me. At their earnest invitation, I sat down to table with them and enjoyed
a hearty meal of soup, meat, bread, etc., in addition to the usual prison fare. These unexpected luxuries were provided for the little party
by the handiwork of Foley, who, being something,
of a cobbler, made shoes from such material as
my boot-legs and sold them to willing customers
in the city, through the mediation of a kindly old
lady who took out and disposed of the shoes,
and returned with their worth in provisions.

At the time of my meeting them, these seven
brave young fellows had just finished serving the
Confederacy three years, or the exact term of
their enlistment. They belonged to the 1st South
Carolina Heavy Artillery, commanded by the
son of the exiled Irish patriot, John Mitchell, and
most of the men were Irish also. Their young
commander, whom they much revered, had been
killed in action.

When their terms of enlistment expired, upon

refusing to serve Jeff. Davis longer, they were thrown into prison, as a recompense for their past gallant services. The young fellows were all single and had no fixed homes. The South had no just claim upon them, as none of their number had ever been naturalized, and consequently, in the eyes of the law, they were still British subjects. Happening to be employed in the South when the war broke out, they were forced, or carried with the current, into the rebel ranks, where they served faithfully during the period named; but now, in view of their ungrateful and unlawful treatment, they were disgusted with their past acts and present surroundings, and were anxious to obtain their freedom and leave the country.

Learning that there was then a British consul in Charleston I drafted a petition for them to that dignitary, setting forth their grievances and asking his protection. I am glad to be able to state that this document had the desired effect, and the young men were soon released. While they remained in jail my good friend and comrade, Captain Whiteside (with whom I subsequently escaped from prison at Columbia), and myself frequently partook of their kind hospitality.

After the term of our paroles had expired, we were transferred and assigned to quarters in two large public buildings, the Roper and the Marine hospitals. In the latter building, Lieutenant

McAdams and myself were room-mates, and being the last in, had to take the poorest apartment in the house—a room of limited dimensions and located in the basement.   It took us a good while to clean this room out so as to fit it for occupancy.   We wheeled out half a dozen barrow-loads of *débris*, which had been caused by a great shell coming down through the ceiling, the building being directly in line and range of our siege-guns on James' Island.   I bunked, or lay, on the floor directly beneath the hole made by this shell.

After being here a week I made a closer inspection of the breach in the ceiling, and found on the extreme edge of the aperture a piece of shell of at least 150 pounds weight, which a slight jar would have caused to come crashing down upon my devoted head.

While here, McAdams found a long, narrow account book, the larger portion of its leaves being blank.   This he hacked in two with an old saw, keeping one-half and giving me the other. In this book, which I still retain, I kept my diary during my flight for freedom.

During the time we were imprisoned in the Marine Hospital, several shells from our guns, which were playing havoc generally on the rebellious city, struck close around us, doing much damage and creating consternation among the prisoners.   Late at night, when not a comrade was astir around me, I have often and alone, from the highest balcony of this large building, watched the awe-inspiring practice of our siege guns upon the city.

Notwithstanding the great danger, I thought this the most pleasing and sublime spectacle I ever witnessed. The calm stillness of the night is broken by a faint distant sound. I look in that direction, and, a few seconds later, a meteor-like object ascends from the horizon, mounts higher and higher, with its bright tail of flame, and describing a curve of over six miles chord, bursts like a torpedo, scattering a shower of fire in all directions.

The gun discharging these terrific missiles was the "Swamp Angel," a seven hundred pounder, and it kept up the fire with great regularity and precision, dealing destruction on the doomed city. I have seen Charleston ablaze in several places at once from these shots, and it was only by the extraordinary efforts of the "fire brigade" that the damage was limited and the scope of the flames circumscribed.

Apropos of these fires, I wish to record an occurrence which simple justice and common gratitude have thus far failed to notice. When man fails to bear testimony to the sweet administrations of kindness and charity, especially when bestowed upon him in his dire necessity by noble woman, then I must say he bears no affinity to such a

grand type of manhood as the beautiful poet,
Schiller, who says:

> " Honored be Woman who beams on the sight,
> Graceful and fair, like a being of light;
> Who scatters around her, wherever she strays,
> Roses of bliss on our thorn-covered ways,
> Like roses of Paradise, which spring from above,
> To be gathered and twined in a garland of love."

The convent where the Sisters of Charity were
teaching school, the revenue from which was their
sole source of income, was one morning entirely
destroyed by fire, the result of a shot from one
of our guns. And this was the time—when the
embers of their ruined home were not yet cool—
we find them ministering to the wants of the Union
soldiers in prison, giving to them money, clothing,
under-wear, tobacco, lemons, oranges, and other
fruits; bearing out their letters and performing a
thousand other acts of kindness and charity.
They never once complained of their own loss,
although it must have been a bitter one; nor either
by word or action did they give preference to
Catholic over any other; in fact, I never heard
them during the whole time of my confinement
there touch upon the subject of religion, and I honored their sublime impartiality. Their gentle
meekness and refinement won the respect of all,
and the influence for good of their angelic visita-
tions upon the officers who for months had not
seen the face of woman, was incalculable and
could not fail to leave a lasting impression.

14

In the latter part of September the yellow fever broke out in Charleston, and large numbers died of it, among them being Captain Sheldon, the commandant of the prison. We thought it remarkable and fortunate that but very few of our men took the dread disease.

Our Government, finding that we were placed under the fire of our guns, retaliated in like fashion with some of their rebel prisoners. This, together with the prevalency of the yellow fever, influenced our keepers to remove us to Columbia, the capital of the State; and thither we were accordingly shipped on October 5th, and on the day following we reached that destination.

On refusing to take a parole we were put in an open field where there was no shelter but a few stunted pine trees, but it will ever be remembered by all who repined there, as "Camp Sorghum." We were driven into this field on the 7th of October, and the humiliation and punishment we had to suffer on this occasion will never be forgotten. It was at the hands, too, of stripling young rebels, sons of aristocratic citizens, who were the cadets of a military academy in Columbia. They were dressed in new gray and formed the rear guard marching us out to prison. Permitted for the first time to have guns and bayonets in their hands, they thought it a safe and convenient opportunity to practice their innate brutality upon the unarmed and wretched Yankees, and they used their bayonets freely in prodding up those unfortunate ones of our comrades who chanced to be nearest them. O, it was sickening to see and hear the poor fellows wince, and cry out under the punishment of the cold steel in the hands of such young spawn. If all our men had seen it, and felt as I did on the subject, these young cubs would have been wiped out regardless of consequences.

On October 25th, Lieutenant Young, of the 4th Pennsylvania Cavalry, was shot dead by one of the rebel guards. The lieutenant, when shot, was fifty yards away from any dead-line, and was quietly sitting at his little fire chatting with his comrades.

CHAPTER XXII.

Escape from Prison—Meeting with Officers—Comparing Routes
—Lieutenant Murphy's Obstinacy—What it Cost Him.

On Friday, November 4, 1864, Captain John
C. Whiteside, of Wyoming, New York, and myself, the former after enjoying the sweets of prison
life for fourteen months and the latter for six
months, took into our heads to encounter the
awful privations and dangers of a journey of
nearly 400 miles, in a direct line from Columbia,
South Carolina, to Knoxville, Tennessee. The
opportunity presented itself to us that day, while
cutting and gathering firewood for the use of our
squad in prison, and it was not a very difficult
thing to do owing to the unenclosed condition of
our prison.

This flight for sweet liberty's sake (ever memorable to me) occupied thirty-one days and nights
in its accomplishment. I should think that on
this trip we travelled on an average twenty miles
each night, making the distance traversed nearer
to 600 than to 400 miles. But, travelling in an
unknown country, without compass or guide,
often making wide detours to escape discovery
by the enemy, subsisting chiefly on raw corn, with

very light clothing and a very heavy load of vermin, it must be admitted that we kept to the
general direction of our goal fairly well, and made
as fast time as could reasonably be expected
under such trying circumstances.

On the same afternoon that we got out of
prison several other officers, perhaps fifty in all,
escaped also. Of this number only a very few
succeeded in getting through. The lucky ones
whom I met in my lonely pilgrimage to the shrine
of freedom were : William Nelson, Lieutenant
13th United States Infantry; V. K. Hart, Captain
19th United States Infantry; Thomas B. De-
Weese, Lieutenant 2d United States Cavalry;
Charles S. Kimball, Captain 1st Massachusetts
Infantry; O. W. Dimick, Lieutenant 11th New
Hampshire Infantry; and Charles G. Davis,
Lieutenant 1st Massachusetts Cavalry.

Comrade Whiteside and myself lay down between two logs in a skirt of woods in view of the
prison-camp until the veil of night hid us from our
numerous enemies. While lying thus concealed
we saw approaching us three escaping officers—
Lieutenants Murphy, Hale, and Halpin. Although very near to where we were lying, they
would have passed without observing us had we
not called to them. They came to where we
were, and we all laid down together.

We then consulted as to the best plan of escape
and the most practicable route to take. I sub-

mitted a plan which had been well matured and carefully mapped out while yet in prison. It was approved of by all present except Lieutenant Murphy, who had a plan of his own, and dogmatically persisted in his comrades adopting it. He proposed that we take a straight course from where we were, and cross over to the left bank of the Saluda river. To this I objected, as there was, in my opinion, a village on that side of the river at this point. This I believed from having heard early that evening the voices of many people there, as though of factory hands just quitting their work.

My plan was to take up the right bank of the river, avoid all enclosures or resorts, and follow a route which I had drawn from a map before escaping.

It was now dark, and the night was calm and beautiful. We started. Murphy, who apparently would rule or ruin, spurted to the front and took his own direction, Hale and Halpin close behind him, with Whiteside and myself reluctantly following. I remonstrated vainly when, a short time after starting, I saw them crossing a fence and getting into an enclosure.

We had not proceeded far within this field when pandemonium was raised about us. The prison-camp was completely aroused. Between fifty and sixty prisoners had escaped. Men shouted, lights flashed, guns were fired, dogs

"Men shouted, lights flashed, guns were fired, dogs howled, and the night was made hideous by discordant noises."—Page 224.

howled, and the night—a few minutes before so calm—was made hideous by discordant noises. This was a nerve-testing time for us. Murphy kept on his headlong course, the rest following. Presently several dogs came charging towards us, with a yelling crowd close behind encouraging them.

Instantly I filed to the left, and for the next twenty minutes ran at the top of my speed in a direction opposite to that taken by the hounds. No luckless pioneer pursued by bloodthirsty savages ever more confidingly appealed to the endurance of his favorite mustang than did I now to my faithful shanks, whose speed I had often tested in years gone by on the bright banks of the river Shannon.

The faithful Whiteside followed me closely and displayed marked running qualities, but Murphy and his companions rushed blindly and excitedly into the arms of their enemies, and were taken back to "Camp Sorghum," to ruminate at their leisure on the self-willed mistake of their leader.

At last, when about exhausted, we reached a laurel thicket, into which we plunged, only to run plump against two men. This was a trying moment. Each party thought the other to be enemies, and prepared for a struggle, but mutual recognitions soon dispelled all fears. The two men were runaways also, and were Lieutenants Wynkoop and Bowles, the latter a Pennsylvania cavalryman. We were glad of their company, and remained together all night, scrambling along, and often falling in our rough zigzag course up the right bank of the Saluda river.   Our immediate necessity was to get beyond the sphere of the despised " Camp Sorghum," for those there in charge were using desperate measures to recapture the escaped and scattered prisoners. Spurred on by this idea, we did our best at getting away.

CHAPTER XXIII.

From my well-worn diary, I extract the following entries:

Saturday, November 5th.—About noon we emerge from the woods well torn with brush and briars, and strike a lonely by-road. We have fasted all day, but are cheerful withal. One of our party has a small sack of rice, but no way of cooking it yet. The day is beautiful and mild, with a warm sun whose most welcome rays partially answered our chilled frames in lieu of fuel, in which luxury our caution will not permit us to indulge.

Night again, and on a brisk march beset with difficulties. We meet with four more runaway officers at eleven o'clock, but permit them to go on ahead, and change our own direction; in fact, we take the back track for about two miles, and in doing so run across a negro. We have a friendly chat with him, but get little information from him. The night is bright and calm and is one not soon to be forgotten by our little party. The

(227)

disagreeable music of deep-baying hounds is heard on every side of us. The whole country appears to be aroused and in pursuit of the escaped Yankees. With renewed efforts, inspired by our besetting dangers, we continue our rapid flight, keeping as far from the noise of the hounds as possible, until weary and hungry we take a rest, hope and will-power alone combating exhaustion. Our only subsistence so far has been a very limited supply of parched corn. We have carried a pumpkin for some time, but for want of a fire cannot cook it.

One precaution which we now adopt is to seek, when day approaches, the retirement of the densest woods and lowest canyons, and there await the return of night before proceeding.

Sunday, November 6th.—As if in keeping with the Sabbath, tranquillity reigns all around us. We enjoy a day of quiet repose and much needed sleep, after which, at eight o'clock P. M., we start briskly forward and make good progress, albeit on empty stomachs. Shortly after starting, and while on a level road, poor Wynkoop sprained his ankle. With profound regret we had to leave him behind to his sad fate. We stopped with him for some time, but he was very unselfish and told us to push ahead and do the best we could for ourselves. We pushed strongly on for several hours, until we came to a river, where we rested after a good night's march.

Monday, November 7th. — Fortunately the weather continues very mild, but we are much fatigued and very hungry this morning. We sleep until noon, after which we descend to the river and take a refreshing bath. We are in a pitiful plight, not a morsel to eat nor a prospect of securing one. We are but three in number now and are all feeling very much dejected. We commence a search for something to appease our hunger and finally espy a small flock of sheep. They are rather wild, but after the exercise of much caution we succeed in getting pretty close to them, when I stood up and let fly a club with all my might at the foremost one, but missed him and frightened the flock so badly that we could not get near them afterwards. This failure on my part did not tend to revive our drooping spirits.

We could see from where we stood a farm-house, about a half mile distant, and started in that direction in the hope of attracting the attention of some of the negroes, and trying if we could get something to eat from them. I was in favor of waiting for the dusk of evening before approaching the house, but Lieutenant Bowles, who was a bold fellow, said he would try it then ; so, urged by the necessity, we permitted him to go. We watched him closely and could see him getting nearer and nearer to the house. We feared he was getting imprudently too near while it was yet so bright. When about a hundred yards from the house he disappeared from view, and then ensued a period of the most anxious suspense. The hope of relief, and the dread of his fate, caused the minutes to appear like hours to us. We waited impatiently a full hour for his return, but in vain. That was the last we ever saw or heard of poor Bowles.

Now Whiteside was my sole companion, and we resumed our dreary march very much depressed in spirits at the loss of our comrade, being totally ignorant and painfully fearful of what his fate might be. I trust he lived to see home, but I have never heard from him since.

One after another of our little party having dropped off, we were now not only staring gaunt hunger in the face, but by reason of our loneliness we were more keenly feeling its pangs. I endeavored to rally the drooping spirits of Whiteside, cheering him as best I could, although I really felt little better than did he, but, like the boy passing the graveyard at midnight who kept whistling a gay air in order to keep his oozing courage up and rising hair down, I assumed a forced cheerfulness of manner whenever I found my companion growing despondent. His faith and fortitude were however superior to mine as a rule, and it was only on very rare occasions that he seemed to lose courage, and then only for a short time.

I must pause here in my narrative to remark that I consider my faithful friend and comrade, Captain John C. Whiteside, to be as noble a specimen of humanity as it has ever been my good fortune to meet. He was the personal embodiment of "charity, fraternity and loyalty," and his morality was of a marked and high standard. "No better than he breathes the air on land or sea."

He was, as I have stated before, from Wyoming, New York. I have forgotten his company and regiment. He had made the ministry his calling before the war, and was the most earnest and effective preacher we had among the sixteen hundred officers then in prison. He was, I believe, a Methodist. Several times while planning our escape, I had contemplated the pleasure I might have if so fortunate as to escape in his company. Though we differed in matters of religion, we had no different ideas of friendship; and I can candidly say that I had no brother for whom I would go farther, or do more, than for the generous Whiteside. I am also sure that I had no brother who could have been truer to me than was he. When I was barefooted in prison he gave me a pair of shoes, the pair he was then wearing being no better than the ones he gave me. They served me well in my long and weary march to our lines.

CHAPTER XXIV.

To return to our sad situation:

In the dusk of that still evening, November 7, 1864, we knelt down and silently and earnestly addressed our prayers to the only source from which we could reasonably expect any relief. How fervently and beseechingly we cast our eyes heavenward! Not a roof or leaf to obstruct our gaze. The blue vault of heaven was the dome of our house of worship. The autumn leaves on Mother Earth were the cushions of our pew. The occasional whistle of a night bird our only choir.

I have never before or since repeated the Lord's prayer so fervently as I did on this occasion, especially that part relating to "our daily bread." Our heartfelt supplications had an inspiriting effect, and we arose with hopes revived and a stronger faith in the providence of God. It now became Whiteside's turn to cheer me up, and he repeated a couplet of sacred poetry:

> "He who fed thee last will feed thee still;
> Be calm, and sink unto His will."

(232)

"Captain," said he, "God has promised to with-
hold no good gift from those who walk uprightly;
He who heard the cry of the young raven will
surely not be deaf to the cry of His needy children."

Under the influence of these and other salutary
lessons we scrambled along, hugging the right
bank of the Saluda river. Our scanty clothing
was badly torn, and our hands and legs were
sorely lacerated by briars encountered while
pursuing our zigzag course, which we did in
almost unbroken silence.

Our destination lay in a northwesterly direction,
and as the river at this point took a northerly
course, we quitted its meanderings and stood out
direct on our proposed line, and had rather rough
travelling for about an hour, when, upon ascending a slight elevation, we suddenly and unexpectedly stood on the banks of a noble river, and
the clear, mellow light of the moon enabled us to
take a satisfactory view of the scene that now
presented itself to our astonished gaze. The
river at this point took a somewhat semicircular
shape, with quite an open space, clothed in rich
verdure, directly in our front, and with a gentle
descent on all sides to the water's edge. The
opposite bank was thickly bordered with stately
pines, towering high and majestic, like mighty
sentinels guarding the stream. The river here
was comparatively broad and smooth, the night

calm and beautiful, and the moon and stars reflected their tranquil beauty in the silent waters before us. I feel inadequate to the task of properly describing this sublime picture; but we felt all its peaceful solitude and solemn grandeur, and were forced to exclaim, in the language of David: "The heavens declare the glory of God; and the firmament showeth His handiwork."

We might have tarried longer at this secluded nook and enjoyed its beauty more, but men who had been fasting four days and nights were scarcely in a mood to appreciate the beauties of nature. So we continued to push ahead as best we could, in hopes of finding something to appease our well-nigh intolerable hunger. Buoyed up somewhat by the reflection that every step forward was one nearer to liberty, we dragged our weary way for about an hour, when we came to what looked like a potato-patch. We halted, and, kneeling down, commenced scratching in the hard and stony ground until we were rewarded by finding a few potatoes. We succeeded in cutting and bruising our hands pretty severely in this operation, but we did not grumble, feeling too thankful for the lucky and much-needed discovery. Had we travelled during the daytime—which we dared not do—we could have seen better where to pick up something to eat.

Having the potatoes, we ventured to prepare a small fire immediately, and roasted a few of them in the coals. Whiteside, with great foresight, had supplied himself with a quantity of matches and salt before escaping, without which all our efforts for liberty, for home, and later to join the boys at the front, would have proven futile, as the reader will readily understand.

Feeling very thirsty after eating, we hunted around for the means to satisfy our longing, and Captain Whiteside soon discovered a small spring of the most delicious water that, as we then thought, we had ever tasted. He had been tapping around with his stick, when he struck a rock, beneath which lay the sparkling fluid. He proved himself a veritable Moses on this occasion. I have often wondered if the rod Moses used for a similar purpose was a hickory one, like that of my friend Whiteside. We each took a deep and refreshing draught. We had not had time to remove from the spring when we discovered by the barking of watch-dogs that we were within a short distance of a dwelling-house. We thereupon moved from the spot with considerable alacrity. This place we named in our memorandums "Aqua Vitæ."

We travelled at a brisk pace from this time on without any incident worthy of note occurring until daylight appeared, admonishing us of the necessity of seeking a hiding-place. As will appear in the next chapter, we properly designated this place "Gooseville."

15

CHAPTER XXV.

Gooseville, Tuesday, November 8, 1864.

This place shall be ever famed in our annals for its hospitalities. Paul was not more rejoiced when he saw the "three taverns" than were we when we discovered this retreat. Lying on the autumn leaves with our martial cloaks (U. S. blankets) around us, it proved a haven of refreshing bliss to us during a period of thirty-six hours. When we arrived here our spirits were overshadowed with gloom, and our bodies exhausted with fatigue and hunger; but when the lowering clouds look most gloomy the benign influence of a propitious heaven will dispel the darkness and show God's power through the unexpected blessings of his gifts.

The few potatoes we secured, as before narrated, merely appeased the hunger of several days previous; but even on this occasion, when exhausted nature keenly claimed some support, we continued hopeful and resigned. Like Wilkins Micawber, we had great faith that something would "turn up." Well, something did turn up in the shape of a plump young goose. I caused his legs to "turn up" in a new-fashioned style. I did it with my little hickory, and that, too, at the first throw.

It occurred in this wise: We lay in a small woods about 300 yards wide, with a strip of cultivated land of about the same dimensions on either side. On our left was a wheat-field; the wheat had been harvested, but considerable remained among the stubble, whereon a number of geese were now feeding. As I lay, with my blanket around me, on a bed of leaves, I heard the cackling of the flock, which sounded like music to my ears. Springing to my feet, I took my shillalah— "that seldom missed fire"—and cautiously approaching the fence bordering the field, I "charged upon that flock of geese," and when about ten yards from them I let fly and hit one, breaking his legs. I was on him in a second, and by pressing on the windpipe prevented his making a noise, and so triumphantly bore my prize back to our hiding-place.

We now set to work plucking the fowl. In my mind's eye I still can see those feathers fly. We carefully concealed the feathers, however, disemboweled, washed, and singed the bird nicely, then, cutting a large slice apiece, we seasoned it, and with the aid of a "spit," or sharp-pointed stick, proceeded to roast our goose. The flavor of that roast, in our opinion, would have satisfied the desires of old Epicurus himself.

When ready for the repast, we thought it eminently proper to say grace. I volunteered to perform the duty on this occasion, although it would seem more in keeping with the proprieties for the Rev. Captain Whiteside to have done so, but recollecting my favorite Bobby Burns, I determined to give the captain a specimen of the Scottish poet's style of grace, and quoted as solemnly as I could:

> "O Lord, who kindly doth provide for every creature's want,
> We bless Thee, Lord of Nature wide, for all Thy goodness lent,
> And, if it please Thee, Heavenly Guide, may never worse be sent,
> But whether granted, or denied, God bless us with content."

We now fell to, and in a very short space of time the bones of his gooseship, stripped of even a suspicion of meat, were all that was left to tell the tale of his sudden taking off.

Present circumstances were fast smoothing our asperity and filling our hearts with the milk of human kindness, and we soon became sleepy. Wrapping ourselves up in our life-saving "U. S." blankets (those talismanic letters! I hope they may always shelter, save, and protect all true citizens of our common country) we were soon in the arms of Morpheus. His majestic godship devotedly performed his duty towards us, and we slept soundly until evening, when we arose greatly refreshed in body and mind.

While discussing the lines of our next move, I

heard a voice come wafting on the gentle breeze:

> Ha! is that a friend? perhaps a foe;
> The former are so scarce I fain would know.
> I reconnoitred, and soon I found
> That "honest Bob" was homeward bound.
> I hailed.   He answered, "Sir, I'm here;
> I am your friend; you need not fear."
> The proof, indeed, of what he said,
> Was a fair supply of meat and bread.
> He was intelligent, bright, and clever,
> And ferried us over the Saluda river.
> The ferry was owned by his master, McNiece,
> Who charged his customers a dime apiece;
> But "Bob" was in charge of the ferry at night,
> And rowed us across with great delight.
> Though no pay he got, it seemed to please him well
> To succor the boys whom his chains would dispel.
> When on the opposite bank from his master's abode,
> With tact he described how we'd find the road
> Which we wanted to travel, as sketched on our map;
> This we succeeded in doing without a mishap.
> Honest Bob was all man in stature and mind,
> With regret we left him in slavery behind;
> But for his fetters, he had a home of some pleasure;
> His accompanying girls thought Bob quite a treasure.
> They looked just like twins—in age, color, and style,
> Showing the whitest of teeth when on him they would smile.

Both of the girls mentioned were fairly good-looking colored damsels of about twenty years of age.   When I hailed Bob, a short time after hearing his voice, they were with him husking corn in a field near by.   Bob came into the woods where we were, and I talked with him alone for several minutes.   He said the girls might be depended on; and it was arranged that when Bob was going home in the evening he should come into the woods and give us a signal by whistling. He did so, and told us the girls had a curiosity to see us, if we had no objection, as they had never seen a "live Yankee," etc. We told him that we would sooner see his colored friends than the fairest ladies in the South, which at that time was true, as the white-faced beauties had almost invariably shaken the black flag in our faces, while on the other hand our sable-hued friends had not on any occasion failed to do the very best they could for us in our distress.

The girls approached with much diffidence and modesty, although our appearance was not calculated to inspire any one with feelings of very profound respect. They eyed us curiously for some time, evidently thinking us specimens of a new species of the genus homo. I should here remark that the owner of these three slaves, Mr. McNiece, was, most fortunately for us, from home on this evening of our visit, the sole occupants of his house on the occasion being our new-found friends. They did not know how soon he might return, and, as a precautionary measure, they conducted us to a safe hiding-place a short distance away, after which they went to the house and soon returned with a good supply of food. We ate heartily of some, and put away the remainder in our canvas haversacks. In parting with these worthy people we had nothing to offer them as a recompense for their kindness to us, except the assurance that within a year from then they would be free. Their term of bondage proved to be even shorter than we had told them, for in the next April, less than the year by several months, the Confederacy surrendered and emancipation became an accomplished fact.

CHAPTER XXVI.

WEDNESDAY, *November* 9*th*.—Having spent the
entire day at McNiece's Ferry (or Gooseville),
where we fared so well, we make a start this
evening in good spirits and in fair marching order.
Shortly after starting, we luckily struck a good
road and one leading in the right direction.
These roads are not much used at night, except
by colored boys going to see or coming from
seeing their girls.

About nine o'clock P. M., after having made a
march of ten or twelve miles, we met with a
strapping negro. He halted at our command and
we had a few minutes' talk with him. He was
going to see his girl and had provided himself
with two large "pone" cakes as a treat for himself and the fair one. The sum-total of all his
earthly cares at that moment seemed to be concentrated in two objects, his girl and his stomach.
Captain Whiteside offered him two dollars for one
of the cakes, but he would not part with it. He
left us soon after, and before he was ten yards
away was vigorously whistling "Dixie." Little

for glory he cared, and appeals to his sense of gratitude were worse than useless.

Nothing more of interest transpired during the night's tramp, and now, as day is dawning, after a march of twenty-five miles, we file to the right and succeed in finding a hiding-place, wherein to remain until night shall again fold her protecting mantle around the weary forms of the two fugitives. It has rained during the last two hours and we are quite wet and very chilly.

DRY HOLLOW, *Thursday, November* 10*th*.—We name our resting-place as above, not being able to procure water either to wash with or to drink. We do not enjoy more than an occasional nap all day; our clothes are soaked with rain and our frames benumbed with cold. Night finds us impatient to be on our way, and as soon as we can prudently do so we start. We trudge along dispiritedly until about ten o'clock, when we meet an old colored man named Dodd. (I kept my diary chiefly in cipher, especially all mention of proper names, so that nobody who befriended us might be compromised in case of my capture.) The negro proved to be a first-rate old fellow, and appeared to derive great satisfaction from our reports of the progress of the war. He succeeded in supplying us with a good supper, consisting of bacon, sweet potatoes and molasses.

Having met with no mishap or adventure during the remainder of the night, we retired at daybreak to the woods, as usual, and slept tolerably well until near evening.

Friday, November 11*th.*—We set out early this evening, perhaps about 6.30. We moved on rapidly and travelled for about half an hour, until we came to a sharp curve in the road, where we were confronted by a white man on horseback. He did not manifest much surprise at meeting us, merely asking if the train had run off the track, and where? We answered, "Yes, at the village a short distance back," and that, in consequence, we were compelled to walk. He appeared satisfied and bade us "good-night." Our appearance at night was not calculated to arouse much suspicion, our garb consisting of soft felt hats, gray blankets and blue pants, the latter now changed to a dull drab color from constant contact with the clayey soil, and the whole outfit showing marked signs of rough usage. The night wore away without further incident.

CHAPTER XXVII.

Saturday night, *November* 12*th.*—The events of to-night proved one of the most trying chapters of my life. After a miserable meal of two or three ounces of half-cooked turnips, we were preparing to again move forward when, upon looking in the direction of the road, we saw a horse and buggy approaching us, the latter occupied by a gentleman. Not having met with so luxurious a conveyance for months, we were much impressed with the sight, and concluded that the occupant must be a person of some note in the neighborhood. However, we did not have the remotest wish to cultivate the gentleman's acquaintance.

But destiny or some other power willed it otherwise, for that night he took back into captivity my worthy and only companion, Whiteside. We permitted him to pass, and then moved cautiously from our hiding-place to the road. Travelling upon the roads was now becoming more

(245)

risky and we acted too rashly in our anxiety to
make better time; but the night was very bright
and we could see a long distance ahead, so securing time to enable us to get over the fence paral-
leling the road, and to get away in case of the
approach of suspected enemies.

While it was yet early—about half an hour only
after nightfall—we saw a house on our left, about
one hundred yards in advance and about twenty
yards from the road. Whiteside and the writer
consulted as to what we should do; whether to
take over the fence and flank the house, or to
proceed cautiously on the road. We foolishly
adopted the latter plan, believing we would not
encounter any but colored folks, in which, however,
we were sadly mistaken.

I have stated that the night was *bright*, but this
poorly describes it; the moon was full, the heavens calm and cloudless and the stars numerous
and brilliant. I have rarely seen a more beautiful night, but bright as it was, neither my comrade
nor myself noticed three or four horses hitched to
a fence in front of the house just mentioned until
we saw their owners come out of the door and
mount them. As they turned their horses in the
direction we were travelling we hoped that they
had not seen us, and hastily crouching down in a
fence corner, we prepared to wait until they had
passed out of sight; they had noticed us, however,
and when they discovered our sudden disappear-

ance their suspicions were aroused, and they rode briskly towards where we lay concealed.

Oh, what a rush of thoughts surged through my brain in those brief moments! My first impulse was to get over the fence and run for it. My next was that we might succeed in bluffing them and avoid the chances of a pursuit by the hounds. We therefore arose and advanced towards them. They were sharp fellows and our replies to their questions were not satisfactory.

One of the party (they were four in number) now proceeded to the house they had just quitted and returned immediately, reinforced by another man with a gun. They questioned us so sharply and were so evidently aware of the character of their capture that we decided to make a clean breast of it; so we simply told them that we were escaping prisoners from Columbia.

We were marched into the house and questioned at more length. The owner of the place seemed to be in good circumstances. He had several slaves, about equally divided as to sex. He proved to be the same gentleman who had passed us in the buggy a short while before. The room into which we were conducted was not very well proportioned, perhaps thirty by fifteen feet, but was very clean and suitably furnished. We were ordered to take a seat on a lounge placed against a side wall. The family were just finishing their supper when we entered.

The gentleman, whose prisoners we now were, was, I learned, a local magistrate. I did not learn his name. He lived exactly seven miles from Laurens Court-House on the National pike. Each mile on this road was defined by well-cut stone posts plainly numbered and lettered.

Poor Whiteside and his companion presented a queer appearance seated upon the lounge with our tattered U. S. blankets wrapped around our emaciated frames, our pantaloons of questionable color, with legs of different lengths and a liberal fringe of frayed material running around their bottoms; hats well ventilated by numerous holes in the tops and sides, and our hair and beards long and unkempt, our faces having been strangers to the touch of a razor for many months previous, heads drooping with weariness and dejection and a general air of abject misery. What a contrast to the pictures we presented when upon dress parade

The gentlemen retired to an adjoining room for consultation and we were left alone for a few moments. While thus alone, I whispered to Whiteside my intention to escape from the house if we were permitted to remain during the night. The Squire, in the next apartment, was preparing to hold his court and grant us the formality of a trial, or at least to examine us closely before returning us to prison. In according us this privilege I thought he was actuated in a good degree

by a desire to display his judicial knowledge and
other varied attainments.

While we were still alone, a door to the left of
us opened gently, and looking in that direction,
we saw first a round black curly head, surmounted
by a red bandanna handkerchief, followed, a moment later, by two large eyes with a good deal of
white in them, looking softly and pitifully at the
captives. The door was closed, and again gently
opened to admit the curious face of another dusky
maid. This last girl was much taller than the
first, and showed considerable of the blue blood
of the South in her veins. Both were decidedly
sympathetic in their glances towards us.

The Squire now entered with a newspaper in
his hand, followed by two of the gentlemen who
had assisted in our capture. Next came in,
through a side door leading from the parlor, the
remarkably pretty hostess, accompanied by two
young ladies. A glance was sufficient to satisfy me
that the three ladies were sisters, the resemblance
they bore to one another being too marked to
admit of any doubt. They were all blue-eyed,
rosy-cheeked, with hair a beautiful auburn, and
forms well rounded and graceful.

All present seated themselves except the
Squire, a man of portly figure and military stride.
He continued walking up and down the room,
holding in his hand the latest available issue of a
newspaper, a sorry-looking sheet containing little

besides war news, and that of a character not the most agreeable to the friends of the Confederacy, as "little Phil" had just succeeded in turning the tables on General Early in the Valley, of which fact we had been made aware from smuggled newspapers while yet in prison.

The first burst of eloquence we had from the Squire was directed to the abuse of whiskey, and how it had lost to them a glorious victory in the Valley of Virginia. He censured Early very severely, who, he said, "commanded the bravest boys that ever fought. These troops," said he, "were whipping and driving before them three times their own number of Yankees in the first part of this engagement, until General Early, flushed with success, dipped too deep in captured Yankee whiskey, and thereby lost a grand opportunity to teach the North a salutary lesson."

I could not at this juncture forbear remarking: "I wish he had captured more whiskey and less men from our side."

This caused a furtive smile from the ladies to be directed toward the dilapidated-looking captives.

The Squire now directed his attention to us and commenced our examination. He first addressed Whiteside, in a quick and imperious tone, and said:

"What is your name, sir?"

"John C. Whiteside," was the reply.

"Where are you from?"

"From Wyoming, New York, sir."

"New York," he repeated, "the receptacle of the slums, the mud-sills and off-scourings of Europe, who, together with your cunning, intermeddling Yankees, have come, like the hirelings you are, to invade our homes and firesides in an effort to overthrow constitutional right and rob us of our property; urged on by such fire-brands and fanatics as old Garrison, Greeley, Phillips, Harriet Beecher Stowe, and others of their ilk. I do not know a punishment severe enough for such ruthless despoilers."

The Squire paused, but my gentle and mild-tempered comrade made no reply.

His Honor was master of the situation, and seemed to realize with some pride the favorable impression he had made upon the ladies. He now turned to me and with renewed force commenced his tirade:

"What is your name, sir?"

"Michael Egan," I replied.

"From what State of the North are you?"

"I am from West Virginia, sir."

"Ah, from Virginia, a State in the Confederacy, then you are an arch-traitor," said he.

"I said from West Virginia, sir, and she is not in the Confederacy."

"Worse and worse," said the Squire; "you add to the crime of treachery that of secession; not like the action of the Sovereign States composing the Confederacy, but like the wilful act of an ungrateful child. The idea of an insignificant corner of the Mother of States and of Presidents separating itself from its parent is simply detestable."

Whether from my name or brogue, or both combined, he drew his conclusions, I do not know; but he suddenly said:

"You are no American by birth, sir."

"No sir, I am Irish by birth, as you seem already to have perceived."

"Yes, I thought so, which fact only tends to aggravate your crime—a traitor and a tory. The action of one whose country and people have suffered for centuries under the oppressive yoke and iron heel of English tyranny, in lending his aid to subject a people to like misfortunes, deserves, sir, the most extreme punishment."

This was too much for me; I was on my feet in an instant.

"I thank you," said I, "for your very complimentary remarks to my companion and myself; we are your prisoners. It's very like the handle of a pitcher, sir—a one-sided affair. I beg to remind you, however, that were we on equal terms you probably would be more careful in the wording of your bill of indictment; more careful in the application of such vile and opprobrious epithets, stupid and unjust ones as they are, as repugnant to my feelings as they are devoid of proof. As to your charge of baseness in an Irishman espousing the cause of the North, I dismiss it with the assertion that the case of poor, struggling Ireland is not a parallel one with this Rebellion, and no amount of sophistry can make it so. It was a love of liberty, and not of tyranny, that caused me to give to the United States my free and willing allegiance. We are here, sir, not to help to inflict injustice, but to aid in upholding unimpaired and intact a republican form of government in a great and varied and expansive country that has not, in all its wide area, one line of natural demarcation to justify the formation of two governments, antagonistic on vital principles and requiring, as they would, large standing armies for their defense.

"Strange as it may now seem to you, sir, I believe you will live to see the day when you will rejoice that the disintegration of the Union was not accomplished. I thank you for allowing me to defend my position, and will conclude by answering your strange charge of toryism. An Irishman of the middle class being a tory is an anomaly, indeed. Where can you cite me one? Of all the 'isms' known to politics toryism has my most cordial detestation. But right here, I would ask, where, during the Revolutionary struggle, was toryism most rampant? I answer in South Carolina, near the Pee Dee, where the gallant Marion was so badly harassed by your

native tories and traitors.   In speaking for myself, I believe, too, that I outline the principles of
my comrade."

"You do," answered Whiteside.

"I hope, sir, your harsh impressions are somewhat modified," I ventured to add mildly.

Yes, there was now manifest a marked change
in our favor, as could be seen by the altered
manner of those present.

"You are not privates?" said the Squire, in-
terrogatively.

My companion replied that we ranked as captains.

The fair hostess now spoke in low tones to her
husband, who nodded assent to whatever she had
said.   It was doubtless something in our favor,
as the little lady at once gave a servant orders to
prepare something for us to eat.   I do not believe the colored cook ever obeyed an order with
more willingness and alacrity than this one.

We were soon called into the dining-room
and plenty of corn-bread, meat and "Jeff. Davis"
coffee (parched rye, ground) were placed before
us.   Flour bread was a rarity in the South at
this time, but our friendly and kind-hearted cook
made a sly visit to the pantry where she found
some, which we lost no time in disposing of.
After our hearty meal, and one that we thoroughly
enjoyed, we returned to our former positions in
the "sitting-room."

The Squire now gave orders to one of his colored servants to procure fresh horses for himself and escort in order to march us back to Laurens Court-House, where, he told us, there were seven other runaway prisoners, in whose company we would return to Columbia. Emboldened by our late kind treatment, I spoke up and said that we were very much fatigued, and begged him to allow us to remain at his house that night, although I had no intention of so remaining, if an opportunity of escape presented itself.

"I presume," said he, "if you were at liberty now you would march more than seven miles to-night."

It was too true to dispute and we were silent.

Now all were ready and we got the word to move.

In describing our outfit, I omitted to mention that we had two good hickory-sticks. When we stood up to begin our march, I leaned heavily on my cane, and walked slowly, with an exaggerated curvature in my spinal column. I was, also, as already stated, prematurely gray, and looked twenty years older than I really was. This latter fact gave my assumed decrepitude an appearance of naturalness.

The Squire and his four friends, all well armed and mounted, ordered us to march in front of them on the road to Laurens. Whiteside and myself walked shoulder to shoulder, about ten yards in advance of our guards. We kept up a low toned conversation for some time, discussing what we should do. I told my friend that if he would make the effort to get away, I would remain with the guards in order to divert a portion of them from his pursuit. He had been a prisoner for fourteen months, while my term of imprisonment had been only six months, and I thought it but fair that he be given the first chance of liberty. He replied, however, that the risk of being shot was too great, and besides, if he did succeed in escaping, he could not make his way alone. I then told him I was determined to make the effort, or die in the attempt. I gave him my wife's address, in case I should never reach home, which then seemed very probable, as eight hundred and twenty miles yet lay between me and my fireside.

My mind was made up to run for it at the first opportunity. I did not turn my head to the right or to the left at any time, but my eyes moved with sharp glances on either side of the road seeking a favorable spot to make a dash. The Squire, meantime, kept up a running conversation with his men, and we now heard him remark to them that if he should call on Mr. Yancey, whose fine plantation we were then passing, that gentleman would quickly respond with himself and hounds. I thought he had an object in making this remark loud enough for us to hear. At all events it had the effect of preventing my going as soon as otherwise I might have done, believing for a certainty that, if I escaped falling by their fire, bloodhounds would be put on my trail immediately.

When about half a mile from the plantation where the hounds were kept I became impatient, thinking I might be passing places more favorable for my flight, perhaps, than I should encounter farther on. I was laboring under a disadvantage, too, but one which happily proved a blessing afterwards; that is, I had a heavy United States blanket on my shoulders. It belonged to Whiteside, he having mine, which was a very light one. We had made the change while travelling in order that he might the better keep up with me, but we had no chance to change back now. Such an act would be sure to create suspicion.

The Squire, at this moment, was entertaining his friends upon the engrossing subject of partridges. He was telling them how he had misled his neighbor Davis, who was an ardent sportsman, by concealing himself in a brushy place near a fence, and whistling in the style peculiar to partridges, thus causing his guileless neighbor to imagine that a covey of the birds was being formed right under his nose.

While the gentlemen were absorbed in this congenial subject, I decided that my time to make

the break for liberty had come. There was a
fence enclosing an open field on my right; a
sparse and level wood on my left, unenclosed;
and my mind was made up. I straightened up,
made one bound, and was away into the woods,
all signs of lameness gone and feeling as though
able to outrun the pick of a hundred men in such
a race, and for such high stakes. I ran in a ziz-
zag manner in order to evade their fire. After
the first volley, one of their fleetest runners dismounted and made after me on foot. Another
followed on a horse for some distance, but returned shortly afterwards (Whiteside wrote me)
minus his carbine and hat, and severely scratched
and bruised by the briars and overhanging
boughs. (See *Frontispiece.*)

The night is still very calm and bright, and the
leaves very dry. I do not take time to look back,
but can hear the leaves rattling in my rear and
conclude that the man on my track must surely
be a good runner. I am not afraid, however, that
I will be overtaken in a long run, if my pursuer
does not catch me in a short one, as I have never
been beaten in a long distance race. My equipments annoy me considerably, being somewhat
cumbersome. I have the heavy blanket before
mentioned, a canvas haversack, hickory-stick,
and a leather belt with a butcher knife in a
sheath attached to it. The knife was given me
by Lieutenant Andrew McNiece, of Philadelphia,
who had bunked with me in prison.

The runner in my rear, on the other hand, is less encumbered, better fed and fresher in every way. But the last few wholesome meals I received are visibly restoring the vitality lost by the starvation of six months in Southern prison pens.

The race continues, and I am getting over the ground satisfactorily until I suddenly strike my foot against a grape-vine, or some other runner, and pitch heavily forward a long distance.

"I have you now, Yank," panted my persistent pursuer.

"Not quite," I gasped, as I sprang up before he could put his hands on me, although his hot breath met my cheek, so close was he. I now start to run as I never did before for the next four hundred or five hundred yards, when I stop to take breath. No stir in the leaves behind me, but I can hear a horseman riding back in the direction of the plantation. I know well his mission. He is going back for the ferocious bloodhounds to put on my track.

When I ran away, I started in a northwesterly direction from the one we were being taken, but now I turn and go in the direction of Laurens Court-House, making a complete circle and running on the pike for several hundred yards in about the same portion of the road I had travelled before escaping from the Squire. This was my "foxey" plan to confuse and delay the hounds and possibly put my pursuers on a wrong scent. I did even better than this. I got upon the top rail of the fence skirting the right of the road, and crawled along in this manner for a considerable distance and then jumped off, making a leap as far to the right as I could in doing so.

I kept up a rapid pace, again circling to the northwest and keeping far enough from the road to elude the hounds. It is hard to realize, and still harder to appreciate the sad position in which I now found myself. After ten or fifteen minutes' hard running, I halt for breath and listen for the yelping of the dogs. Glad of the stillness I renew my flight, and ten minutes or so later halt again for a brief rest. The brightness of the night helped in my capture but I find it a blessing now, giving light to my path.

It was fully an hour after my escape before I heard, as I trotted along, the deep baying of the hounds away off to my left. The sickening sound had a heart-sinking effect on me for a moment, as I pictured in my mind the barbarous brutes in the act of jumping for my throat. I soon rallied, however, my good butcher knife and trusty hickory-stick being no small factors in bracing up my drooping spirits.

I now directed my course through such portions of country on my route as were impracticable for horseback riding, well satisfied that if the hounds made rapid progress, which they

were most assuredly doing, the footmen would
be far in the rear. On I went until I came to
a river on my left. I first thought of plunging
in and swimming to the opposite bank, but decided to keep on the right shore in the hope of
again coming out on the National pike, on which
I wanted to travel. Nearer and nearer came the
relentless hounds; their deep baying could now
be plainly heard, and far in the rear the faint
shouts of the footmen could be distinguished.
The night was now far advanced and the moon's
rays were not so brilliant, so I kept running down
close to the water's edge, where the trail was more
open and easier followed. The shore was covered
with a fine, light sand which was very agreeable
to my tired feet.

The river here followed a straight course for a
great distance ahead, and I could see quite plainly,
making it comparatively easy for me to travel in
the dim light of the morning. Looking ahead a
short time later, I discovered a light far in advance and apparently close to the river front. I
concluded it was the fire of some picket, or party
camping out, and at once decided to flank the
position. But the hounds, the hellish bloodhounds, were getting uncomfortably nearer. One,
greatly in advance of his mates, was almost upon
me. I stopped running, put off my blanket, looked
to my knife, and rested for the inevitable encounter.

It soon came; the dog, as he neared his human game, ran the faster. I faced the brute, with his glaring and bloodshot eyes looking like two balls of fire, and extended jaws from which were dropping large drops of saliva; and as he sprang for my throat I came down with a crushing blow of my cudgel upon his forelegs, breaking them, and as he fell from the blow, I again struck him with all my might upon the skull. Finding I had effectually disabled him, I picked up my blanket and tying it around my neck, I took to the river immediately. I thought I would have to swim, but found it could be waded, although not without an effort to keep my feet, as the water came up to my arm-pits, or was about four feet four inches deep. I managed to keep my blanket from getting wet, and scrambling up the other side concealed myself in some brush and watched, in safety, the approach of the remainder of the dogs.

They soon came up and I could faintly discern their dark forms circling around their disabled leader. Presently one picked up a trail somewhat farther in advance of the point at which I had crossed, and the other hounds at once followed him, and I could hear them as they went flying along down the river shore on the scent, perhaps, of the parties who had lighted the fire before spoken of, some distance ahead.

I now clambered up a woody bluff overhanging the river and, shivering with cold from my en-

forced bath, I start ahead briskly to restore circulation and get my bearings. In about half an
hour I was delighted to find myself on the pike
again, and the first milestone I came to was
marked: " To Laurens C. H.; 17 miles." This
would seem to indicate that I had travelled twelve
miles in a straight direction from the point where
I had so unceremoniously left my escort; and by
adding the circles I made to this, it would make
my run between seventeen and eighteen miles. I
continued on the road for about three miles more,
when day was pretty well advanced, and I filed to
the right and into the woods to look for a hiding-
place.

CHAPTER XXVIII.

WE will now return to Captain Whiteside, who found himself (as he states in his letter to me) in a very uncomfortable position. Two men remained with him, while the others devoted their attentions to me. When the pursuing party returned, after their fruitless chase, they were so highly incensed at my escape that his life hung on a thread for some time. He escaped being shot through the intervention of one of their number, but they all vehemently avowed that if they had succeeded in overhauling "that infernal flying, gray-haired Yank" (with which name they kindly christened me) they would have "riddled him with bullets."

SQUIRREL FLAT, *Sunday, November* 1*3th.*—Having no pencil, pen, or ink, and not wishing a blank in my diary, I keep my record for a few days in my own blood, by opening one of the small veins in my left arm, and using a goose-quill, sharpened and pointed with my indispensable butcher-knife. This kind of treatment is calculated to try an iron constitution. I am chilled through after my cold plunge in the river at a time when I was in the height of perspiration, and am fatigued, footsore, and heartsick after my terrible race.

This is the most desolate day I have yet spent. all alone, suffering under accumulative misfortunes, and not knowing the moment I may be called upon to undergo afresh a similar ordeal. The sun is coming out bright and strong, and its warming rays are very welcome, but it brings a danger with it also. The woods all around and near me are alive with barking squirrels. If hunters seeking this kind of game should be attracted this way I can hardly hope to escape being seen, as the place is very level and open, with little or no brush in it.

How many times, while hunting, would I have been delighted to alight upon such a spot, but now the frisky little creatures were a source of great annoyance to me, more especially as I could plainly see some habitations a short distance away. But a due observance of the Sabbath or a respect for Sunday laws, perhaps, was in my favor. The advancing day and increasing heat are conducive to sleep, and, having nothing to eat, I approach the sleepy god with heavy eyelids and an empty stomach, and pass away to dreamland, where I revel in a sumptuous feast, spread in a gorgeous banqueting-hall, with old Epicurus and his court.

Night comes again, and with it a realization of my deplorable situation.

On the march again, though weary, footsore and badly used up generally. Have had nothing to eat all day and no prospect of anything. When on the road a while, like an old stage-horse I limber up and make tolerably good headway until about midnight, when, while plodding along a path through the woods, faint and hungry, hope and energy both exhausted, my foot came in contact with something soft and hairy. I stooped down and found an opossum, dead, as I supposed. If not too long dead I would, in my present condition, be compelled to eat it. I rolled him over, and found him rather limp for a dead animal. I now took hold of him carefully by the tail, lifting him up, and found him quite warm. Persons not familiar with the nature of this little animal would scarcely stop to investigate his condition, but I had previously witnessed his dissimulations, and was not to be so easily fooled. Taking him to a convenient log, I cut off his head with my invaluable butcher-knife.

This discovery was one of the most evident acts of providential aid ever manifested towards my unworthy self. I do not consider this and many other interpositions of divine protection to be due to any merit of my own, but entirely to the pure and earnest supplications of my devout and loving wife and our three little innocent children, whose petitions to the throne of heaven were day and night, during the whole period of my imprisonment and escape, offered up for my safe return.

I left the path for some distance, until I heard
the rippling of a little stream, near which I lighted
a fire, luckily still having a few of the indispensable matches with me. I now skinned and cleaned
the 'possum, and, cutting a good-sized steak, I
placed it on a pointed stick and commenced
roasting it before the fire, the fat falling upon the
coals in the operation. Every drop of this precious juice I was sorry to lose, but I had no means
of saving it. The flavor arising from that savory
roast was more pleasing to my olfactories than
the scent of water to the thirsty camel approaching an oasis in the desert. Having had no meat
whatsoever, if I except the maggoty bacon used
for grease while in prison, my enforced abstinence
created a consuming desire for fatty meat entirely
unknown to persons who have not had a simi-
larly rough experience.

After my meal, and being by this time greatly
refreshed, I moved from "Opossum Run," got
upon the path again, and looked for my guiding-
star. Finding this and faced to the northwest, I
pursued my course for about an hour, when I came
to a large farm-house, its appearance and sur
roundings denoting a degree of opulence. Cautiously reconnoitring for some time, I at length
approached one of the outbuildings and rapped
gently on the door. It was timidly opened by an
individual whose color gave me immediate relief.
It was past midnight when I appeared before the

occupants of these humble "quarters"—a strapping young buck and a buxom, kinky-haired girl. They were badly scared at my unexpected and no doubt somewhat startling appearance. By the flickering light I could see their rolling black eyes exchange furtive glances at each other and at me. I relieved their suspense by asking if they had ever seen a Yankee soldier.

"No, sah; neber," replied the buck; "but I hear'n massa tell a hull lot about de Yanks, an' as how de Confedits kill an' whip dem at Manassa', an' den Bull Run dem ter Washatin, an' most capture Massa Linkum, an' as how dere is a hull army o' Yanks in de prisons down Souf."

The girl looked proudly at her sable Adonis, and said: "Yes, sah, I hear'n my missus say de same ting."

"Well," said I, "they have both told you a good deal of truth. It is true they have a great many Yankee prisoners, and they are treating them very badly; in fact, starving them slowly to death. I am one of them—not a dead one, it is true, but pretty nearly so. I concluded a few days ago that I would not stop with them any longer, so I ran away and am now making for the Union lines. Their story is a very old one, however. Were they to tell you of more recent events, it would put a different phase on the matter, and make you colored people feel very good. They have not told you of the great battle of Gettysburg, where General Lee and his great army were defeated, and thousands of their men were killed and captured after three days' hard fighting from July 1 to 3, 1863. They have not told you that Atlanta, Ga., is taken by the Unionists, and that one part of the Yankee army is going right through the Confederacy; nor how the great Union General, Phil. Sheridan, made General Early and his men fly so fast in Virginia that he left all his cannon and guns behind him."

"Yah, yah, dat's good," exclaimed my attentive listeners.

"These things," I continued, "occurred before I stole out of prison at Columbia. At present I do not look much like a Yankee soldier in the field does, but I have been nearly seven months starving, and have, as you see, almost no clothing." I concluded by assuring them that, in my opinion, they would all be free within a year from then. They appeared to believe me and hoped for the early arrival of the day of jubilee.

The girl then set to work and soon had me something to eat. I never saw a happier pair of darkies. I did not attribute it to the anticipation of their near deliverance, as they could not realize or appreciate that properly, but rather to the possession of good health and animal spirits, coupled with a natural aptitude for deriving solid pleasure from their inborn vivacity; and

being free, as they were, from the cares and responsibilities that usually beset their otherwise
more fortunate white brethren. This pair joked,
giggled, and "sparked" in my presence without
much restraint.

I now begin to fell the need of rest very much,
and after a hearty meal I asked the girl if there
was any place near-by where I could hide until
next morning. After some reflection, she said
that in the large barn she thought I could be
stowed away behind the plows and harrows. So
thither I was shortly conducted by the girl.

CHAPTER XXIX.

Monday, *November* 14*th.*—Ensconced in a corner of the big barn and shielded by a good deal of trumpery, I lay down on some sacks, with some others thrown over me, and slept soundly. It was the first roof I had slept under since my escape and for a long time before.

About eight o'clock A. M. the door opened and the colored girl who had befriended me the night before came in. She brought with her some bread and meat, which I proceeded to consume with startling expedition. I find the day very long and feel very uncomfortable with an oppressive sense of confinement, and wish for the approach of night.

At about eleven o'clock A. M. the door again opened. This was not the time of day for a friendly visit, and I felt somewhat perturbed in consequence. I heard the rattling of chains in disagreeable proximity to my hiding-place, and was in a quandary as to what to do. I finally obtained a glance at this unwelcome visitor through an aperture, and was not very kindly impressed with his appearance. He was a large white man, and walked heavily, weighing probably two hundred and twenty-five pounds. I thought that he had discovered me, perhaps, and was preparing to tie me or attempt to, with a chain. To my great relief, however, he soon found what he was looking for and departed.

Late again in the afternoon the negro girl got an opportunity to visit me and bring something more to eat. I felt rather impatient at to-day's delay, but the rest and food were really essential to my system at this period of my progress.

Before leaving here, where I have been so kindly treated by this poor, good-natured slave, I deeply regret that I have not some of the money of which my captors robbed me, that I might give her some substantial token of my gratitude.

The weather is growing disagreeably colder, and I feel the want of gloves. To supply this want, the kind-hearted negress procured some pieces of old cloth, and in a short time had made a pair of "mits" that served me well for some time afterwards.

I wish to put myself on record right here as a warm champion of the much abused colored race. Although generally ignorant and uneducated, yet how intuitively noble, kind, and brave have they acted toward me and other unfortunate comrades under like circumstances ! By betray-

ing us to their masters they would have been
duly rewarded and appreciated, while if found
giving aid or comfort to escaping Yankee soldiers it would insure to them punishment, the nature of which I leave the reader to infer. Hence
their undoubted bravery, as I see it, in addition to
their other virtues.

I am, as I learn, just five miles from Greenville,
South Carolina, but have no assurance that I am
on the direct course, as my guides, the stars, are
hidden from view by the clouds, which are dark
and heavy, and threaten rain. There is every
sign of disagreeable weather ahead for some time
to come. I keep up my march this dark and
dreary night until about midnight, and, just as a
drizzling rain sets in, I espy at a short distance
from the road a farm-house with comfortable surroundings. Just before reaching the house I got
over the fence and into the kitchen garden, where,
after groping around for a few minutes, I un-
earthed three or four good-sized turnips. I now
noticed a small cabin, some twenty or thirty yards
from the house, and I decided to try my luck at
the humbler abode. Approaching, I rapped gently
once or twice, when a voice on the inside called
out:

"Am dat yo', Jake?"

"No," I replied; "it is not Jake; but I am a
friend. Please open the door."

In due time the door opened, but not before the

occupant, a middle-aged man, had struck a light. He came to the door in his bare head. He was of medium height, of stout build, and had an intelligent face. My visit and appearance somewhat mystified him, and it was plain he did not know what to make of me. I then showed him the significant letters, "U. S.," on my old gray blanket and also my old blue pantaloons.

He smiled kindly, and said :

"I understand, sah; but sometimes de Confederates hab some of dem tings, an' try ter pass off fo' Yanks, ter see if we'd help dem."

This man, whose name was Jim Reese, and who was a slave of a Mr. Murray, was the most intelligent colored man I met with during the period of my escape. I was not long in convincing him of the genuineness of my personality. He was a kind of head man or leader among the negroes in his neighborhood, having a smattering of education and considerable mother-wit. He was a good house-carpenter, and generally very useful to his master, who had paid a large sum for him a few years previously. When I entered Jim's cabin I was wet and chilled, but a bright fire was soon burning, which, with Jim's cheerfulness, caused me soon to feel quite at home.

I asked him if he could cook a turnip.

"Yes, sah," said he.

I took a couple from my haversack and handed them to him. As I did so, he showed his white teeth as a broad smile overspread his good-natured countenance.

"I kno' whar yo' got dem tarnips; yo' done got 'em in Marse Murray's gardyin."

"Well, Jim, I guess you are about right," said I; "it may look like I have been making free with Mr. Murray's property, but the gentleman is 'sound' I hope? I feared it might inconvenience him were I to arouse him from his slumbers to secure his permission."

The darky indulged in a suppressed laugh, and went to work with a will to prepare something better than turnips for my meal.

After eating I plied Jim with a number of necessary questions in relation to my route. I had two points marked on my map as of equal practicability—Walhalla and Pickens Court-House—but was undecided in my mind which I should adopt. I appealed to Jim, and he said that I must not attempt to go by way of Pickens Court-House, as Captain Charles Perkins, of the 16th South Carolina Infantry, was there, and that I "would hab a mighty bad chance o' gittin' past dar; Walhalla am de bes' way."

I saw the soundness of Jim's reasoning, and decided to adopt the latter route. He then gave me explicit directions as to my course to Walhalla, at what point I should strike the railroad, and when I did so I was to keep upon and follow it.

"The fust big trussel-bridge yo' come to," said

he, "is jus' eighteen miles from heah, and on de left-hand side ob it yo' will see a big plantation. Dey hab a great lot o' cullud folks dar; my Jim is one ob dem. His name is Jim Reese, too. If yo' find him, and tell him dat I sent yo', he will do de best he kin for yo'."

I was extremely fortunate in finding this well-posted darky, as I was surely going astray in the early part of the night.

I passed two or three hours very profitably in Jim's company, and he gradually became more interested in my welfare. I was a mile away from the direct road to Walhalla, and would have to cross the country in a northeasterly direction to find it. My colored friend described fully how I should go, but the night was very dark and I was in doubt about finding the country road referred to. A happy thought then struck Jim, which relieved me of my trouble. He said he was in need of some white paint for a building he had just completed, which he would have to procure at a small village lying in the direction I was to take, and that he would accompany me as far as the road. Going over to his workshop for a vessel to take with him for the paint, the dogs, which had hitherto remained perfectly quiet, now set up an unearthly howling. It took Jim some time to quiet them, but he finally did so.

He now acted as guide, and in a short time we reached the main road. I was well posted as to

my route now, and after a friendly farewell to my
trusty friend, I moved ahead with a comparatively
light heart, feeling quite improved in health and
spirits. It was about half-past three o'clock in
the morning when I bade my friend good-bye;
the road was in fair condition and pleasant to
travel on, and I was making about four miles an
hour, when I espied in my front two men going
in the same direction as myself. I thereupon
slackened my pace a little, thinking it not prudent
to encounter them while in doubt as to whether
they were enemies or friends. They kept looking
behind and at me continually, which, as will be
seen later, was natural under the circumstances.

I now found that they had checked their pace
also, which action on their part made me somewhat apprehensive of coming trouble. I felt for
my knife, a highly useful article, as the reader has
by this time learned. I was not at all desirous
of using it upon my fellow-man, and I thank God
I have never yet done so, but self-preservation
being the "first law of nature," I was determined
to give a good account of myself should the
emergency require it.

The men in front were walking still slower, so
I put on a bold front and walked rapidly forward
until I came up with them. Each was carrying a
heavy club. I do not know what the size of
Hercules' walking stick was, but I am sure that
these two young giants, who would not have dis-

graced the sireship of that famous son of Jupiter, carried canes in perfect keeping with their enormous bulk. I discovered, on closer examination, that if Hercules denied their paternity, Ham could not, an agreeable fact which relieved me greatly.

I spoke first and said:

"Good-morning, boys."

They replied very sullenly and eyed me suspiciously for a while.

I asked if they were going far.

One answered. "A little this side of Slabtown."

I took this to be slang, or an evasion, but afterwards found that there was such a village a short distance ahead. In a short time a few mutual confidences passed between us:

"Ain't you a Yankee officer?" asked one.

"Why do you think so?" I queried in return.

"Don't mean no harm, sah; but we just met tree off'cers 'scapin' from prison, an' tought you might be one, too," said the spokesman apologetically.

I had no further object in concealing the truth from them, and admitted the correctness of their surmise. They then became very friendly and told me their troubles. They were, like myself, fleeing from captivity, but with this difference: they had never seen the dawn of freedom. Their names were, they said, Willis and Stephens. The former was six feet high and weighed about two hundred and twenty-five pounds; the latter was about five feet eleven inches, and would weigh not less than two hundred pounds. Both were about twenty-four or twenty-five years of age, and some white blood coursed through the veins of each.

The cause of their running away was brutal treatment received at the hands of their respective masters, for the crime of going to see their dusky sweethearts, on a neighboring plantation, too early on the Saturday evening previous. Willis told me that he was the property of a Mr. McCullough; that a son of McCullough's, who was an officer in the rebel army, and then home on a furlough, had tied him to a stump with a chain and unmercifully lashed him with a "black-snake" whip. Stephens, on his part, had received equally as severe punishment from his master

So we find these two young darkies, who lived not far apart, deeply sympathizing with one another and deciding to make a joint effort to escape into the Union lines. When I met them they were about eighteen or twenty miles from the plantations of their masters, and were hurrying forward to the "land of promise."

We continued together for some time, making good progress and chatting familiarly the while, but I was not at ease. I had often before reflected on the desolateness of being alone while travelling in an unknown country, but now I would have much preferred it to my present company.

Pursuit of them in the morning was certain, and the manner of it, I felt equally certain, would be with horsemen and hounds. My chances if captured under ordinary circumstances would be slim enough, but being caught in the company of runaway negroes would most certainly insure my quick despatch, and possibly that of the poor slaves also. But whatever chance of life they might have owing to their commercial value, I could expect none, as the presumption would be too strong that I was conducting the negroes away, an unpardonable offence in the South in those days. Therefore I told them we should have to part company, explaining to them the great risk I ran in continuing with them.

They begged most piteously to be allowed to remain with me, promising to serve me as long as I wished after getting through. I told them that there were no unpaid servants at the North; that they were at liberty to go where they pleased there, and nobody would dispute their right. They told me, however, that they were afraid they could not find their way, as they would be compelled, as a matter of course, to travel entirely by night and confine all their queries for information to the colored people along their route, who would not, as a rule, know any more about their proper course than did the fugitives.

I fully appreciated the sad predicament of the unfortunate negroes in this particular, as even intelligent and well-posted officers had frequently failed to make their way safely through that long tramp; but I could not allow my sympathies to jeopardize my own safety without in any way insuring theirs, so bidding them "good-bye," I spurted ahead, determined to leave them behind. They had travelled fast and far that night, and I expected to have no difficulty in distancing them; but to my surprise and annoyance they still followed close at my heels, making prodigious efforts to keep me in sight. Our strides on this occasion would compare favorably with those of a Weston or an O'Leary.

The race continued on these terms until dawn of day, when I filed from the main road into an open woods. Before doing so, I looked back and found the persistent darkies in full swing after me. After penetrating a little farther into the woods, I came to a halt under a large tree and waited for them to come up. I thought it useless to show anger at their action, and so became resigned to whatever fate might have in store for me.

"What do you intend doing in case you are pursued and found here?" I asked.

"We shall fight for our lives," was the resolute reply of both.

"I like your pluck," said I, "for that is your only alternative."

I then instructed them in what they should do,

placing each under a tree, so that in our positions we formed a triangle. When the hounds should come up, all were to lay on thick and heavy upon their legs with our clubs until we disabled them, and then run from the horsemen, who by this time would in all probability be upon us, we dodging behind trees as we ran to escape their fire.

The runaways appeared to understand their parts and were willing to perform them. With their great hickory clubs, and the power to wield them which they possessed, I thought them fully capable of felling an ox if needs be.

The morning was calm and the air salubrious, although boding no good health for us. We could not think of lying down or of going to sleep, as pursuit of the two fugitive slaves was a certainty, and the natural and most direct route northward the first one their pursuing masters would follow. If well posted, these runaways would have taken a more circuitous course at the start, as being the one most likely to baffle their masters.

About nine o'clock, and when we were beginning to hope that our fears were unfounded, we hear far away in the rear the sickening sound of the barbarous Siberian-hounds.

> At first we fancy they, perhaps, are on another trail,
> To civilization and to sporting fame more in accord;
> God send such luck, we pray, and may it now prevail;
> In our sad plight, blacks and white alike, lean on the Lord.

But our hopes are ebbing fast, our spirits sinking low;
Upon the breeze comes wafting a sound too well we know:
Louder yet we hear it, that deep-toned hellish cry;
The darkies grip their clubs more tight, prepared to do or die.

Away five hundred yards or so, their noses near the ground,
In Indian file, come dashing on the gaunt and cruel hound;
With increasing speed we see them come, two hundred yards away;
The negroes' faces now grow white—they think of Judgment Day.

But God, who heard the raven's cry, as comrade Whiteside said
A nimble creature of His make put in her covert bed,
And when the dogs came bounding on to where this rabbit lay,
She jumped right up before them and bounded quick away.

The leading hound sets up a yelp and after " bunny " goes;
Around and round we see them run, our little friend and foes;
We breathe a prayer of silent thanks to Him who doth ordain
Protection to all children that in His path remain.

18

CHAPTER XXX.

PARTING FROM THE RUNAWAYS—DISCOURAGED—A CLOSE SHAVE—
MORE FRIENDS—ALMOST CAUGHT—THE THIRD SCARE.

I HESITATED no longer, but now told Willis and Stephens in plain terms that we must part for good. Before leaving, however, I gave them a good general idea of how they should go: to Walhalla; to Franklin; to Rabens' Gap; over the Blue Ridge Mountains in North Carolina to Cage Cove, East Tennessee, and thence to Knoxville, where the "boys in blue" were.

I lost no time in getting away. I crossed over and ran for some distance on the trail which the hounds had taken in coming down, and then took off to the right, keeping in the least frequented places I could find, until I was about two miles from where I had left the negroes. I could hear the hateful, discordant yelping of the dogs gradually dying out and I felt much relieved. That was the last I saw of the two darkies; I hope they reached the North safely, but there were many chances against their doing so. I managed to get a little sleep during the afternoon, but it was unrefreshing and unsatisfactory, being broken by dreams of imaginary perils.

(284)

Tuesday night, November 15*th.*—Fatigued, hungry and foot-sore. For the first time, I regret that I have made the awful trial. Saw several fires in the woods with small parties around them. After travelling for about two hours, very slowly at first, but improving a little as I progressed, I heard the pesky hounds again, but from the direction and distance of the sounds I did not apprehend any danger. How often have I heard with delight the deep-toned and mellow music of the hounds and, boy-like, joined with them in the exciting fox-chase. Many a long fast and severe drubbing have been my punishment, when a lad in Ireland, for playing truant to follow the Erycourt and Bannagher "packs;" but now I am sick of the music I once thought so thrilling.

Plodding along, ruminating on my hard luck, I start the ascent of a hill of some steepness, and at a point where the road took a sharp turn to the left, I see a cross or branch road a short distance in front. Scarcely had I made this discovery when I was challenged with:

"Who goes there?"

I made no answer but continued to advance towards the sentinel. Misfortunes were crowding too fast upon me, and for a moment I thought of giving myself up, and so ending the heart-breaking worry, fatigue and never-ending struggle for food. But a second later my mind underwent a complete change. It was now death or no surrender, and, turning, I dashed away down the declivity in the direction whence I came, just as a whistling bullet passed by my ear as a parting salute.   Leaving the road, I now took to the fields and ran for a long distance contrary to my direct route, oblivious to any physical defects resulting from fatigue or other causes.   There was no pursuit, however, and I soon after checked my pace and again changed my course.   Doubtless the sentinel who fired upon me thought the disturber nothing more than a speculative darky out in quest of a chicken, and perhaps indulged in a smile as he saw him split the wind when his musket cracked.   After a good many roundabout movements, I came upon the road again, on which I continued without incident, until once more I turn off and seek a hiding-place.

Wednesday, November 16*th.*—About twelve o'clock, midnight, while gliding along at a fair gait, being pretty thoroughly warmed and limbered up, I espied on my left a commodious and comfortable-looking dwelling, and at a respectful or convenient distance from it could be seen a small cabin.   I approached the latter cautiously, but rapped confidently.   I was becoming well posted as to where I should be the most likely to find friends.   Nor was I mistaken now.   The door opened and a thoroughbred African, stout and well built, with a large shock of thick, black, woolly hair, peered curiously at me.   I explained to him the reasons for my late call; told him that I had met, a day or so before, a very fine old colored man in the person of Jim Reese, with whom perhaps he was acquainted; adding that my experiences with the colored folks thus far had been pleasant ones, etc.

He invited me in, stirred up the log fire and told me to come nearer to it. He then retired to an adjoining apartment. I could hear some movements and low whisperings on the inside, and presently my friend returned, and said:

"If yo' have no 'jections, de odder uns inside (nodding to the door of the inner apartment) would like fo' to see yo'."

"All right," was my reply, cheerfully; "I am satisfied, if my appearance does not frighten them."

"Joe" (for that was his name) went inside again, and soon returned followed by another darky much taller and more slender than himself. This latter negro was very shy and respectful, although there was quite a strain of humor apparent in the twinkle of his eye. He, in turn, was followed by the eldest of the inmates, a man probably fifty years of age, and evidently the head of the household. In a short time there were four men and two women in the room. They were all plantation hands and very ignorant.

From the account given me they were receiving rather rough treatment at the hands of their

master. They were rarely permitted, they told
me, to leave the plantation, and then only for a
short distance, and of course knew nothing of how
the outside world was getting on. Of the great
war then in progress they had heard a little, and
had a faint idea of its cause, but they could not
realize or appreciate the stream of human blood
that was being spilled in that deadly struggle, of
which they and their race were a moving though
innocent cause.

What little information they did possess was
altogether one-sided. The Yankees were invariably getting whipped and the rebels were always
victorious. I took the opportunity to relate a
chapter of our side of the story, describing as
best I could some of the late victories of the Union
forces, and predicting a speedy termination of the
war with the slaves all free. They listened atten-
tively and appeared to derive a great deal of satisfaction from the news.

"Oh, golly, Joe, do yo' heah dat? an' Massa
Henry say all de time dat de Yanks am gettin'
whipped," remarked the slim fellow, throwing up
his hands and indulging in the most comical
suppressed laugh imaginable, in which all present
joined heartily.

By this time they were all in good humor and
intent on being hospitable. Said one:

"Boss, I s'pose youse hungry, ain't yo'?"

"Yes," I reply, "but I'm used to it."

"Well, we ain't got much," said another, "but we'll knock aroun' an' do de bes' we kin fo' yo'."

In a short time they placed before me some corn-bread and fat pork (the only food they had), but I relished it, and ate plentifully of it.

I now took leave of these kind and good-natured chattels, being well rested and thoroughly warmed, and started on my way, if not rejoicing at least decidedly improved in condition and spirits. Half an hour later I came in view of the railroad that I had been anxiously looking out for. After travelling for about a mile on the track I came to a trestle-work spanning a ravine. I thought perhaps this might be the locality where Jim Reese had directed me to find his son and namesake, although it did not quite correspond with the description he had given me. I discovered a cluster of cabins on the left, and selecting the poorest looking one of the group, I approached and rapped. I was answered in a shrill voice from the inside, with :

"What yo' want out dar?"

"I want to get in."

"We don't 'low no men folks in heah."

"Can't you let me in for a short time while I talk to you?"

"No, sah, yo' go on way from dat do', yo' heah?" indignantly.

"Is there a colored man named Jim Reese on this plantation?" I asked.

"Go on ober to de big house ober dar; de men folks will tell yo'."

The cabin to which the girl directed me was the best-looking one on the premises, and I had serious doubts of the prudence of arousing the inmates. Sure enough I did awaken the wrong man this time, the first and last mistake that I made of this kind. When the door opened, there stood before me a large white man, over six feet tall, with full bushy whiskers of a fiery red color and carrying in his hand a shot-gun. Promptness and tact alone (qualities I cannot, as a rule, lay claim to) could save me now.

"Have you a colored man named Reese in your 'quarters,' sir?" I asked in a quick, business-like manner.

"No, sir," was the curt reply.

"Beg pardon; sorry to have disturbed you, but I have been misinformed," said I, at the same time turning around and in a loud voice calling out, as if addressing a party at a distance from the house, "Move on, John; he is not here." This all took place in a very short space of time and if "John" did not move on, I know I did, and that too in double-quick order. I continued on the run until well out of sight and gunshot distance when, finding no pursuit, I proceeded more leisurely.

While tramping along some time later I saw a camp-fire in the woods about one hundred yards from the railroad. I was almost certain that it was the camp of some runaway prisoners, like myself, who had made a fire to cook their food and to warm themselves. I could not think of any other cause for a camp in such an isolated location. Leaving the track, I went in the direction of the fire, determined to give my supposed foolhardy comrades a scare. The leaves were dry and crackled under my feet, so I walked slowly and cautiously until I could see by the flickering light a half dozen recumbent figures around the dying blaze.

Upon getting nearer, I noticed that they had erected a rude structure of logs, with no roof, probably ten by twelve feet square and three feet high. This latter fact caused me some uneasiness, so I got down on all-fours and crept still nearer, but came to a dead stop on making a discovery. Those were no harmless walking-canes resting upon the logs and pointing in my direction. No, I was only ten yards away and could not be mistaken; they were guns. That their owners were, happily for me, in the tender embrace of Morpheus is the reason, perhaps, that I am left to tell the tale.

The intended joke had recoiled upon myself, and I was the scared party. I craw-fished back as stealthily and nearly as lightly as a cat, keeping my eyes bent in the direction of the sleepers until I was a safe distance away and again upon the railroad. I concluded that the soldiers composing this party must have been detailed to cut firewood for the use of their army.

CHAPTER XXXI.

An Inquisitive Stranger—Meeting with Six Escaping Officers —A Cruel Blow—Alone Again.

BREATHING a sigh of profound relief, and meditating on the incidents of the night, I proceeded on my way, with my head down, and picking my steps on the cross-ties. I had not gone far when my attention was attracted by hearing footsteps in my front. Looking up, I saw a man approaching; as he neared me, he said:

"Good-morning, sir."

I returned the salutation, and kept slowly moving ahead.

"You are travelling late," said the stranger.

"Yes; a little like yourself in that respect," was my reply.

He showed a disposition to move after me, and said that he would like to ask me a few questions. I told him, in reply, that I hadn't time to accommodate him just then, and added: "I am not inquisitive myself, and do not recognize your right to be so."

He seemed for some time undecided what to do, and stopped where he was until I had gone a good distance. He was quite a stout fellow, and

I feared at one time that we were going to have an encounter.

It was approaching daylight when I got upon the long trestle-work previously spoken of by old man Reese. It was not yet light enough to see the plantation on the left, and I crossed entirely over the structure, and reached a thickly wooded place on the northern end before I discovered that the place I was in search of lay on the opposite end. I sat down on a log in the woods, in view of the railroad, undetermined what to do. I was fast losing the chance of seeing young Reese, from whom I expected to get some needed assistance.

Day was breaking now, and I could see the plantation. As it would not be practicable to go to the place in daytime, I must act quickly or not at all. I started to retrace my steps, but when about half-way over I saw in the dim, uncertain light of morning a squad of men coming towards me. Here was a predicament in earnest. I could not jump off, and running on the narrow ties was out of the question; I therefore determined to brave it out. We met full abreast, and halted and looked at each other. The first words uttered were:

"My God, Egan; is that you?" spoken with a decided accent on the last syllable of my name. The speaker was Lieutenant Thomas B. De-Weese, of the 2d United States Cavalry, and his companions were Captains V. K. Hart and Charles S. Kimball, and Lieutenants William Nelson, O. W. Dimick, and Charles G. Davis, three from the regular army and three from the volunteer service, all of whom I have mentioned as meeting in another part of this book. We were all feeling decidedly uncomfortable until we made the mutually pleasing discovery that we were comrades and fellow-sufferers, engaged in the same hazardous mission.

To one who, like myself, had passed through so many trials in my lonely tramp, the companionship of these gentlemen was an agreeable change indeed. I realized, as never before, the truthfulness of the divine proposition, " It is not well for man to be alone." I abandoned my intention of seeking young Reese, and returned with my companions to the woods.

Thursday, November 17*th.*—A nice, pleasant day, and I found it doubly agreeable in comparison with those lately spent by me in loneliness and solitude. We had a refreshing wash, but very little to eat. We found a shady dell, where we enjoyed a calm and uninterrupted repose of some hours to prepare us for the night's march. It was strange, but fortunate, that we had an officer with us who had a fair knowledge of the locality we were now in. Lieutenant DeWeese, having been an assistant-engineer on the division of the railroad we were following, some years before the

war, was the guide of his party, and continued to
act as such to the end; his route, however, was
the same as the one I had mapped out, and was
following with comparative accuracy at the time I
met his party.

As evening approached, and while preparing
for the night's march, the six officers held a private conversation among themselves.   I thought
it rather strange that they did not wish me to
hear what they had to say, but I soon learned the
topic of their conference.   When they had finished
talking, they came forward and told me that they
were sorry to inform me that we should have to
part company, as their party was already too
large, and that any further addition to it would
endanger their safety.

To say that this announcement stunned me but
faintly describes its effect.   I can liken it to nothing but the sensation one experiences when a
little cold steel is being inserted into the region
of one's short ribs.   I realized, however, that there
might be a grain of truth in what they had said,
and even if I had not realized this I was too proud
to permit my feelings to be shown in my face or
manner, and simply replied:

"What you say is doubtless true, gentlemen;
large bodies move slowly.   It is not my wish to
further impede your progress or endanger your
safety by my unwelcome presence among you.
I am 'as independent as a wood-sawyer.'   I was

equal to the situation before I had the pleasure
of meeting you, and I am fully as competent now
to continue so ; you may either precede or follow
me, as you elect."

They went ahead, and I remained standing
where I was until they were long out of sight, but
I could not help feeling as though this last was
indeed " the unkindest cut of all."

Reader, I appeal to you : was there any chivalry, loyalty, or fraternity in this unmerited slight
put upon me by my fellow-comrades, at a time
when such an action would be most keenly felt?
The addition of one man to their number could
hardly in reason be considered a very large factor
in their sum of danger.   You will see later how
they also came to this conclusion.

Finally, I started on my weary and now doubly
lonesome pilgrimage, and had been on the march
about an hour, keeping on the railroad track and
in the direction of Walhalla, when I saw a light
from a fire some distance ahead on the edge of
the track.   About the same time I noticed, a few
yards in front, some men on the track approaching me.   I got off to the left, and lay down in some
scrubby brushwood, and awaited their advance.
As they filed by me, six in number, I recognized
the officers with whom I had parted an hour
before.   They had evidently seen the light in our
front some time before I came up, but must have
halted to rest or hold a council, thereby enabling

me to overtake them.   At all events, they were
now beating a retreat.   When nearly opposite
where I lay they got into a field, made a wide
circle, and flanked the fire ahead.   On the other
hand, I kept right on, going slowly and cautiously
as I neared the blaze.   It proved to be a bonfire
lighted by some children, who were even then
playing around it.   I passed unnoticed.

Finding that I was now unexpectedly in the
lead, I determined to keep it.   To do so I increased my gait, putting my whole heart into the
effort, wounded pride and self-pity urging me on.
The night was pretty far advanced and a drizzling
rain had set in, when I came in sight of a long,
straggling village.   It was Walhalla.   I could see
a number of street lamps extending away into the
perspective, and concluded that it would scarcely
be safe to venture through the town.   Accordingly, I took the woods to the right, making a wide
detour, and coming out far northward of the town.
Just as I landed upon the pike, here running
parallel with the railroad, I again met my recent
friends, the officers.   They had passed right
through the town without mishap, and had by this
means succeeded in catching up with me.

It was now breaking day, and the rain increasing to a steady downpour.   The "big six" filed
to the right, but I went straight on, hoping sincerely that I might not meet them again, lest they
should think I was seeking their company.   After

going two or three hundred yards farther, and finding the woods.too open, I penetrated the timber for some distance before I pitched my tent (the blanket I carried) under a large tree, the gnarled roots and overhanging boughs of which kept it sufficiently high from the ground to afford me some shelter from the rain.

CHAPTER XXXII.

Friday, *November* 18*th*.—Heard some desultory
shooting near by, a by no means agreeable sound
in these open woods. By a great effort I succeeded in lighting a fire and roasting a couple of
sweet potatoes. It has poured down rain incessantly all day. I am completely drenched,
and suffering hardships not often encountered;
hungry and wet; drowsy and much in need of
sleep, yet too chilly and uncomfortable to succumb to somnolency. As night approached the
rain increased; gloom, then utter darkness and
desolation as if in keeping with my deplorable
situation, seemed to pervade my surroundings.
No darker night ever enveloped man.

I moved off, groping my way in search of the
pike I had quitted at daybreak, and for an hour
or more I was like one playing at "blindman's
buff," stumbling and falling in my efforts to find
the road. At last I sat down, completely bewil-
dered. When leaving my hiding-place I had left
a small fire there; now, if I could find it, I would
try to study my bearings better. After some

19   (299)

more wanderings, stumblings, and falls, I de-
scried the flickering spark again:

> That little spark, bright silent friend,
> Fresh courage to my heart doth lend;
> Though flickering low, and dying out,
> It starts a hope, removes a doubt.
>
> From pensive study at its blaze,
> A clearer dawn breaks through the maze
> Of utter darkness, woe and damp,
> And once again I start my tramp.

I was more fortunate this time in getting on
the pike. I supposed it to be the one I was seeking, but after travelling some time I became dis-
satisfied with the direction it was taking; it circled
too much to the right, and could not be the one
I had diverged from in the morning. However, I
resolved to continue on it until I got better information, or found a highway leading more to
the left. I had to move slowly, using my cane
like a blind man, in the inky darkness.

About nine o'clock P. M. I saw a light glimmering through the murky atmosphere. When
nearer I found it came from a large farm-house.
On the opposite side of the road, to the left of
this dwelling, was a barn of good dimensions.
This I entered and found a large quantity of un-
husked corn. The corn was of the very best
grade. I shelled some of it and placed it in my
haversack, feeling glad in my deplorable condition to get even it. In fact, this kind of food

was the chief article of diet that I had during the
month of my escape.

While standing in the barn and looking across
to the opposite side, I could see a house presenting all the home comforts of farm-life. It was
cheerfully lighted up, with a warm fire of logs
blazing upon the open hearth, and all the surroundings indicated peace and prosperity.
What a contrast to my deplorable fix, and the
lonely situation of my young wife and babes on
our little farm in the wilds of West Virginia!

I dare not go to this house, but very naturally
judged that the owner must have a large number
of colored servants ; so I waited patiently until the
lights were all out before reconnoitring for the
negro "quarters." It seemed a long time to wait,
but finally all was still and I emerged from the
barn and passed to the rear, over a fence and
into a kitchen garden, when I saw at its foot a
house of humble pretensions, from the small
window of which a dim light was burning. I
advanced to the door of the cabin and rapped.
It was opened at once by a robust, middle-aged
colored woman, who was accompanied to the
door by another female much younger than herself. They were both surprised and somewhat
scared at the appearance of their singular-look-
ing and late visitor. The younger woman spoke
first.

"Who are you, and what do you want?"

" Do not be afraid," I replied, " I am a friend."

I then told her my circumstances ; that I had waited until the white folks at the large house were all in bed; that I was hungry, tired and wet, as was plain to be seen, and needed some assistance. The elder negress was nervous and fearful, and plainly reluctant to give me any countenance, but I soon talked her into a more sympathetic frame of mind, and she stirred up the fire and invited me to sit down near it. I did so without further ceremony, and soon my soaked clothing was steaming and rapidly drying. The two women retired for a short time while my clothes were drying, and soon I could hear a partly suppressed conversation in an adjoining room.

After its termination the pair returned, followed by another girl and two sturdy " bucks." The newcomers eyed me with undisguised curiosity, but appeared kindly disposed. They listened to what I had to say with attention and evident interest. The negress who had opened the door in answer to my knock appeared to be the head of the household, and now gave orders to the girls to prepare me something to eat. They went to work at once to do so, and I could see them getting ready on a scale entirely unknown to me for months. In return for their kindness I informed them as best I could of how things were going on in the outside world; of the progress of the war, of their consequent near approach to freedom, etc.

To my surprise these faithful servants doubted my word. One of the girls said:

"Missus tole me dat you treated de cullud folks mitey bad in de Norf; an' dat you couldn't whip de Souf, nohow."

It was plain that this slave loved her mistress, and had an implicit faith in her statements. In fact none of this party seemed to yearn for freedom while enjoying this evidently kind treatment from their owner.

"If all slaves, or servants, were treated as kindly and humanely as you evidently are," said I, "we should, possibly, have no war now. But good masters die, and then the servants may have bad times with somebody else."

"I hope my missus won't die," exclaimed the innocent creature.

"I hope not," was my rejoinder, "but we must all pay the debt of nature some day."

By this time there was placed before me a bountiful meal consisting of bacon, flour bread, apple-butter, fresh milk, etc. It would surprise a delicate person were he to see how much of this substantial fare I disposed of. My friends then filled my haversack with meat and bread, and being thoroughly warmed and dry, I was in prime marching order. Before starting, I made some necessary inquiries of one of the men regarding the roads along my route, and carefully noted the instructions he gave me. His knowledge was merely local, but it was very essential on account of the darkness that prevailed. He said I was to leave the pike I was then on and take a diagonal course to the left. I surmised in the early part of the night that I was going a little astray, but the result showed that in falling in with these darkies I had struck the right place after all.

I left these contented and kind-hearted people with feelings of deep gratitude. Taken in general, I believe the negro race to be very sympathetic and kind.

It was not quite so dark now as in the early part of the night, and I soon succeeded in getting on the road to the left, of which the darkies had told me. Being satisfied that I was in the proper path I tramped along contentedly, but had not gone far when I saw a fire about twenty-five yards ahead, and probably six or seven yards from the road. My first impression was that it must be the fire of some wagon train that had encamped for the night, and I took my usual precautions in finding out, and again made the discovery of my late lukewarm acquaintances. They were huddled around the blaze and the steam from their dripping garments was ascending in small clouds. As they sat there they presented a drowsy and woe-begone appearance, and looked as though they had been fasting a long time. I conceived

the idea of giving them a little scare before I
passed by; so, when close up, I gave the word to
"charge" in a loud and authoritative tone, as
though addressing a squad of men. The escaping Yankees showed no "white feather," however,
but remained quietly seated until I advanced.
They recognized me and inquired how I had
fared since leaving them, and all appeared agreeably surprised at my good luck.

I was not very communicative, however, and
was preparing to move on when I bethought me
of my full haversack and their empty stomachs;
and, although I felt that they had acted heart-
lessly towards me, I could not bear to see them
hungry, so I divided the contents of my sack
equally amongst them, and felt a good deal better
for having done so. I then moved on, but the
entire party, without exception, united in entreating me earnestly to remain with them. A conflict
ensued between wounded pride on the one side
and extreme lonesomeness on the other; but at
last I submitted to their urging, and cast my lot
with them for the through trip.

There are many who, doubtless, would not have
done as I did in this instance, and I have a proper
respect for that type of manhood, but, although
high-spirited and sensitive, my anger is but short-
lived. They were very agreeable in their man-
ners now, asking me many questions in relation
to my tramp and success since parting from

them. I was brief in my replies, saying that I had made no great effort; that it was luck; that I was an odd number, etc.

It was still raining, dark, and growing colder, but all were in as good spirits as at any time since the escape.

CHAPTER XXXIII.

Saturday, *November* 19*th.*—We resume our march; the weather simply wretched. In the darkness Captain Hart fell into a deep chasm, but luckily received only slight injuries. About an hour before day we aroused a young darky who got us something to eat; he also conducted us to a neighboring hen-roost, but we failed to capture any of the fowl. It has been raining incessantly and getting much colder; all things considered, this is the most wretched night we have yet experienced.

After leaving the negro we came to a rapid stream, swollen by the late hard rains. We climbed a bluff overlooking its banks to look for a more favorable crossing-place, but had to return to the point from which we first approached it. All stripped but each hesitated to go in, not knowing the depth. I took the water first; but Nelson, young, stout and brave, was in immediately after and spurted ahead. I presume he thought it scarcely proper that the only gray-haired man in the party should be the first to try the depths of the turbulent stream. It took us breast-high and tested our best ability to keep upon our feet. The water was cuttingly cold and chilled us to the marrow. When on the other side, the getting into our pantaloons and shoes with wet feet and sandy legs was a cold and uncomfortable operation. We proceeded until daylight without anything of note transpiring.

Sunday, November 20th.—Shortly after nightfall, and while on the march, we came in sight of a commodious and fine-looking residence. A careful investigation shows that there are no white gentry about the premises. The housekeeper (or, more properly, the mistress) is a quadroon. She learned from some of her underservants of our presence, and sent word that she desired to see us. One of these servants, a pert, loquacious girl, told us very confidentially, for such a short acquaintance, that "de massa" liked the young lady housekeeper "berry much." Her master was not married and the mistress of his household was his slave, yet her authority was supreme about the house.

The owner of these people was not, as good fortune willed it, at home at the time of our visit. The appearance of his mistress, a splendid-looking brunette, tall and shapely, with lustrous, mild black eyes, as beautiful and as graceful as the

queen of a fairy extravaganza, was a great surprise to us. In her treatment of us she proved
as good as her looks. For our better safety,
we were conducted to what is set down in my
diary as the "Travellers' Rest." We fared
sumptuously here, getting chicken, sweet potatoes, apples, etc., and even tobacco for those who
wished to use it. An occasional oasis like this,
in our wide and dismal desert, was a much-
needed stimulation.

The night had grown bitter cold, with a
severe frost, when we again started. Our progress was very slow, soon being stopped by another stream of no small dimensions. We did
not make more than three or four miles in all the
night and were staggering from loss of sleep.
We decided to camp near the river front.

Monday, November 21*st.*—Still embarrassed
about crossing the stream, though very anxious
to proceed. The weather has grown still colder
but the day is bright; we get some beans and
corn, which we cook and make a hearty meal.
We cut new hickory canes and throw our old
ones away. Whenever on our long march we
met with a fine hickory sapling suitable for a
walking-stick, we would cut it down and discard
our old ones. This was the practice of all of our
party except DeWeese. He brought home the
cane he first started with from prison. He was
an expert carver in wood, and an abstract history

of his escape was cut in plain characters on the bark of his cane. While the other officers, like the writer, kept a book record of the events of their flight, he carved his in enduring wood, to remain for all time a curiosity and heirloom in his family.

As night approached, we became determined to cross the river at all hazards. At the point of our encampment it was fifty yards wide at least. We had no idea of its depth, but made up our minds to swim it if needs be. DeWeese called it the "Cullaloo." Stripping off and tying our clothes high up around our heads, we plunged in. It was freezing and snowing now, and the water was bitterly cold, but we at last succeeded in crossing the "angry flood" and devoutly hoped that we should not soon again be called upon to undergo another such test of endurance.

The ordeals undergone for the past two days have been a severe tax upon our reserve vitality. Half an hour after our cold and enforced bath, we came in sight of a rapid stream. Whether it was another river, or the same one whose numerous meanderings we had to cross several times while keeping to our northwest course, I could not say. However this may have been, the hard and bitter fact remained that we must again face the ordeal.

Once over, we realized that we were beginning the ascent of the rugged mountains of the Blue Ridge in North Carolina, whose swollen streams

were too frequently impeding our progress.
Travelling grows more difficult, and in addition
to other impediments the frost proves a severe
punishment to Lieutenant Dimick and myself, as
we are nearly shoeless. The hard rough road
and jagged stones feel like spikes to our poorly
protected soles. All are now badly in need of
something to eat. Dimick and myself made
great efforts to capture a stray sheep which we
discovered in an enclosure near our path; but
we failed to secure it.

Later, I was successful in finding a negro
"quarters." I find black Jim, who is suffering
severely from the toothache (a rare complaint
among the darkies). Jim makes us acquainted
with two or three of his friends, including a buxom
young girl. They appear to be well taken care
of and to have plenty to eat, and when this is so,
they are generally found to be contented and
happy. All of them show us as much kindness
as possible, but "Betsy" is the most assiduous
and successful in providing for our wants. Lieutenant Davis, in recognition of her efforts, and
as a compensation for what she had given us, made
her a present of a gold finger-ring. After eating moderately we still had a little remaining,
which we carefully packed away in our indispensable haversacks.

Tuesday, November 22d.—We secured a nice
resting-place. The day is pleasant and agreeable

and we enjoy our repose to its fullest extent.
We also greased our shoes thoroughly with some
tallow procured from the negroes last night, the
first process of the kind that they have undergone since starting upon our journey, and one
which they much needed.   And then we go
sound asleep.

Soon each heavy-laden brow gently fell;
Who closed last his eyes, I cannot tell;
And who first did blink an owlish wink
At departing day, I cannot say;
I slept so sound, on that damp ground.
In dreams I'm off to the field of strife,
Where drops so many a precious life,
Of comrades dear in their country's cause,
For the flag and for our country's laws.

In that same sleep, I had a dream,
I did not then divulge the same,
As only lovers of fireside bliss
Can rightly feel a dream like this.
I thought I was back in Glade Run water,
With my wife, two boys and little daughter,
The eldest child but six years old,
My heart was home in that loving fold,
While little arms with childish delight
Were clinging to papa so close and tight;
But I woke to a cold embrace that night.

CHAPTER XXXIV.

Lost Again—Dimick's Feet Give Out—Bidding him Good-bye—
His Unexpected Reappearance—Challenged—Capturing Geese.

As night approached, my companions and myself prepared to move. When others rest from the labors of the day, and " the ploughman homeward plods his weary way," we take up a lonely march to our Mecca of freedom. Nothing unusual occurred during the night's tramp, except the appearance of a hard frost, which together with the rough travelling and interminable streamcrossing made our tramp one never to be forgotten.

Wednesday, November 23d.—We made an early start and continued until we came in sight of the small village of Clayton, which we flanked. Our commissary stores are now entirely consumed, and all of our party are very hungry. Dimick reconnoitred a neighboring negro "quarters" for supplies, but returned emptyhanded. Lieutenants Davis and Dimick again tried it with no better success. Hope seemed to centre on me, and I do not recollect of having failed in a single instance to procure food of some

(313)

kind. This time I brought relief after a short absence.

The night has grown so dark that we have small hopes of making any further headway while this darkness lasts. After marching and counter-marching for a couple of hours we become satis-fied that we have lost our way, and finally decide to lay up for the remainder of the night. It is freezing hard, and yet we are very thirsty ; we try industriously to procure some water but fail. It appears to be either a feast or a famine with us as regards water. In the morning we discovered that within ten feet of where we lay there was an abundant supply of the limpid food. As another addition to the night's unpleasantness, I found my trousers badly torn, and having no drawers or lining, I find myself badly off indeed.

Thursday, November 24th.—While it was yet day, a couple of our party set out in search of the road, which we unfortunately lost last night, and succeeded in finding it. We moved out early in the evening in the direction of Franklin, and found the road very rough, and marching on it very painful. Not long after starting, we sighted two small wagon-trains and successfully flanked them. Later on we passed three sportsmen with hounds, presumably going coon-hunting. 'Tis fortunate, we think, that the game sought for is not biped " coon," like ourselves. In the earlier days of our flight, the fellows of these modern Nimrods paid us more attention in this respect.

And now comes another sad trial. Dimick's
shoes are at last completely worn out, and he is
literally walking on his "uppers." It was painful
to see him flinching and suffering as his tender
soles pressed the sharp rough ground. He is
the heaviest man in our party, weighing probably
one hundred and ninety pounds. He had no
blanket, but used instead a well-worn United
States overcoat, minus the cape. We were all
anxious to travel fast, but had to check our speed
in order to not hurry him. Presently we stop
and wait until he cuts off a portion of the skirt of
his coat to bind around his sore feet. After an
hour's hard marching this temporary protection
also gives out, and we wait until he has again
fixed up his feet. He hobbled along after this
last make-shift, suffering severely in his efforts to
keep up with us.

At last he said he could stand it no longer and
would have to give up, or go on more slowly
until he could procure something to put on his
feet. No wonder he had to succumb: the poor
fellow's feet were fearfully cut and bruised, and
were bleeding profusely. With genuine regret
we all shook hands with him and bade him good-
bye. I was the last to part with him and felt
miserably sad on the occasion. All of my comrades, also, were very sorrow to have to abandon
him ; but Dimick, it will be seen, suffered more
from mental than bodily torture after we had left

20

him behind. His complete isolation and the extreme lonesomeness of his situation over-balanced the pain he endured from his bleeding feet, as was shown by the almost superhuman efforts he must have used in running after and overtaking us, which he did in about three-quarters of an hour after bidding us a supposed final good-bye. We were, of course, agreeably surprised to find him with us again, and we thereupon slackened our pace to conform to his necessity; and out of humanity to our unfortunate comrade we soon lay up for the remainder of the night.

Friday, November 25th.—On our march to-night we find the country through which we were passing becoming more populous; and the dogs begin to give us considerable annoyance.

It was some time after midnight, perhaps two o'clock A. M., when we got into the village of Franklin. In passing a few houses in the suburbs we were not positive that we were getting into the town, but as we proceeded we found the buildings becoming more numerous. We then concluded that we must be in about the centre of the town, and that it would be about as safe to advance as to retreat. Why we had acted so thoughtlessly as to make an attempt to pass through such a dangerous place I cannot tell. I had little to say on the subject.

The town was silent and dark, and we glided along in Indian-file. The village consisted of apparently one long main street. When a couple of squares farther on, we could see a faint light glimmering in the distance, as if at the head of the street. We still kept on and the light grew brighter. Suddenly we were halted, the voice sounding loud and clear on the still air; but such a challenge! Our well-drilled officers are not likely to ever forget it. The words of this picket can hardly be written so as to spin them out as they were delivered.

"H–a–l–t! w–h–o c–o–m–e–s t–h–e–r–e?" he drawled.

The answer from our leader came with promptness, decision and ready wit.

"Will Willis."

"C-o-m-e h-e-r-e t-i-l-l I s-e-e y-o-u," was the next demand of the guard.

"Oh," replied DeWeese, "if you are so particular, I don't want to pass," at the same time making a right-about, and from quick to double-quick was the order of our retreat. From the sleepy, half dead-and-alive manner of our challenger, we entertained fair hopes of securing a good start, but thought it almost certain that we should be pursued. The reader is safe in surmising that I was not, by any means, last in this retreat. I vaulted over a fence, passed through a kitchen garden, without taking the time or trouble to scratch for possible potatoes or turnips, and on to the rear. I found myself alone, but reasonably

satisfied that I had made good my escape.   I
continued in a circle and came out at the northern
end of the town, and there luckily rejoined my
comrades. Doubtless that old "home-guardsman"
reflected deeply on what a wayward, naughty boy
that "Will Willis" was to have been out of bed at
such an unchristianlike hour. We did not slacken
our speed much until we felt that we were at a
safe distance from the town, and then daylight
sent us to cover.

SATURDAY, *November 26th.*—Our slumbers are
very much disturbed and our spirits greatly depressed by the frequent firing of small-arms and
the ominous cry of hounds. We are all in a deplorable condition, for the want of a change of
clothing, especially of inner garments.

Night, and our time for marching. We feel
mystified as to where we are going, and after
travelling about five miles in a hap-hazard direction we met a citizen. He informed us that we
were but four miles from Franklin. Then he
directed us to the right road, and, unobtrusive
gentleman that he was, asked us no questions.
It was raining a little at the time of our meeting
and quite dark, and he did not seem to notice
anything unusual or suspicious about us. This
darkness, and consequent absence of the stars,
was the cause of our going astray. We are again
feeling the pinching pangs of hunger, and think
ourselves fortunate in the possession of a few ears
of raw corn.

Away after midnight, when passing a farm residence, we noticed a good-sized pool of water. This pond in itself was not particularly attractive, but on its placid bosom there floated objects of absorbing interest and attractiveness to me. The moving forms were those of geese, and my late acquaintance with that species of fowl was highly conducive to a desire, on my part, for a renewal of our intimacy. The boys passed on, unmindful, but Dimick and the writer tarried. The geese, however, kept in the middle of the pond with ill-mannered pertinacity. If we are to succeed in capturing any we must not be afraid to wet our feet. I took deliberate aim, fired my stick and then took to the water instanter, Dimick closely following.

> And of that pretty flock of geese,
> God forgive us, we took one apiece;
> And putting them gently under an arm,
> We squeezed their necks to prevent alarm.

We soon caught up with our companions, who were, as may be imagined, well pleased with our success.

The night is now far advanced and growing darker. We have not yet found the right road.

CHAPTER XXXV.

SUNDAY, *November 27th.*—At daylight we traversed the woods round about for some distance, looking for the road. At last becoming assured of our bearings, we went into camp. The sun was then coming out bright and strong and the day promised to be one of the finest we had enjoyed for some time.

We are up in the mountains now; the country is rough and thickly timbered, chiefly with chestnut. In our hiding-place we feel quite safe from intrusion and can look upon and enjoy some wild and romantic scenery. From where we build our fire we can see and hear a cascade of the prettiest outline. The volume of water is not large, but is clear as crystal, with the spray sparkling like many-hued gems, as it falls, in the morning sunlight. The water tumbles over three different natural projections, like steps, of a uniform distance from one another, and of the same inclination and degree of uprightness. The whole might properly be called the "Stair Falls."

As raw corn has been our chief subsistence

lately, the mess we are now preparing is quite a luxury. One member of the party has a little tin bucket and in it is boiling corn on a comfortable fire. The rest of us are making goose feathers fly, and as many hands make light work, it does not take us long to pluck, singe, disembowel and wash the geese. Each man then helps himself to a liberal slice and proceeds to broil it over our camp-fire. We wash down this healthful and appetizing meal with copious draughts from one of the mountain springs, and the sum of our earthly happiness is complete.

My increasing nakedness now demands some attention, as a little longer extension of this kind of life will compel me to return to the primitive costume of Father Adam, unless some measures can be taken to arrest the rapid destruction of my garments by the brush and the briars. To check the growing evil I borrow a needle and thread from one of our men, and soon a visible improvement was made in the continuity of my "make-up."

Dimick also has been quite busy. His feet are the greatest source of trouble to him, and the application of goose grease is very soothing to his poor soles. Since his shoes gave out he has used a great quantity of rags in tying up his feet. His overcoat, which originally was very long, its skirts extending below his knees, has been undergoing during the past few days a startling and ludicrous metamorphosis. Two days ago the left skirt commenced to shrink visibly, giving Dimick the appearance of careening heavily to the starboard, but yesterday the right side entirely disappeared, only a few shreds remaining close up to the arm-pits; and to-day—must I record it—the remaining portion of the opposite tail has followed its fellow, and now the heavy and cumbersome army greatcoat of a few days ago has become a trim and natty pea-jacket, giving to the fat and good-natured lieutenant the appearance of an overgrown schoolboy.

To-day is one of our "skirmishing" days. The warm sun, the safe retreat, and above all the pinching necessity of the disagreeable occasion, gave us busy employment for some time. The above is hint enough on the delicate subject of "skirmishing" to any of my readers who have languished in the South as prisoners of war.

Lieutenant Davis reports having seen an old citizen in the woods to-day.

Night.—We descend this chestnut range of mountains, and at the base we strike a narrow road and follow it, but finding it to lead toward the southwest we go slowly and cautiously. We meet a gentleman and three ladies on the road, but let them pass without their seeing us.

Here Dimick makes the discouraging discovery that he has forgotten his haversack, which contained the entire supplies of our party.

We now come to what we suppose to be the Little Tennessee river, and turn with the stream towards its northwest source. The weather has again turned cold and the night dreary. We have no fire, are very hungry, but have nothing to eat.

Monday, November 28th.—We are in a thickly populated district, and are very uneasy, for which reason we lay up all day without fire, cold and hungry. The latter is becoming a chronic complaint in our little band. This constant exposure in such weather as we have had is trying even to an iron constitution. May God sustain us!

Friendly night again, and we are once more on the tramp. But ill-luck seems determined to stick to us, as we lose our way again, returning after a half hour's march to where we had encamped. We start again, and clamber up and slide down an exceedingly steep mountain shortly after making our second attempt, suffering many cuts and bruises in so doing. On account of the pitchy darkness we make but little or no headway, and all are feeling much discouraged in consequence. I now proposed that we detail one of our number to seek information as to our route from the inmates of the first isolated farm-house we should meet, but I was overruled. We lay up in a deep canyon, thoroughly disheartened.

Tuesday, November 29th.—Our party cannot agree upon any given course to follow. Being in

a thickly wooded and rough country bordering on
East Tennessee, we might now travel in daytime
without much fear of arrest, but we have been
wandering up and down all the morning looking
for some sort of a road, and not finding any we
sit down discouraged under a large tree. The
day is nice and warm, and we take a good wash
in a pool of clear water. We have no bread or
meat, or anything but a little raw corn to eat. In
a gloomy mood we hold a council, and I renewed
my proposition of yesterday, saying I thought it
imperative that we should secure some information at once, and did not think there was much
risk in the part of the country we were then in,
believing there was a goodly sprinkling of loyal
citizens there.

Dimick was the only one who favored my views,
and, although in the minority, we became resolved
to carry them into effect. Lieutenant Dimick,
cool, brave, and unpretentious, now started to go
to a house that could be seen at some distance,
and with no other habitation within three-quarters
of a mile of it. I advanced near enough to watch
his movements. I saw him approach the house
and speak to a small boy outside, after which he
entered an outhouse, or barn, near by. He remained inside for some time, and when he
emerged from the building he was accompanied
by a man. Dimick performed his duty well, and
our plan proved a complete success.

The stranger approaching us is a stout, well-built man, about thirty-five years of age, and dressed in a suit of good homespun cloth. His name we learn is Henry P. Grant, and his home Brown's Creek, Macon county, North Carolina. He is a fire-tried Unionist, brave, prudent, determined, and inflexible. All the ingenuity of the rebel authorities failed to make him fight against his country and flag.

By reason of his well-known principles, he was under the necessity of watching and hiding night and day, in season and out of season, in order to keep out of their clutches. To-day he thought he was captured at last when Dimick darkened the door of the barn where he was husking corn. His little son was posted on the lookout while his father worked, but Dimick appeared before him so suddenly the little fellow did not have time to give the alarm. Grant and Dimick tell us that they each eyed the other suspiciously, thinking that each confronted an enemy, and both prepared to fight before surrendering; but when, instead of enemies, they discovered they were friends, their friendship was warm indeed.

All of our party are now made acquainted with Mr. Grant, who is in entire sympathy with us. From where we stand we are in sight of his house, but safe from observation. It is only three o'clock P. M., and Grant is anxious to relieve our distress and give us the shelter of his hospitable roof at

once, but there is a slight obstacle in the way—
there is an armed rebel soldier in the house.

The question of a method for surmounting the
difficulty at once becomes the subject of a council,
in the deliberation of which our friend Grant took
the leading and chief part.   The first decision, and
a most natural one the reader will agree, that we
arrived at was that Mr. Grant should at once
return to his home and procure something where-
with to appease the cravings of our consuming
hunger..

On making known the circumstances to his
wife that estimable lady, the faithful and worthy
companion of a good man, entered at once into
sympathetic unison, acting and planning with her
husband for our aid and comfort.   The first result
of his interview with his wife was his quick return
to us with a bountiful supply of wholesome and
substantial food.   We ate somewhat sparingly,
thinking it not prudent to eat much at a time
after our long fast.

CHAPTER XXXVI.

AMONG KIND FRIENDS—A REBEL SOLDIER IN A QUEER ROLE—NEAR-
ING THE END.

OUR HOST now tells us about this rebel soldier
who is quartered in his house. His name is
Burton McQueen. He is a good-looking, stout
young fellow, of about eighteen or twenty years
of age, and belongs to the "Thomas Legion,"
which is doing post duty fifteen miles from where
we are. The boy is home for a few days on a
furlough to see his widowed mother, made so by
the death of her husband, who was impressed into
the rebel service, and who was killed in action.
Her boy is the widow's only natural support remaining, but he cannot support her now. Mr. and
Mrs. Grant appear to be her main stay at present.
She occupies a house adjoining that of the kind
and hospitable Grants, who are assiduous in their
attentions to the lonely widow. So it is no
wonder that the poor woman is greatly attached
to this worthy couple.

Young McQueen returns to his command to-
morrow morning. The Grants are anxious to
give us a cordial reception in their own house to-
night, but this cannot be done without the knowl-

(327)

edge of the McQueens.   We therefore conclude to confide our situation to the widow, and delegate Mr. and Mrs. Grant to perform the delicate duty.

The result of their mission to Mrs. McQueen exceeds our most sanguine expectations.   They found upon broaching the subject cautiously that the widow was in hearty accord with them in their desire to assist us.   She had, it seemed, no real sympathy with the Southern cause; or if she once had, the loss of her husband and the constant dangers of her son had turned that feeling to a far different one.

The boy, in her hands, was as clay, and soon all is well, and when night came we were conducted to the house, a very comfortable one notwithstanding the numerous raids of the hungry enemy, where we were introduced to Mrs. Grant, with whom we all cordially shook hands.   Seated around a spacious and well-swept hearth, with old-fashioned andirons supporting logs of hickory, ash and beech which composed the incomparable fire, a new life seemed to be infused into the members of our party, as was not strange under such cheering and home-like influences.

Mrs. Grant was bustling about like a true housewife, intent upon preparing us a nice meal. In a short time the table was spread with a snowy white cloth, the viands piping hot were placed thereon, and all were invited to draw up their

chairs and set-to. Our worthy host, who had retired a few minutes previously, now returned,
bearing a good-sized flask in one hand and a
drinking-glass in the other. Standing before us,
he said:

"Gentlemen: Before you begin your meal I
wish you to honor me by partaking of something of my own manufacture, which I have here.
In your present condition, a little tonic, it seems
to me, would not hurt you; it is pure apple-
brandy."

He then approached the writer, and in handing
him the beverage hoped that his venerable friend
would set the example. How many of my readers under such circumstances might have refused
the kindly offer of our host, I am not prepared to
say. If any, they possess, in a marked degree,
an abstemious virtue that I can lay no claim to,
although I have never indulged to excess.

It was suggested that a toast was now in order,
so I poured out a moderate portion of the sparkling fluid, and holding it aloft, said:

"God bless our country and perpetuate its
union! God bless our good President Lincoln,
and give him wisdom and years to finish the
grand work he has begun; and may we all, and
especially our worthy friends here in North Carolina, live to see and enjoy the fruits of our many
sacrifices and our devotion to the cause of freedom
and liberty. A long time between drinks; God
bless us all."

Supper over, and all being in the best of humor, it was suggested that it would be only proper and courteous for some of our number to call upon Mrs. McQueen. Lieutenant DeWeese and Captain Hart were chosen to perform the duty, and were introduced by Mrs. Grant to a comely and pensive matron of about fifty-five years of age. The general subject of our conversation was the war, and its widespread scourges, which phase of the subject we dwelt upon at considerable length. We received, before we left, many assurances of friendship from the widow.

What a happy change in the situation of our little party! A few hours ago we were lost in the mountains, our spirits well-nigh broken, and we staring gaunt hunger in the face. Now, surrounded by kind friends, our wants attended to, and our hearts beating joyfully with the thought that we shall not again suffer the privations and heartaches that we have daily and hourly undergone since the first day of our long and hazardous flight. We realize, now, that we are fast nearing the end of our journey.

It has been decided that we shall start in the morning in company with young McQueen, who is returning to his command, and who has volunteered to act as guide through the woods and mountains. After spending the happiest evening of many months, we retired to sleep and dream, under the protection of a roof, the first covering of the kind for, lo, these many days.

So passed the auspicious twenty-ninth of November, 1864.

Wednesday, November 30th.—Bright and early, kind Mrs. Grant prepared us a dainty and substantial breakfast. After we had taken a refreshing ablution, our host made his appearance with the suspicious-looking bottle of last evening and, if I am not mistaken, all the boys took the "oath" again. After breakfast we took leave of Mrs. Grant and the widow McQueen, and turned our backs on the fair haven of Brown's Creek.

Upon leaving all of us were provided with a full day's rations in our haversacks, and Mr. Grant accompanied us for about two miles to where he had another farm. The house thereon was unoccupied, and was used in winter to store apples and other farm products. When there, he gave us all the apples we could carry, and bade us good-bye.

We have never seen or heard from him since; at least I have not.

We were all now in prime marching order, and started out briskly and with light hearts, including our friend Dimick, whose soles had at last been covered by the kindly thoughtfulness of Mr. Grant. We had a jolly time on the march, cracking jokes and singing snatches of our camp songs, and even taking turns carrying the musket of our

21

rebel guide. His was a strange case, presenting as it did the startling anomaly of a man,
sworn and armed to shoot Yankees, acting as
their friend and guide. It is questionable if anything similar to it occurred during the war. He
conducted us in safety a distance of fifteen miles
on our journey in the broad open light of day,
and to within fifty yards of the outposts of his
command, which place we reached shortly after
dusk, and so close were we that could hear the
soldiers enjoying themselves with music and
dancing. Our guide's reason for bringing us so
close to the rebel camp was because our only feasi-
ble route lay in this direction. I do not know how
my comrades felt, but I recollect distinctly to have
been considerably perturbed when I discovered
our near proximity to the enemy. The man
could have easily given us up, and by so doing
be assured of favorable mention, and probable
promotion, for his zeal; but he proved true to his
mother and faithful to his promise.

Burton McQueen's case may be a subject for
debate and wide divergence of opinion. Many
will claim, no doubt, that he did right, and that
his action was commendable; while others, with
fully as strong argument, will prove that his action
was traitorous and in direct violation of his oath
of allegiance. In justice to the young man it is
but fair to state, however, that he was not in the
Confederate service from choice. He was im-

pressed into their ranks, as was also his father. The matter, therefore, narrows down to the question whether compulsory obligations should or should not be binding. At all events our Confederate guide not only piloted us safely the distance before named, but in leaving us gave important directions as to where we should cross the next river; also where we were to find a loyal family named Welsh, who would assist us.

After a kindly parting with our friend in gray we started on double-quick time, and did not slacken our speed until we had covered a good five miles. Although not a word was spoken on the subject, our minds were alike filled with one idea. Would our guide betray us at the eleventh hour? This thought urged us forward, and not until the river lay between us and the camp of the enemy did we feel safe and were we heartily disposed to do the young fellow justice. Such, however, must always be the fate of one who, like him, violates a solemn obligation.

As indicated by our late guide we shortly came to the point of the river where we were to cross. It was at or near the confluence of the Tuckasee and Tennessee rivers, and was fully one hundred yards wide, making the crossing a fearful undertaking. Had we not been so well used to this business we might have hesitated to enter such a broad and rapid current; but stripping to the buff, we waded into the rushing stream. The water was intensely cold and very deep at points, but we made the passage safely, with our garments badly soaked.

Although not aware of it at the time, we had, happily, crossed our last great barrier. We wrung the water out of our clothes, put them on, and started briskly to restore the circulation in our benumbed frames.

A quarter of a mile from the river we entered the house of Mr. A. B. Welsh. We had been led to believe that this gentleman was a friend, but we found him quite cool and somewhat suspicious at first. In those trying times the loyal frontiersmen were required to be as innocent as doves and as wise as serpents to steer their course safely. The family were surprised when we told them that we had swum the river, and after learning who we were, and how we had suffered, their hearts warmed towards us. Mr. Welsh for a time kept up a semblance of Southern sympathy; but his better half was stoutly Union in her sentiments.

About this time I found I had sustained quite a loss; my trusty butcher-knife was gone. Before removing my clothes at the river I had unbuckled my belt containing the knife, laid it down on the bank, and forgot it afterwards. I was determined to return and recross the stream to secure it, but Mr. Welsh promised to send his son, a young man, for it early the following morning.

The young fellow went, but failed to find the treasure, and it was then too late for me to go back. I felt the loss keenly because of its associations and the protection it had afforded me, but it transpired, happily, that I did not need it much afterwards, as we were getting into a friendly section.

Our day's march from Grant's to Welsh's was about twenty-two miles, and we fully appreciated the hospitalities of this happy home, where warmth, cheerfulness and kindness reigned, and every moment's interchange of views and feelings produced a warmer current of reciprocal friendship. Our treatment so much resembled that which we had received at Grant's, that to enumerate their many kindnesses would be merely a repetition of what I have already said. The same cleanliness existed and the same expedition was used. The only marked difference was in the conversational powers of the respective housewives. Mrs. Grant was quiet and of a rather retiring disposition, while Mrs. Welsh kept up a running stream of small talk while preparing our supper. Having a loving and interesting family herself, she was curious to know how we were situated.

"Are you married?" she asks one.

"No, ma'am."

"Is your mother living?"

"Yes, ma'am."

"May God hear and pity the cries of the mothers of this country!" she piously ejaculated.

She had a question and a pious and appropriate ejaculation for each.

My comrades were all young men, and I believe unmarried. I was then about forty years of age, and in answer to her question said I was married and the father of three children, aged respectively two, four and six, and my wife but twenty-two years old. Surprise, sympathy and censure were then equally blended in her manner and remarks, but sympathy ultimately predominated.

When supper, a most inviting one, was ready, the sprightly little lady whispered mysteriously to her good man, and he retired and directly returned with a decanter containing some first-rate apple-jack of his own make. Like our friend of last evening, giving the preference to age, he first passed the bottle to me. After our meal, to which we did full justice, we learned from the family that they were subject to frequent nocturnal visits from their rebel neighbors, who suspected them of sympathy for the Union, and of harboring Yankee refugees.

It was thought advisable under these circumstances that we should sleep out in the brush rather than in the house. When we made a move, however, Mrs. Welsh spoke a few words to her husband, who then came to me and requested that I should remain in the house, as she had a good bed for me. I thanked her, saying that I was a stranger to such luxuries, and declined the offer, giving as a reason that I thought it safer to be with my comrades.

I shall never forget with what kindness she persisted upon my remaining, urging that the night was cold ; that I needed rest, and that she thought the change would do me good. I then was forced to tell her plainly my real reason for refusing. I could not go into her clean bed, for, breathe it softly, I was lousy, as indeed was every man who was confined in rebel prison pens. Strange to say this disgusting announcement did not cool her charity, or cause her to cease her kind importunities. At last I submitted reluctantly, after devising a plan to prevent the infection of the bed by the disgusting vermin. I divested myself completely of all my "duds," and tying them up in my blanket made a bundle which I placed in the middle of the uncarpeted pine floor, and then crept into bed in the presumable fashion of Father Adam before the era of fig-leaf night-shirts.

I was soon asleep and enjoyed a most refreshing slumber until morning. We all ate a hearty breakfast, which was made doubly pleasing by the untiring efforts of our kind friends to make us comfortable. Mr. Welsh and his son got their rifles and hunting-traps and proposed to escort us up the mountains. When starting, all of us received a liberal day's rations, as on the day before. Father and son each had among his supplies a canteen slung over the shoulder ; one contained Sorghum molasses, and the contents of the other was at the start but a surmise. Through the kindly guidance and protection of the Welshes we escaped two parties of armed rebels.

CHAPTER XXXVII.

ARRIVAL AT CAGE COVE, TENNESSEE—TUCKALEECHIE COVE—AL-MOST THERE.

THURSDAY, *December* 1*st.*—After taking leave of Mrs. Welsh with feelings of genuine regret, we started briskly, leaving the valley of the Little Tennessee and striking out boldly for the Great Smoky, one of the highest mountain ranges in North America, guided by Welsh and his son. In our ascent of the mountain we met with several tiny streams, rapid, sparkling and limpid; their banks bordered thickly with balsam fir, the water clear and cold, and as pleasant to the taste as it was pure in appearance. Our guides tell us that the water of these streams is equally as cold in summer.

Following the course of one of these mountain brooks until noon-time, we arrived at a point commanding one of the finest views along our route—a broad table-land where a mound of earth had made a natural dam, obstructing the current of the bright living waters and forming one of the prettiest little lakes imaginable, its sides fringed with a thick growth of laurel and spruce pine, and in their front a frame of moss-grown rocks of countless shapes and sizes. On a pretty elevation near the water's edge we called a halt and held an informal picnic, and such a one as I have never since enjoyed, although the cold-sliced ham with bread and molasses, washed down with apple-brandy (which one of the canteens was now found to contain), might not be considered, under other circumstances, a remarkably sumptuous repast.

Our genial surroundings shed a new-found happiness upon the members of our little party. We are breathing a healthier atmosphere and enjoying a greater security than heretofore, enabling us to travel in daylight and converse with one another without much restraint, and feeling that we are fast nearing our deliverance ; so, with thankful hearts, we eat, drink, and are merry, not fearing for the morrow. After our enjoyable collation we shook hands and reluctantly parted with the Welshes. They turned and retraced their steps down the mountain's side ; we continued to ascend its rugged heights. After travelling for an hour, we stopped and cast a long last look of grateful emotion far down into that hospitable valley lying below us, where dwelt a noble type of Irish-American patriotism.

The good water, the bracing air, the quantity and quality of our rations, has had a visible effect upon all of us, and by nightfall we arrived at the summit of the mountain, calculated by one of our party to be 6,476 feet above the level of the sea.

We selected our camping-ground, gathered some dry leaves, put down our blankets and prepared for undisturbed repose. We can now indulge in talking aloud; for nearly a month past we have been schooled to whispering:

> Fearful lest some evil breeze our covert should disclose,
> And lead to our recapture by our ever watchful foes.

Miles away from the habitation of man we go to rest, conscious of the unlikelihood of our being disturbed, except possibly by some wild denizen of the forest. We build a fire as a precaution against this latter danger, and then go to sleep. Far in the night, when our fire was smouldering and almost out, we were startled from our slumbers by a mighty rush among the dry leaves, followed a second later by the snorting and bounding away of deer.

Friday, December 2.—We find ourselves now on the State line of North Carolina and Tennessee. The soil of the mountains is very rich; the earth is black and loose and heavily timbered. Cage Cove is five miles from where we stand, with a continued steep descent the whole distance. It is the first settlement we find in Tennessee, and our hearts beat joyfully when we find it inhabited by the truest types of Union men. Oh, how delightful to find ourselves among friends once more!

The men here on the border have had to pay dearly for their loyal principles, but they are a brave and determined set, and often make it decidedly unpleasant for small bands of horse-thieves and other marauders who come among them, as we discovered when at the foot of the mountain, and before we entered the Cove. We there entered a narrow bridle-path, upon which, after travelling but a short distance, we came to a halt, attracted by a fresh-dug grave, in which were imbedded two upright posts, to which was nailed a small board bearing the following inscription in rudely painted letters:

"LET THIS BE A WARNING TO ALL HORSE-THIEVES
AND GUERILLAS."

Much property of these loyal citizens had been taken away or wantonly destroyed, and a number of their best men had been murdered by parties of marauding guerillas. Only a month previous to our arrival a gang of rebels had galloped into the little settlement, and murdered one man and mortally wounded another, the former a Mr. Gregory and the latter a Mr. Shields. Mr. Gregory's son, we learned, was one of the rebel party, and the parasite was well aware that his party were going to murder his father.

The Cove extended westward as far as one could see, and was completely encompassed on the east and south by large mountains. It was level and fertile, and had been a happy and prosperous little settlement before this unholy and fratricidal strife.

As we emerged from the woods and found ourselves in the Cove we felt highly elated by the knowledge that at last we were among friends. But that newly made grave should have admonished us to act prudently upon entering the village. We numbered seven, and were wild, stalwart-looking fellows, all armed with stout hickorysticks, which at a distance might be taken for more dangerous weapons. As we approached the first house a young girl appeared in the doorway. The house was yet about 200 yards in our front, and to the right of us. At the sight of the damsel several of my companions raised a mighty shout, whereupon the girl suddenly disappeared within, apparently badly frightened.

I felt very indignant at such imprudence, which was calculated to create a false and unnecessary alarm, frightening the worthy people without reason, and, being in those days of a somewhat impulsive and hasty disposition, I indulged in some cutting remarks as to their newly found bravery and culpable lack of judgment.

They were evidently much hurt by my remarks, and maintained a silence and reserve for some time afterwards. We now noticed a man mounted upon a white horse, some distance in advance of us, riding into the centre of the town, and we then realized that he was giving the alarm to the set-tlers that the rebels were in the Cove.

We proceeded to the next house, where we found only women and children. We explained our circumstances and who we were to them, and they at once set about preparing us something to eat from their scanty store. We asked them to send word as soon as possible to their neighbors that we were friends and not enemies.

After the excitement had subsided, and when we were comfortably disposed of in the house, my comrades held a whispered consultation apart from me, and at its termination advanced and de-manded that I should apologize for the insulting language I had used towards them.

"Gentlemen," said I, "I am sorry you feel so much hurt by what I consider a deserved rebuke for a rashness so evidently alarming to these worthy people; I cannot apologize, so you will have to decide as to the best way to redress your imaginary grievance."

These officers, whom I have earlier introduced to the reader, were gentlemen of undoubted bravery, refinement, and education, and were well qualified for their successful and arduous journey. Three of them were of the regular army and the other three of the volunteer service, selected by

"He was willing to show the marauders who infested his neighborhood what 'Old '79' could do."—Page 345.

the former as suitable companions in the effort to escape.

Thinking that seven men were too many for this poor woman at whose home we were to entertain, a few of our number went to a neighboring house. I was one of the party that remained. We were just sitting down to a much-needed and very welcome meal when the startling report reached us that the rebel raiders were really in the Cove. I favored remaining and taking the chances where we were but was overruled; however, I did remain until I had somewhat appeased my appetite and secured something in my haversack.

We then started for a low, log block-house, situated in a small clearing in the woods, accompanied by twelve well-armed and determined Union men. Among these brave men of the border was a Mr. George Rowan, seventy-nine years old, and famous as a hunter who hardly ever missed a "buck," even when on the run. He was active, light of foot, muscular, and willing to show the marauders who infested his neighborhood what old "79" could do.

At last it is found that it was our entry that had caused the alarm, and we returned to the settlement.

Saturday, December 3d.—After being right royally entertained by our friends of Cage Cove we prepared to depart. I was so fortunate as to

secure the loan of a horse from one of the settlers.
It was agreed that one of the citizens should
accompany us as far as Knoxville as a guide, and
should bring back the horse and some articles of
necessity from the city for the settlers.   We also
took a memorandum of some notions intended
for the ladies, and ammunition and other articles
for the men, as a partial return for their kindness
to us.

We struck out for Tuckaleechie Cove, four or
five miles distant, which place we soon reached,
and found all good and loyal men there.   We
stopped at the house of a Mr. Campbell, and were
very kindly treated.   Here I met Mr. Samuel
Wetzel, from my State (West Virginia).   He
knew me, and did all in his power to make us
comfortable.   He even gave me his horse to ride
to Knoxville, and I transferred the one I rode to
Lieutenant DeWeese.

Sunday, December 4th.—Half a dozen men
of this second Cove mounted their horses and
came with us for about twelve or fifteen miles, in
order to put our foot-men across the many wide
and rapid streams along our route.   During the
day's tramp we passed through a fine and richly
cultivated country, and at noon we ate our lunch
upon the banks of a beautiful stream within ten
miles of Knoxville.

When about six miles from the city, our guide
pointed out the residence of a Mr. Brown, who

appeared to be very comfortably situated. We found Mr. Brown very reserved, and reluctant to admit us at first, but he afterwards treated us very well. He was true to the Union cause, and had two sons in the United States army.

Being now well fortified inwardly, we feel invigorated both in mind and body, and look forward eagerly to our reunion with our gallant comrades in arms, from whom we have been so long and so unwillingly separated, and to reach whom we have made such mighty efforts and endured so many privations.

When at last we came in sight of the glorious old flag, the Stars and Stripes, waving grandly on the fort at the southern end of Knoxville, it was not to be wondered at that we raised a shout whose tones reverberated from valley to hill, and returned with the pleasing assurance of the advent of our longed-for deliverance. The videttes were on the alert, and at our appearance thought no doubt that the enemy was approaching. We were challenged and closely questioned by the pickets, and then conducted to the town by a corporal of the guard. When near the town, and still in the vicinity of the fort, we observed evident marks of recent fighting, which had occurred, we learned, only a few days previous to our entry.

22

CHAPTER XXXVIII.

ARRIVAL AT KNOXVILLE—GOVERNOR BROWNLOW—INTERVIEWING
PAYMASTERS—CHATTANOOGA—A SPARRING MATCH—LOOKOUT
MOUNTAIN—THE GERMAN SOLDIERS—SHERIDAN'S RIDE.

ARRIVED at Knoxville, we saw some four or five
gentlemen approaching us. They were evidently
all officers except one. The civilian wore a suit
of dark-colored, plain-cut clothing, and I recognized him at sight, although I had never seen him
before. Walking straight over to where he stood,
I said:

"You are Governor Brownlow, are you not?"

"Yes," he answered, "but I do not recall your
face."

"We have never met before," said I, "but the
last book I have read claims you, sir, as its able
author; and its frontispiece is a well-executed
steel engraving, so perfect a likeness of yourself,
indeed, that I could not possibly mistake the
original."

This was the famous "Fighting Parson," then
Governor of Tennessee, who proved as true to
the Union as he was to the Gospel, and as ready
to confirm his position with the sword too, if needs
be. His intelligence, bravery, influence and pa-

(348)

GOVERNOR WILLIAM G. BROWNLOW,
"THE FIGHTING PARSON."

triotism, more than any other single cause, helped
to restrain his State from going wholesale into the
Confederacy. While I am taking a short glance
at the great Governor of Tennessee, his friends
are scrutinizing us with somewhat humorous curiosity; and no wonder they do so, for we presented
a decidedly ragged and unkempt appearance and
were almost barefooted. What was once Dimick's
old blue overcoat is now the funniest-looking
garment possible to imagine. As I have already
stated, it was at first a very long one; but when
his shoes played out, before we reached Franklin,
he commenced at the bottom of the skirts and
kept clipping them off to protect his bare feet
from the sharp and frosty ground, until now, when
we arrive in Knoxville, he has remaining only two
sleeves, or parts of them, and a strip of the body
probably twelve inches long; this veritable "cut-
away" on a big, tall, good-natured, gallant fellow
like Dimick, was calculated to make even an
anchorite laugh.

I took from my haversack an ear of corn and
showed it to the Governor, as a specimen of the
chief article of diet upon which we subsisted
during our long race for liberty. He called the
attention of his staff (his son, a lieutenant, being
one of them) to the kind of luxury we fared on.
All were very sympathetic, notably the Governor
himself, who gave orders that we should be properly attended to and cared for. His orders were

carried out punctiliously and with cheerful alacrity; we being conducted to a commodious building, where a warm bath was prepared for us.   In
a short time each came from the healthy ablution
regenerated, and as happy as a brave young soldier when donning his first shoulder-straps.

The city was full of good stories of the governor, one of which I must tell.   Long after every
other American flag had been hauled down in
Knoxville, he courageously kept his flying.   On
one occasion a Louisiana regiment *en route* for
the front halted in the city.   Seeing the Brownlow
flag flaunting defiance in the breezes, they sent two
men to cut it down.   The parson's daughter answered their summons and, learning their errand,
drew a revolver from her dress pocket and, leveling
it at them, defiantly replied:

" Come on, sirs, and take it down ! "

As they backed off before her determined advance they said something about getting more
men to do the work, to which she sneeringly
answered:

" Yes ; go and get some *men;* you are not men."

On the following day, wishing to pay some
grateful attentions to our kind friends of Cage
Cove, we procured some needed articles, including
boots, shoes, powder, gun-caps, etc., and sent
them back with our late guide.

Being out of money we applied to a paymaster
who was at this time in Knoxville, for some of

"Come on, Sirs, and take it down!"—Page 352.

the back pay due us, but he refused. We thereupon telegraphed Major Clark, United States Paymaster, then in Chattanooga. He answered us
promptly, saying:

"Come on; it will give me pleasure to relieve
you."

On Wednesday morning, December 7th, we
started for Chattanooga by train, but had a slow
ride, not arriving there until 5.30 o'clock P. M.
We put up at the Crutchfield House, kept at this
time by a Mrs. Bishop. It had the poorest accommodations that I ever received at any hotel
charging $3.50 per day. The rooms were without
fires and almost barren of furniture. We even
had to make a deposit of fifty cents each for the
privilege of using a towel. The hotel was crowded
with a promiscuous gathering of civil and military
dignitaries and hangers-on. All seemed to have
plenty of money and seemingly were bent upon
spending it. The presence in the town of three
United States paymasters was probably the cause
of the unusual plethora.

In such a motley crowd, as was but natural to
suppose, "John barley-corn" flowed freely, giving
loquacity and vivacity to the veteran braves, and
courage and self-importance to the civilians.
There was present a young man of the latter
class, who was conspicuous among all the assem-
bly for his style and bearing. He boasted of how
he had disposed of a young pugilist the evening

before in a soft glove encounter, and displayed at the same time a set of gloves, as if to say, "Who will try them on with me?" In the absence of other amusements, the "manly art" was generally practiced by our men during the war, especially so when large bodies of troops were quartered together for any length of time.

The room in which we were assembled was quite a spacious one, and had a large stove at its centre for heating purposes. No one seemed disposed to put on the "mits" with the young man, who exhibited fine physical proportions, and looked a formidable antagonist. Although I kept shady for some time, I was determined that he should not retire untried. Finally I suggested quietly to one of my comrades to introduce me for a friendly pass with the redoubtable youngster. As he did so, all eyes were directed towards me, and a great many present treated my acceptance of the defiance as a joke, and laughed good-naturedly, as did also the young athlete himself. The contrast was quite striking between the youthful and blooming giant and the gray-haired and somewhat cadaverous-looking old man.

My opponent smilingly tossed me the gloves, and we were soon in position. When I stood before my man I had no misgivings, but I sparred cautiously for a while, until I got an opportunity to use my right, causing him to spin to the left. I followed this up a second later and while he was yet on the move, with a blow from the "kithogue" on his left ear, which sent him crashing against the stove before mentioned, and we had a time gathering it up hastily to prevent a fire. There was no disposition on the part of the young fellow to renew the encounter.

The remainder of the evening passed very pleasantly, and I made a great many new acquaintances.

The next day I received five months' pay from Major Clark, being about one-half of the amount due. The other officers were paid also. Major Clark would have given us more but we would not accept it, as we were running a risk in carrying even so much, especially those of us who later volunteered to cross the enemy's path again, via Cumberland Gap and Wild Cat Knob, in order to reach Cincinnati.

On Friday, the 9th, the medical director procured ambulances and had us conveyed to the summit of Lookout mountain, whereon there was then an officers' hospital. The place was well kept, with beautifully laid out grounds, and its situation and the ample supplies in store made it an eminently admirable place for convalescents. The treatment received there also proved highly conducive to the building up of the shattered health of many a gallant veteran. The journey thither was one of almost continuous ascent from Chattanooga to the top of the mountain, and consequently our progress was slow and somewhat tedious. We arrived about dinner time, and were cordially received and treated in a characteristic soldierly fashion. We enjoyed our dinner and other little attentions, with the relish of those who had long been denied such luxuries.

There was another feature connected with the neighborhood that occupied our thoughts in no small degree. We were now looking upon the wild and natural fastness where the famous battle "above the clouds" was fought. As we look out upon this famous battle-ground with the appreciative eyes of old soldiers, we feel an involuntary thrill of pride at the wonderful achievement of the Union forces on this memorable occasion. What a galaxy of military genius and chivalry represented our army here! With such leaders as Grant, Sherman, Sheridan, Hooker, Thomas, Geary, Wood, Dodge, Granger, the Smiths, Ewing, Carlin, Davis, Palmer, Osterhaus, Howard and Brannon, it is no wonder that those able and trained generals, Bragg and Longstreet, with their gallant army, flushed with their late success at Chickamauga, and occupying as they did a position of vastly superior natural advantages, could not withstand the resistless onslaught of the Union troops.

Saturday, December 10*th*, was a wet and disagreeable day. Heavy clouds encompassed the mountain, cutting off from our view the valley

" 'The wild and natural fastness where the famous battle 'Above the Clouds' was fought.'"—Page 356.

below. But everything was pleasant and comfortable within the hospital, where there was a good table of substantial fare, and clean and warm sleeping accommodation, all furnished for the moderate charge of $1 per day.

The ward to which we were assigned was occupied chiefly by officers of German birth or descent, and they presented such a picture of happy congeniality as I have seldom witnessed. They appeared to have to eat everything desirable and palatable to the German taste, and seemingly no stint of the beverage so dear to the heart of the thoroughbred Teuton. Seated on their cots, which were drawn up to form a circle for the occasion, with packs of cards between them, and each with a meerschaum pipe between his lips, making the atmosphere of the ward redolent with smoke, they looked and acted the picture of genuine and complete contentment.

Having incidentally touched upon the subject of the German soldier, I would here say that their proverbial thrift and industry, their admitted soldierly qualities, fraternal intercourse and loyalty to one another, and their well-established jealousy of any infringement on the laws of liberty and justice, are such as to be, in my opinion, well worthy of emulation.

We remained up until a late hour in the entertaining company of these hospitable comrades, who had many war reminiscences to recount, which were, of course, entirely new to us, on account of our remoteness and complete isolation while in prison. We, in turn, described to them the luxuries, the pleasures and the hospitalities we uniformly enjoyed while the guests of our friends in the " bright, sunny South." And now we seek our peaceful couches, when the muse, in one of her mistaken freaks, taps on my dull cranium, and so I think :

For hardships and dangers passed, comes a partial reward at last,
    In our right royal reception at Lookout mountain,
Where the pure and bracing breeze doth fan the lofty trees,
    And sparkling falls the water from the fountain.

With pleasure and with pride we hear of Sheridan's ride
    From Winchester, twenty miles from his command,
Whom he found in full retreat, scared and badly beat,
    But at once he brought them to a royal stand.

Then his waving sabre flashes, as through the ranks he dashes,
    While cheers of inspiration rend the plain.
He shouts " Right about, my boys, we'll give Early a surprise,
    And send him back far faster than he came."

When the aides received the word, their horses soon were spurred
    Into the broken ranks, extending left and right,
Then to the front and rear they rapidly repair
    With instructions to push into the fight.

The response is free and fast as they hear the bugles' blast,
    To the charge, in martial notes resounding,
Then on the double-quick, through bullets hot and thick,
    Unchecked our gallant troops came fiercely bounding.

Now Early's whole command here made a stubborn stand,
    But from centre to circumference it was shaken.
At last they wheel about, their retreat becomes a rout,
    With five thousand of their number prisoners taken.

Their cannon, too, and rifles, with many lesser trifles,
  They sustained amongst their heavy loss.
Some rebels make a plea that Early took a spree,
  But, in truth, the noble Sheridan was his "boss."

And now we see it plain, how a single man may gain
  A great victory from seeming dire defeat.
Among all the shining stars of the votaries of Mars,
  General Sheridan is the hardest yet to beat.

CHAPTER XXXIX.

For months prior to the date of our arrival
within the Union lines, Knoxville and Chattanooga had been the rendezvous of escaping prisoners of war from every rebel prison within a
radius of six hundred miles, all of whom made
these places their objective points. The majority
of them were now anxious to get home; some to
stay there, but more to rejoin their commands at
the front as soon as possible. Among the number
most anxious to return to the North were Major
Clark and his two assistant United States paymasters; but how to do so was the absorbing
question.

Generals Thomas and Hood were at this time
engaged in a deadly conflict at Nashville, on the
line of the railroad over which we would be forced
to travel to reach our destination. It was questionable when the line would be open for traffic,
and our party had already grown impatient.
There remained therefore but one practicable,
though exceedingly dangerous, course left to us;
that was to make the trip overland by way of

(362)

Cumberland Gap and Wild Cat Knob, to Cincinnati.

This route would involve eight days' marching and being unguarded by our troops for at least a hundred miles, the journey would be attended with considerable risk to so small a party as ours proved to be. This latter fact was owing, in a great measure, to the backwardness of a majority of the men, who had been incarcerated for many weary months in Southern prisons, to incur unnecessary dangers, especially so as they were now in the enjoyment of comparative luxury and among friends.

None of the six officers with whom I escaped volunteered for this hazardous trip over the Cumberland mountains, preferring to remain where they were, and bear the ills they had, rather than fly to others they knew not of.

On Sunday, December 11th, after a hearty breakfast, we took leave of our kind comrades at the military hospital on Lookout Mountain, and, accompanied by several other officers, walked leisurely down to the city. The day was fine and the road good, being a gradual descent all the way. We found the exercise very agreeable and exhilarating. Arrived at Chattanooga, we found a telegram, dated Knoxville, from Captain Albert Grant, in which he informed us that he was organizing a determined little force to make the trip above mentioned, and asked us to get all the volunteers in Chattanooga that we could, and to come to Knoxville immediately.

We went to work, and by nightfall had quite a respectably sized squad ready for departure next morning. We found no improvement in the accommodations at the Crutchfield House. When ready to retire, we were shown to a dormitory as large as a barracks and as cold as an iceberg. The beds were as hard and as flat as gridirons. The covering of each consisted of a sheet and a *comfort*, but what a misnomer for that holey and wafer-like article! The furniture in the room consisted of a rickety and three-legged chair, which I fear one of the boys mistook, next morning, for kindling wood.

We left Chattanooga for Knoxville early Monday morning, December 12th, but owing to the bad condition of the railroad caused by continued neglect of repairs, our train was compelled to run very slowly, and we did not arrive at Knoxville until about an hour after night.

Captain Grant was awaiting us at the depot, and received us very cordially. We were quite well pleased with the genial manner of the vivacious captain upon this, our first acquaintance. He informed us that we could secure quarters at the United States hospital. We accordingly went to the place named, but were not admitted. Our next move, guided by the captain, was to the Franklin House, where we were fortunate enough to secure good accommodations, and where we passed a very pleasant evening in the company of a jovial party of officers, among whom our new commander was acknowledged to be the most jolly. He appeared to be considerably elated at the prospect of commanding an expedition to be composed of so many commissioned officers, many of whom far outranked him.

The next day, Tuesday, December 13th, was spent in completing all necessary arrangements for our march over the mountains. By night-fall we had procured a supply of cast-off arms and accoutrements, together with some broken-down horses and mules from the quartermaster at Knoxville. This officer, before delivering these supplies, required vouchers in due form from some responsible member of our party, for the safe convoy and proper rendering up of the property to the government upon our arriving at Cincin-nati, or sooner, if practicable.

Captain Grant, I understood, signed the receipts presented to him, thinking it no doubt a mere for-mality in this case, as the material received was of such a character, being almost valueless, as to lead him to believe that it was of little use to the government or to any one else. When, there-fore, we arrived at the little town of Crab Orchard, in Kentucky, where the good-natured captain de-livered up the property in his charge, he was so pleased with the success of his expedition over the wild and rugged mountains that he neglected, thoughtlessly, to secure proper receipts from the quartermaster at Crab Orchard. Like the quarry-man, however, who lost the contractor's crowbar and who on the following pay-day informed a friend that he had found the missing tool, and being asked by that individual, "where?" replied, "in the boss's ledger;" so Captain Grant a short time afterwards found his big crowbar in Uncle Sam's ledger as a "bar" to his back pay, which, owing to his long imprisonment, amounted to a considerable sum.

On Wednesday, the 14th, arms, ammunition and accoutrements were issued to us by Commander Grant. He also made an assignment of a few of our number to the different positions in the little force. He designated me to take charge of the rear guard. Among the latter I recall the names of a few, as follows: Captain Fuller, Lieutenants Thornburg, Conn, Good, Coleman, Applegate and Tinker; Sergeants Gordon and Crow; Privates Carlisle, Sells, Westfall, Bowers, Nelson, Munnell, Darcey and Monlan; and citizen Davis.

The first-named officer, Captain Fuller, of the West Virginia State Militia, together with Private Darcey above mentioned, and two other comrades, while away from their command on a scouting expedition, were captured by four rebel raiders. The captain related, and his story was fully corroborated by Private Darcey, that while being marched to prison through the mountains of North Carolina, the party called a halt one day about dusk, at a deserted cabin on the summit of the mountain; they made a fire, cooked their food, and soon after lay down and fell asleep, the Confederates foolishly neglecting to guard their prisoners. Captain Fuller, however, remained wide awake and, at the proper time, gently awakened his comrades, and whispered to them to secure the guns of their escorts. This they quietly did and at last, when the "Johnnies" awoke and rubbed their eyes, they found themselves the victims of a bold Yankee trick.

Captain Fuller now told his ex-captors that his and his comrades' safety demanded that they be summarily disposed of. This announcement scared them badly and they begged piteously to be allowed to go unharmed, promising to take any obligation required to not make any alarm, or attempt their recapture. As a matter of fact, there was little chance of their being able to do so in the wild and isolated region in which they were. After administering most solemn obligations to each, and taking the guns and side-arms of the crest-fallen "Johnnies," Fuller and his party departed and made good their escape to Knoxville.

As we rode out of Knoxville at ten o'clock A. M. we presented a rather motley and incongruous

23

appearance in our variegated uniforms and with our rusty firearms, and astride of animals in all stages of disease and decrepitude. Military distinctions in our party were, in a great measure, lost sight of during the period of our journey. The major and the sergeant, the colonel and the corporal, rode familiarly side by side on terms of the greatest intimacy, sharing each other's burdens and privations with true brotherly solicitude.

It required no little courage to face such a road as we now had before us, of about two hundred miles in length, and through an almost unbroken wilderness.

About an hour after starting one of our team mules lay down with the proverbial deliberation of his species, and no amount of coaxing and beating judiciously divided availed to bring him out of the mire. With some further effort he was released from his harness and extricated from the mud, and replaced in the wagon by one of the pack mules, and we moved ahead again.

Throughout our journey, whenever any of the teams would stall, or get into particularly bad places, which, as may be surmised, was quite often, our men would cheerfully place their shoulders to the wheels, and so keep the tired animals up. By these means, together with the good care taken of the stock, we were enabled to make surprisingly good headway.

Being busy attending to the duties assigned to

me, on this difficult trip, I here quit my diary entries for good until I rejoin my company before Richmond.

I believe it was on the eve of our first day's march that we came to a rapid stream, the descent to which was steep and winding. The opposite side was high and closely wooded to the water's edge; a most favorable time and place for the enemy to attack us would be here, while we were fording this river. It was getting dark as we approached the stream, and we could discern several flickering lights in the woods in our front and on the opposite side of the current. Our advance checked up long enough to enable us to get into more compact shape, and for a brief consultation among the officers.

It was decided to feel for the enemy, or to awaken him if found where the lights indicated. To this end several well-aimed shots were fired in that direction, without awakening any response. We then took to the river, which proved barely fordable, passed over safely without molestation, and encamped for the night on a level space about a half mile beyond the river, where we picketed our animals and disposed of the wagons in such a manner as to afford us the best protection in the event of an attack.

We also had guards properly placed around the camp with a schedule of reliefs, and used every precaution to guard against a surprise. The presence in our midst of three United States paymasters made us more watchful than we otherwise might have been, knowing that the enemy, if aware of their proximity, would naturally be greatly interested in the capture of such a booty as these gentlemen might reasonably be supposed to have in their possession. Happily this night of our greatest apprehension passed without interruption. Our trip, aside from its dreary tediousness, was devoid of any particular interest as regards incidents, if I except the following humorous episode, though at one time it promised to be tragic in its character.

In the organization of our somewhat diversified band, in which the colonel or the major was liable to be called upon occasionally to perform the duties ordinarily appertaining to the private, it was not to be expected that a very strict system of discipline could be maintained, although, as a rule, rank and grade were temporarily waived in passive submission to the gentleman who had assumed command. The one exception to this arrangement was Captain Todd, a small, vivacious young fellow, full of life and spirits, and possessed of considerable good nature, though at times a trifle headstrong. When passing a small settlement in the mountains, the houses of which presented the external appearance of possessing some home comforts, Todd and one or two comrades made an incursion in the direction of the abodes and confiscated, as contraband of war, whatever articles caught their fancy, and were easily portable. When these acts of pillage came to the ears of Commander Grant, he became virtuously indignant at such a flagrant breach of discipline, and forthwith he sought out the doughty little captain and severely reprimanded him for his offence.

Todd was on his dignity in a moment, and retorted to the censure in terms anything but complimentary to the dignity of a commander who, as in this case, was honored with the control of as many commissioned officers as a brigadier-general. Crimination and recrimination were hurled at each other by the thoroughly infuriated officers, who were already grasping the hilts of their rusty swords. At this critical juncture several officers interposed, and a truce was called. So ended for that day what appeared to be a near approach to a bloody encounter. That night when the two belligerents sought their couches it was only to brood over their respective grievances of insult and injured dignity, which grew larger the more they were thought of, until by morning both gentlemen were in a state bordering on frenzy. As a result, a challenge passed between the two officers as soon as day permitted the hostile interchange. As to which of them issued the sanguinary document I am not prepared to say, but I believe it was Captain Todd.

By this time the entire command had become apprised of what was transpiring. The majority of us looked upon the matter as a huge joke, but all were prepared to prevent if necessary any such foolish passage-at-arms. The humorists of our party derived a great deal of enjoyment from several interviews obtained under the guise of deeply concerned friendship with the challenged party, who had, under the rules of the code, the choice of weapons. He was asked what weapon he preferred; if he named a revolver, one of the jokers would interpose, and with great seriousness inform the duellist that his opponent was a dead-shot   If the sword was mentioned, another friend would volunteer the information that with that weapon the challenger was invincible, and so on all through the list. Another objection to such a method of settling their grievances, and one that appeared to have been momentarily lost sight of, was that one of the articles of war in the book of army regulations expressly prohibited, under a severe penalty, any resort by officers to the code of honor.

I cannot say which of the points raised as a bar to bloodshed had the most potential effect, but I am safe in stating that, after this latter intimation, our peaceful interpositions were not so strongly resisted by either of the valiant gentlemen. For two or three days following the issuing of the challenge the dying embers of the hostile blaze would flicker up again, but at last it died out completely in boyish forgetfulness, leaving but slight traces of this amusing interlude to an otherwise weary journey over the worst road in all creation.

We found a detachment of our troops at Cumberland Gap, and enjoyed in consequence more repose and creature comforts there than at any place since leaving Knoxville. Cumberland Gap is a natural stronghold; wild, rocky, and precipitous to such a degree as would enable a small body of troops to withstand an army. Henceforth to the end of our journey travelling was safe and pleasant, and nothing occurred during the remainder of the trip worthy of mention.

Our minds were now alike concentrated on the sweet thoughts of home and friends, and when we reached the first railroad station a partial separation among the members of our band took place, and at Cincinnati a complete breaking up of the party. So far as I am concerned it was almost a final one, having seen but one of our entire number since, and that was Captain Grant, whom I met some years later in the city of Washington, he still being in trouble with the government authorities regarding his non-accounting for the stores furnished him for our expedition.

When I arrived in Cincinnati about the first thing I did was to telegraph my wife that, God permitting, I would see her in three days from date of message, which would be Christmas, 1864. I was at home according to promise. My unexpected return and gaunt and pallid appearance looked so much like a resurrection of the dead that some of my friends, and, indeed, one of my family—my eldest son—questioned my identity. Of course this state of affairs was merely momentary, and soon we were gathered around the festal board, laden with a bounteous Christmas dinner, which, as may be surmised, we discussed with joyful hearts and good appetites.

CHAPTER XL.

AFTER a long and painful absence, covering a
period into which were crowded incidents of such
character and number as do not fall to the lot of
most men, I am at last at home in the bosom of
my little family and surrounded by kind friends,
all glad to have me with them again and anxious
that I should remain. Having "exchanged" myself by running away from prison, there was
nothing to prevent my remaining quietly at home,
watching events until all the danger was over, and
then, reporting to the proper authorities, rejoin
my company at the close of the war.

But, as before stated, my strongest incentive
to undertake the many hardships connected
with my escape from the South was not so
much the thoughts of the endearments of home
as the hope of rejoining my command at Chapin's
Farm, before Richmond. This I did ten days
prior to the expiration of my leave of absence of
one month granted by the Secretary of War to all
escaped prisoners, and this fact should be accepted

(375)

as sufficient evidence of my unaltered determination to do my full duty to the end.

About the middle of February I again parted from my family and started for the front. I could not help feeling that my chances of returning were very slight indeed. It was easy to perceive and natural to expect that, as the struggle approached its final and conclusive blow, the conflict would be continuous, fierce, desperate, and much circumscribed in its scope, and for all these reasons doubly dangerous to the participants of both armies.

As a member of a skirmishing company I expected to occupy an active and advanced position in the front, where, if there was any work to be done, we were sure of being among the first called upon to assist in its performance.

Filled with these thoughts, I prepared a day or so before my departure a few lines of farewell to my wife and family, with instructions that the seal be not broken except in the event of my death. This letter, of course, has never yet been opened, and still remains among my papers.

When passing through Washington, D. C., on my way to rejoin my company, then with the Army of the James, I neglected to call upon "Honest Abe," our martyred President, with whom, as is well known, the humblest soldier in the land was always sure of securing an audience and a cordial welcome. Had I imagined that I should never again have that honored privilege I assure the reader I would not have overlooked it then.

The Army of the James, Major-General E. O. C. Ord commanding, was encamped on the plains at Chapin's Farm, confronting Richmond. A few days after my arrival there, on the 17th of February, 1865, the 1st Division of the Army of West Virginia, embracing the 10th, 11th, 12th, and 15th West Virginia Infantry Regiments, was incorporated into the 24th Army Corps, Major-General John Gibbon commanding. Our regiments formed the 3d Division of this corps, commanded by Brevet Major-General John W. Turner; the 1st Brigade of this Division was composed of the 10th, 11th, and 15th Regiments, under command of Brigadier-General (later Brevet Major-General) Thomas M. Harris; while the 12th Regiment was incorporated in the 3d Brigade, under command of Colonel William B. Curtis, of the 12th.

All of the boys of the company appeared glad to see me after our long and somewhat eventful separation. I found them, on my return, well seasoned veterans, with a record made during my absence that was a source of pride to both the men and their captain.

Wherever and whenever there are large bodies of troops encamped for any considerable period, as was the case here at Chapin's Farm, at the time of which I write, there will often occur laugh-

able incidents, originating in the wild exuberance
of some of the younger men, seeking a means of
whiling away the tedium of camp-life. One of
these little episodes took place shortly after my
return to my company, which has often since
been laughingly recalled to my mind by many of
the men who participated in the mirth-provoking
race.

The line officers not having much to do, were
wont to devote a goodly portion of their time to
the self-pleasing task of adorning their persons
as becomingly as was possible under the circumstances. It was about this time that "paper
collars" appeared on the market, and when the
officers found these little articles in the list of the
sutler's supplies, they eagerly purchased his entire stock, and lost no time in arraying themselves
in their best uniforms and adorning themselves
with one of these immaculate delusions.

When I found all my brother officers thus ap-
parelled, I too followed the general lead, rather
than appear odd. These innovations, however,
were looked upon with high disfavor by the rank
and file, and so, shortly after the appearance of
the delusive parchment choker, the men instituted
a regular and determined raid upon the obnoxious
collar, and soon countless bits of white paper
could be found strewn about the camp in all
directions, remnants of the shattered pride of the
officers.

One day, during the progress of this crusade of extermination, I was sitting in my little "quarters" engaged in some writing and arrayed in one of the hated little neck-bands, when my attention was attracted, by a mighty shout in my immediate neighborhood, to a large crowd of men approaching in the direction of my quarters. I soon learned of their object, and immediately became resolved for fun.

Jumping up, I loosened the breast buttons of my jacket, and as the foremost despoiler appeared at the entrance to my tent I made a rush in his direction, like a headstrong pig, but, stooping under his arms, I escaped his clutches. Once outside in the open ground I straightened up and started away from my determined pursuers over a field as level as possible, and of hundreds of acres in extent.

It is difficult to imagine a more exciting chase than now took place. At first the large number of my pursuers was appreciably augmented by fresh recruits, but soon the crowd dwindled down and the contest remained only to the best and more determined runners. These often and often succeeded in putting their hands on me for an instant, but by an active turn or sudden twist I threw them off and sped away. One by one the men abandoned the chase until I was free to rest, and finally to return to camp, where I found a great crowd awaiting me, of whom I requested.

the honor of being permitted to wear the collar of which they had failed to divest me. I am pleased to be able to state that my request was cheerfully granted, and I was ever afterwards un-molested in the exercise of my right to wear the article in question.

The next move of any importance of our division was on the 26th of March, 1865, when we were ordered to Long Bridge, on the Chicka-hominy. The place of our encampment had been at New Market, whither we had gone a few days before to aid General Sheridan to effect a cross-ing of that stream on his way from the White House to the south side of James river; but on our arrival at the designated point we found that General Sheridan had already effected a crossing several miles below. The division then returned to New Market, where it received orders to pro-ceed at once to the left of our line at Hatcher's Run, to co-operate in the general movement against the enemy.

The 1st Brigade, 10th, 11th, and 15th Regi-ments West Virginia Infantry, under command of General T. M. Harris, was the first to strike the enemy's lines at an angle where two of his forts were concentrated near Petersburg. In ap-proaching these outer forts Companies A and B of the 15th Regiment, Captain Dovenner in charge of the former, and the writer of the latter company, were ordered by General Harris to ad-

vance as skirmishers, which we at once did, driving
in the enemy's outer posts.

In marching in advance here we passed the
late encampment of a portion of the enemy re-
cently engaged in the conflict with our forces.
The scene that presented itself was a horrible one
to look upon. The ground was cut up in many
places by newly made graves, sticking up from a
number of which could be seen the ghastly heads
of the hastily and imperfectly buried soldiers.
The woods and ground for a good distance surrounding the late rebel camp were also badly
shattered and cut up by our shot and shell. I
was afraid the awful spectacle would have a dam-
pening effect upon the ardor of our boys now
going in, who were expected to give a good account of themselves. The sight had no apparent
bad effect, however, and they performed their
duty, as usual, without faltering. We kept
steadly on in front of these forts, compelling the
enemy to fall back to his trenches.

Being now as far as we could go without making
regular targets of ourselves for the enemy's
sharpshooters, protected behind his breastworks,
I halted my company, and ordered the men to lie
down. We found ourselves in an open field at
the time I gave this order, without the slightest
protection of any kind, even while lying prostrate
on the ground, and a number of my men were
badly wounded while thus exposed. Fearing a

sudden approach of the enemy from an unexpected quarter, and in order to see perfectly all
that was going on in front of and behind us, I
remained standing and in consequence had
several narrow escapes. For a short time, while
in this exposed situation, I had the slight protection of an isolated sapling of about seven
inches in diameter, and probably fifteen feet in
height. Such as it was, it undoubtedly saved
my life from a bullet which otherwise would have
taken me full in the breast.

During this day my clothing was cut in five
different places, and one of my boots became
pretty well filled with blood from a flesh-wound
in the calf of my left leg, which, though painful, was
not serious enough to cause me to discontinue
the usual performance of my duty. We were
doing no practical good in our present open situation; we had complied, as far as I understood
them, with our instructions, which were to advance, feel for, and locate the enemy; and now to
remain longer in the position we then occupied
would, I calmly believed, be more censurable
than praiseworthy. I therefore ordered my company to fall back.

I may have been influenced in making this
move as soon as I did by the entreaties of one
of my men, who called my attention to the fact
that we were under a cross-fire, and urged that I
ought to order a retreat. We fell back to the

main body, which soon after moved forward in grand line of battle confronting the two forts, which now opened fire upon us with grape. It was in this movement that I received the wound in my leg referred to above.

On reaching a low ground not far from the most troublesome of the two forts our brigade halted. We were directed to keep up a sharp fire upon the enemy whenever he showed his head over his breastworks. By this means we checked his destructive fire very materially, and were enabled to hold our position without much trouble or serious loss. About this time we received orders from our general to be more sparing of our ammunition. Being senior officer on the line, I complied with the instructions by ordering the skirmishers to slacken fire; but I soon found that to continue inactive must be at the expense of the lives of my men, as they now commenced to fall all around me, being picked off in safety by the enemy's sharpshooters. So, thinking it better to save lives than powder and lead, we renewed our practice to the extent previously indulged in, with an immediate good effect; but now General Turner rode out to where we were, and in an angry tone ordered us to cease firing altogether. His orders were repeated and obeyed, but the moment they were so a perfect fusillade of shot poured into us, giving the general a better understanding of our position.

24

I do not know how he escaped the shower of leaden hail which fell thick and fast around him. On his perilous retreat back to the main body he called out to us to keep up a slow fire, but to husband our ammunition. We did so, and performed some nice sharpshooting on our part, for the remainder of the afternoon, when we fell back, under orders, on the main body. This preliminary engagement occurred on the 1st of April, 1865, and during the night of that date we enjoyed but little repose, being under arms all night.

The death-like stillness that reigned during the early hours of the night gave no intimation of the stern work about to be inaugurated on the morrow. It was the calm, however, that precedes the storm. To many a hero whose thoughts, doubtless, were on a smiling home and fond friends, if in this immediate and mighty conflict he might be spared to see the one and grasp the warm hand of the other, it proved a last night before the great dawn of the resurrection. Many of these brave boys, whose patriotism predominated over every other feeling, were seen by us on the following day to gallantly and unselfishly mount the breach unbidden, and to face the steel of a desperate foe at least five times their number.*

---

* The heroes of the storming of Fort Gregg.

About two or three o'clock in the morning of April 2, 1865, there burst upon the ears of the armed mass of expectant listeners such a thunderous sound of Bellona's pent-up resources as never before or since reached the eager hearing of her chivalrous votaries. A simultaneous advance on the enemy's works throughout the length of the whole line extending several miles was now inaugurated.

All of the many appliances of modern warfare, from the great siege-gun and other monster cannon down to the death-dealing Gatling gun; the sixteen-shooting breach-loading rifle, carbines, muskets, and even six-shooting navy revolvers, were here brought into combined and terrible requisition by the determined and frenzied forces of the two great contending armies engaged in the last supreme struggle of a long and bitter war.

This was indeed a moment to "try men's souls," and many of the participants in the awful event never recovered from the nerve-shattering ordeal. One very stout-looking soldier named Reese, a private of Company G, of our regiment, became a raving maniac on the instant, from the great and unexpected shock to his nervous system caused by the tremendous and sudden roar of cannon and outpour of musketry on that memorable morning. In his wild ravings he continued to cry out, as he walked aimlessly up and down near me:

"Put up your sword; put up your sword; let us shed no more blood; the war is over, the war is over."

For some time after the thunderous opening of hostilities by the cannon from the batteries on our right and left we were compelled to stand inactive, awaiting the break of day before moving on the forts in our front, one of which lay on the opposite side of Hatcher's Run; the other protected by deep and wide trenches which surrounded it, and which the enemy had flooded with water to further impede our entrance.

When the faint dawning of day gave us light to see our way, "Forward March" was given. It was a general move all along the line, and it was grimly understood by every one that earnest business and no faltering was now to be the programme. We were not to be denied admittance to their inner circle much longer, and so, when we came to the water, which was intended to check our aggressive advance, we tarried not on the brink of that Rubicon to think, but plunged right in, and the trees and *débris* which the enemy had cut down and thrown into the water, and which were now floating there, designed as another obstruction to our advance, proved rather a benefit instead, affording us as they did a chance to get from one fallen tree to another, and by holding to the limbs a number of the foremost men scrambled across without getting wet.

While making this difficult crossing our comrades on dry ground in our rear diverted the fire
of the enemy within the fort from us considerably.
The first over did not even wait to be reinforced
by those immediately following them, but went at
once directly to the fort. This little band was
very much scattered and entirely exposed to the
fire of the enemy, who had us under such close
range that a plucky resistance on his part must
have inevitably caused great havoc amongst us.
As it was, however, they became panic-stricken,
and threw away every impediment to their very
expeditious flight.

While thus engaged I had not much chance to
take notice of what was going on at the fort next
and to the right of us; but it was carried at the
same time and in much the same manner as was
ours. In both of these forts there were large
numbers of men and much war material captured.

After the successful taking of these works our
scattered command formed in proper shape and
in line of battle, and soon moved forward in grand
array, facing the three last and greatest works of
the enemy at Petersburg, Virginia, viz., Forts
Gregg, Whitworth, and May. These forts were
nearest our extreme front, in the order named.
From our point of approach the forts formed an
imperfect triangle; Forts Gregg and Whitworth
were, if on a direct line, about two hundred yards

apart, but the latter retired about fifty yards from the former, while Fort May, the last and greatest of these forts, was about six hundred or seven hundred yards to the rear, and in about the centre of the other two forts.

Before making the assault on the two nearest forts we were halted for the purpose of making a reconnoissance. While thus halted we were within easy range of the enemy's sharpshooters, who commenced making it decidedly unpleasant for us. Soon we noticed, on a gently elevated plateau to our right, a splendid troop of handsomely equipped and richly caparisoned horsemen cantering briskly forward in a diagonal direction to the front. It was a thrilling, and, in a soldier's eye, an admirable sight to see such "shining lights" thus expose themselves to the discretionary action of the enemy, who, had he been so disposed, could have annihilated the larger portion of that distinguished party. This was General Grant and his staff making a personal observation of the field before us. After an apparently satisfactory inspection the general and his party rode leisurely back to the point whence they came.

This calm and dignified exhibition of intrepidity was well calculated to engender a great respect and pride in the minds of the men for such brave leaders. At the time of this action of General Grant's there was nothing to prevent the concentration of the enemy's fire from the three forts upon him and his conspicuous party. Why the enemy did not do so may be food for reflection. It was, indeed, an unexpected and deferential act of courtesy, which justly earned the reciprocal kindness extended one week later at Appomattox.

Soon after General Grant and his staff fell back the 3d Division of the 24th Corps, under the command of Brevet Major-General John W. Turner, was ordered to advance on the two forts in front of us. The 10th, 11th, and 15th Regiments, West Virginia Infantry, constituted the 1st Brigade of this division, and was under the command of Brevet Major-General Thomas M. Harris.

In advancing, the 1st and 3d Brigades had a fort each to encounter; the 1st on the left and confronting Fort Whitworth, the 3d Brigade on the right in front of Fort Gregg. In moving on a right line the 3d Brigade became engaged first, as Fort Gregg was, as I have before stated, the most advanced in position. As we neared these works the enemy's fire therefrom became very fierce and destructive, and the two brigades halted at nearly the same time and lay down.

At the time of lying down I found myself, with two men of Company K of our regiment, a few yards in advance of the remainder of the troops of our brigade; these two boys kept steadily on at their work of loading and firing at the heads of the enemy whenever he exposed himself to fire at

us.   I assisted by biting cartridges for them ready
to ram home, and, while thus employed, a bullet
passed through my left sleeve at my wrist, and
came out at the elbow; on glancing involuntarily
behind me after this narrow escape I saw two men
lying dead, one across the other, the uppermost
having just received a bullet in the centre of his
forehead.   Whether or not this bullet was the one
that first passed through my sleeve I can only
surmise.

In our advanced position I had a distinct view
of what was transpiring on our right at Fort
Gregg, and never have I witnessed anything to
compare with that bloody struggle for its possession on the one side and retention on the other.
While gazing at this desperate hand-to-hand encounter going on upon its ramparts I lost all
thoughts of personal danger under the excitement
of the moment, and lay spell-bound, waiting the
final issue of the struggle.   A few of the men of
the 3d Brigade nearest Fort Gregg were seen to
make a sudden break and climb the breastworks
of the rebel stronghold, only to be immediately
bayoneted by its reckless defenders.   Another heroic band, bearing the Stars and Stripes, instantly
followed, and a moment later proudly planted the
beautiful banner high on the rebel ramparts.   I
cheered immediately, and the shout was taken up
and repeated by comrades all around me; but,
alas! our joy was but momentary; a second

"Another heroic band instantly followed, and planted the beautiful banner high on the rebel ramparts." Page 390

later the Union flag, together with its noble defenders, fell, and in its place stood the Bars and
Stars.

And now, unbidden, another handful of men
scaled the fort, and once more the rebel insignia
is hauled down and our colors again float triumphantly in the blood-charged breeze. And so the
flags alternated, carrying with them in their rise
and fall the hopes and fears of the thousands of
overwrought onlookers; but at last the officer in
charge of this gallant brigade gave the word to
charge, and in they went, with an irresistible rush,
maddened at the slaughter of their late comrades,
and determined to avenge their deaths. That
onslaught could not be checked, and though the
reckless rebels fought to the bitter end the struggle was soon over.

At the same time that the general advance was
ordered on Fort Gregg, General Harris gave the
word to charge on Fort Whitworth. This latter
fort was the larger one and had more than twice
the number defending it. General Harris did
not say " Go," but " Come, boys," and was the first
to shoot ahead himself. I had no idea, at that
time, that he was such a runner as he proved to
be. I considered myself, in those days, a fair
athlete, but in the race to this fort I could not get
one foot ahead of our gallant general. We both
got into the rebel works at about the same time,
and in close company with a few of our fleetest

men. I went in bareheaded, losing my hat by a missile from Fort May directed at us to cover the retreat of about half of the rebel defenders of Fort Whitworth. We found upon our entrance the remaining half, with one exception, submissive captives ; this latter was the youngest member of the crowd, and he was the last to quit shooting at us. Even after he had been disarmed, he kept shaking his little fist defiantly in our faces, and offering to fight all the Yankees in the field, single-handed and alone.

In passing I wish to state, without attempting to make invidious comparisons, that in every action directed by General Harris, of which I have any knowledge, I became more and more impressed with his cool and accurate judgment, his pronounced ability and undoubted courage. Whenever he moved he did so at the opportune moment, and then his movements were rapid and decisive, doing the work assigned him nobly and with a saving of life at once commendable and in perfect keeping with the spirit of true military ethics.

All of the rebel works but one, Fort May, were now carried ; but after the severe fighting of the previous two days a cessation of hostilities, apparently by mutual consent, succeeded, and we had time to look about us, and take a view of the havoc done in the recent struggle. I can compare the appearance of Fort Gregg to nothing but a slaughter-pen. The blue and the gray were there promiscuously heaped together. Their kindred blood commingling presented a sight that could not fail to impress one indelibly with the horrors of a civil war.

I was informed that the defenders of Fort Gregg were sons of the Green Isle, which fact I can readily believe from their stubborn resistance to our troops. Among those found therein wearing the blood-stained blue I recognized some of the 23d Illinois, the remnant of Mulligan's Irish Brigade. One of the latter, named Dwyer, with whom I had been talking only a short time before he went in, was found among the slain. I question if half a dozen of the defenders of the fort survived its capture.

Late in the afternoon General Grant again made his appearance at the front.

Now he had Lee, with all of his command, encompassed within that little spot at Petersburg comprising Fort May. I thought this must be the "last ditch," as with our superior force we could easily keep him there, until our large available supply of artillery was trained upon him, when, in my opinion, he could be brought to unconditional terms.

Apart from my own circumscribed vision and meagre sources of information I do not know what disposition was made of our forces on the night of the 2d of April. I was awake and on duty all of the night, and, as far as I could learn, was nearest to the enemy's works; sufficiently near, at all events, to plainly hear the moving of wagons and see the flickering of innumerable lights flitting back and forth through the rebel camp, presenting unmistakable signs of an evacuation.   I lost no time in reporting my observations and conclusions to my immediate commander.

All night long these evidences of flight continued, and when daylight came it revealed the mortifying fact that General Lee and his entire command had quietly decamped.

CHAPTER XLI.

After breakfast and other preliminaries, we started after the light-footed enemy.

During our week's pursuit of Lee nothing worthy of special mention transpired until we arrived in the neighborhood of Rice's Station, Prince Edward county, Virginia, where we succeeded in getting into such close quarters with the enemy that he offered a vigorous objection by opening a brisk fire upon our advance. The rebel fire was so obstinate that our heavy line of skirmishers was held in check, and the repeated and loud commands of General Harris to the skirmishers to advance were unavailing. The general, losing patience, came to me and asked how many men I had. When I had told him, he ordered me to advance with them and take charge of the skirmish line in our front.

I prepared to obey, and just at the time that my men were in proper alignment and ready to move forward, an officer, splendidly mounted and accompanied by a staff of fine military appearance, rode up to where we were. Although the gentleman had not seen me during the previous eight or nine months, I was flattered to find that he recognized me, as he held out his hand and grasped mine. This was the gallant General George Crook, whom I had long revered.

The esteem of such men as Generals Crook and Harris should, to a certain extent, make even cowardly men brave, and we now felt very proud as we moved off in nice order and took charge of the skirmish line which afterwards did its work handsomely, pressing the enemy back until the shadows of night secured to both sides a temporary respite. Even after nightfall we advanced some little distance farther and straightened and strengthened our lines. At early dawn next morning we advanced on quick time after the elusive enemy. But he did not wait for us but left his temporary entrenchments in a great hurry, leaving some things of value to him behind, including medical stores.

In the pursuit of Lee from Petersburg to Appomattox, embracing a period of a week, there were only a couple of encounters with him, one at Sailor's Creek, on the 6th, with the cavalry, and the one mentioned at Rice's Station with infantry; and it may be inferred from the few engagements had with him, and the distance covered, that there was fast time made on that march. The last day's tramp will be admitted to be a fair test of the

APPOMATTOX COURT-HOUSE.

sterling qualities of our men. Their endurance and determination will be understood in the record they made of thirty-five and a half miles without halting, except for a short time to eat.

On this trying occasion it was admirable, considering the heavy weights they had to carry, the hard fighting, little sleeping and forced marching of many days previous that they had undergone, to see how few of the brave boys faltered or fell back. One of the most potent reasons for the almost superhuman efforts of the men was found in the uniform kindness and encouragement to the rank and file by General Ord, who often during the day expressed his sympathy for them, and said:

"I promise you, boys, that this will be the last day's march you will have to endure."

They believed him and responded with renewed exertions. If it had not been for this encouragement on his part, there would have been far less of our number in Lee's front on the next morning, April the ninth.

An incident of this last hard day's march will be my excuse for again introducing to the reader my orderly sergeant, Lawrence May.

While trudging wearily along, two of my men came to me and told me that Orderly May's feet were badly cut up and bleeding from the effects of marching in a pair of new boots. I dropped back to where the poor fellow was, and at once

noticed the evident signs of his sufferings in his
noble but painful efforts to keep up.

"Orderly," said I, "I see your feet hurt you
badly."

"Just a little, Captain; I can get along all
right," was the uncomplaining reply.

"I wish you," I replied, "to get into one of the
ambulances; that is what they are for, and you
are plainly not in a fit condition to walk."

"I never rode in one, sir," said he, proudly,
"and I hope I sha'n't have to now."

Knowing the soldierly pride of which May was
possessed in so marked a degree was what held
him back from complying with my request, I did not
urge him further; but, unknown to him, I watched
him closely, and as the torture from his boots increased, he could not conceal his terrible sufferings from anybody. My heart ached for him and
I became determined to relieve him in some way.
Realizing and appreciating the heroic and uncomplaining spirit of the man, and wishing to spare
his feelings as much as possible, I went to our
regimental surgeon, Dr. Walter S. Welsh, and
explained matters to him, and requested that he
issue direct and imperative orders to May to go
into an ambulance.

The orderly was at all times subordinate, but
in complying with this order, he did so as reluctantly and with as shamed a face as though he was
on his way to the gallows.

We had scarcely gotten him well disposed of within the wagon when he was again in the ranks, persisting vehemently that he was all right and well able to walk. The humiliation attaching to his position in an ambulance appeared to him to be a greater torture than were the pinchings of his boots, and so he refused to remain longer in the wagon. When his boots were removed the next day, after the white flag came out, they were found to be thoroughly soaked with blood.

During his term of service, of nearly three years, May was never sick; never absent, but always at his post; he was unoffending, modest, virtuous, and gentle; and as true in the performance of his duty as is the sun in his course. This man has never received a pension and would not, I believe, under any circumstances, ask for it; and so it is that many a faithful servant of the government is neglected, because through diffidence and modesty he neglects himself.

We are at last confronting Lee at Appomattox Court-House.

The action here of the corps to which we were attached has been briefly given in the State Adjutant-General's report for 1865, and is, in the main, correct. The only fault I am inclined to find with this report is that it does not, as in fact such a general summary of the event could not well be expected to do, go quite far enough; and it is

25

these unintentional omissions that the writer seeks
to supply.

The report referred to is as follows:

"In the pursuit of Lee's army, which followed,
the 24th Army Corps bore a conspicuous part,
and the West Virginia troops, by their gallantry
and endurance, elicited warm expressions of
admiration from the commander of the corps,
General Gibbon, as also from Major-General
Ord, commanding the Army of the James.

"It was the 1st and 3d Divisions of the 24th
Corps that formed a line across Lee's front on
the morning of the 9th of April at Appomattox
Court-House, and brought from that commander
the flag of truce which resulted in the capitula-
tion and disbanding of the rebel Army of Northern Virginia, having marched on the 8th and
morning of the 9th thirty-five miles to gain that
position. This line was formed across the road
to Lynchburg, on which Lee was retreating, and
but for which he might have continued his
march.

"The troops from West Virginia also claim
with pride the honor of silencing the last battery
that General Lee ever had put in position; this
was effected by a skirmish line sent forward by
General Harris, under Captain James A. Jarboe,
of the 10th Regiment, armed with Spencer seven-
shooting rifles, closely sustained by the brigade.
Of this battery two or three guns were captured."

"Of this battery two or three guns were captured."—Page 400.

Who captured them?

Very early on the morning of the 9th we were taking a hurried breakfast while encamped in a plowed field, at one end of which ran a narrow lane. I was very near this road, and while busy trying to heat my coffee I noticed a lone horseman riding out from the direction of a stone house in our rear to where we were. The horseman was an officer in fine uniform and astride of a splendid horse:

"There goes Sheridan," shouted the men.

Anxious to get a closer look at this American counterpart of Marshal Ney I left my coffee, and ran up to the lane whereon "little Phil" was riding leisurely along and alone. He was going in front of Lee's army, which was heading for Lynchburg. I never saw a fairer picture of health and composure. His features were faultless in my partial opinion, but it may have been that the final result, then so near its accomplishment, lent an added charm to his expression. How sad to learn that at this writing (July, 1888) such a shining light is so nearly extinguished! From all accounts this bright life is fast waning and descending towards the horizon below which so many of his compatriot luminaries have lately disappeared.

In less than ten minutes after Sheridan had ridden past we received orders to march quickly in the same direction. We did so at once.

On coming in Lee's front, and after emerging from a skirt of woods, we came into an open field of triangular shape, containing perhaps ten or twelve acres. Here was General Sheridan at the head of a small force of his cavalry, in the front and on the flank of which were woods, and in that position the enemy's infantry had every advantage of our cavalry. But General Harris was at hand with his infantry and we soon saw our immediate commander in close conversation with the little "Field-Marshal;" the result of their conference was that General Harris at once detailed a strong line of skirmishers to operate against the enemy in these woods. He called two officers to take charge of this line; their instructions were separate and distinct. One of them, Captain James A. Jarboe, of the 10th West Virginia regiment, as brave and as good a man as was on the field, was assigned to the left of the line; and the writer received instructions from the general to take charge of the skirmishers on the right of the line. I did not at any time while confronting the enemy receive orders from Captain Jarboe, but always immediately and directly from General Harris, who was very close to me most of the time, and cognizant of every move as soon as made.

Reaching the woods mentioned, we engaged the enemy's skirmishers and drove them steadily back. Their officers in trying to rally them assured the dejected and despairing "Johnnies" that there was nothing in their front but cavalry.

"By G——," was the desperate reply, "you'll find that they are knapsack cavalry."

Incidentally the appellation embodied in the above remark does not appear inappropriate in view of the marching qualities then exhibited by our men.

The enemy finding their skirmishers thus driven back, hurried forward two brass field-pieces, which they were placing in position about two hundred yards in our front at the time we emerged from the woods. General Harris, who was near me, ordered an advance, when we went in on double-quick for the battery, which started at the same moment in more than double-quick time for the rear. While this chase was in progress General Harris, with a heavy line of battle, was moving up briskly some distance in the rear of his pursuing skirmishers. The rebel battery in our front continued retreating to the enemy's main body as fast as the old horses attached to the pieces could move; but meeting a strong fence in their front they were forced to halt for a few moments, enabling us to overtake them. They therefore abandoned their guns and two of their horses; I tarried long enough in the pursuit of the rebel skirmishers to cast a wistful glance at a little artillery saddle which formed a part of the trappings of one of the abandoned horses; and then over the fence we went, after the fast retreating enemy. Five minutes had probably elapsed after the capture of the artillery pieces when the "white flag" came out directly in our front.

The scene that followed its appearance has often been so graphically described that I have not the hardihood to attempt it here.

After the cheering and excitement had in a measure subsided I bethought me of the little saddle. Returning to where the horses were, I removed it and later placed it in a trunk and sent it home. I have never parted with it, and regard it, justly I think, as the real trophy of the "last ditch." It was exhibited by the Grand Army of the Republic, together with other curiosities and mementos of the late war, at the Pittsburg Exposition, in 1879.

General Grant being about seven miles in the rear when the "white flag" appeared, we had a long and impatient wait before the brave remnant of Lee's army marched passed us after being paroled for all time. During the interval of waiting I made use of the opportunity to convey to the members of my little command an idea of the feelings that such an event as the present one engendered in me. I told them that I was hungry (as indeed they all must be) and had but few crackers remaining, but those few I proposed to divide with our late enemy, but who now and henceforth were our friends, with but one country and one flag. This family feud was over and I sincerely hoped forever. The sooner its grievous wounds were healed by manly forgiveness and kind words the better for all concerned. There are few survivors of the late struggle who have suffered more, personally, from the treatment of the enemy than I; but on this day I would cheerfully give the brave though mistaken fellows the hand of eternal friendship; and more to the same effect.

How pleased I was to discover later that in exhibiting this conciliatory spirit to a fallen foe I was only anticipating the wishes of General Grant, as was shown in his liberal treatment of General Lee, giving him horses, mules, and side-arms and twenty thousand rations besides.

Compare this magnanimous action of a victorious leader with the brutal exactions demanded under kingly rule, and gracefully say, with me: Long live and God bless our glorious Republic.

As the disbanded army, now without a head, was passing before us, heading for Lynchburg, at a go-as-you-please gait, our brave boys carried out the suggestions made to them by their officers, by sharing with the defeated "Johnnies" the contents of their haversacks, and by using such pleasing and friendly expressions as: "We're all going home now to the girls we left behind us;" "Good-bye, boys," etc., etc.

General Harris, with his command, marched

from Appomattox to Lynchburg, where the bulk of
Lee's disbanded army concentrated before starting for their respective homes. From Lynchburg, where we distributed rations among the
needy soldiers, we proceeded to Richmond. We
were among the first troops to occupy the Southern capital after its evacuation, and we were surprised to find, upon our entrance, such a large
portion of that beautiful city in ruins and ashes.
The devilish incendiaries were, not the invading
Unionists, but those whose duty it should have
been to build up and protect it. Were it not for
the determined and successful efforts of our men
the conflagration would have been general and
entirely destructive to the city.

We retain some pleasant recollections of Richmond during our stay there. There seemed to
be no stint of money among our boys, so every
day while we remained gayety and good-fellow-
ship seemed to be effectually dispelling the previous gloom; acquaintanceship and genial intercourse were fast obliterating the embittered feelings engendered by the war. Soon the places
of amusement began to reopen their doors, and
resume their wonted attractions; business houses
displayed their wares and commenced a lively
competition for the patronage of the Yankees;
and things generally again took on their old time
look.

I do not recall an instance during the two

months we were in Richmond of the slightest insult being offered to any of its inhabitants by our men, which remarkable fact was unprecedented in history and a noble line of conduct in victors, and quite contrary to the many warnings of the leaders of the late rebellion, in their highly colored harangues to their credulous people on the subject of an invasion of the South by Union troops, which dire calamity was sure to be followed by a policy of extermination, confiscation and assaults upon the honor of their wives and daughters, etc., by the "Northern Vandals."

While encamped near Richmond we were visited by two gentlemen who had occupied positions of distinction in the executive branch of the Confederacy, and who were, prior to the outbreak of the war, well acquainted with a number of our men ; one was Judge Draper Camden, of Clarksburg, West Va. ; the other, Mr. Jonathan Bennett, of Weston, West Va., who had been the late Auditor-General of the Confederacy. Both gentlemen felt, under the changed condition, somewhat timid, especially Mr. Bennett, who, by reason of his course during the war, was not popular in the section of country whence he came, and from where several of our companies, now doing duty here, were raised.

I extended every possible courtesy to the gentlemen during their visit to our camp, and as we walked through the grounds together my presence, I am pleased to state, was sufficient to insure them from all indignities, or any unpleasant remarks.

On the 14th of June, 1865, our regiment was mustered out at Richmond, and our fares paid to Wheeling, where on our arrival we were paid off and finally discharged.

ROSTER

OF

COMPANY B, 15TH REGT. W. VA. INFANTRY VOL.

Names.	Rank.	Age.	When mustered into service.	Remarks.
Egan, Michael	Capt.	36	Sept. 1, 1862.	Taken prisoner of war, May 9, '64, escaped Nov. 4, '64.
Nicholas, William J.	1st Lieut.	27	" "	Promoted to Capt. Co. D, Oct. 27,'63.
Detamore, John W.	2d Lieut.	36	" "	Promoted to 1st Lieut.
Power, Patrick	1st Sgt.	26	" "	Promoted to 2d and to 1st Lieut.
May, Lawrence	1st Sgt.	38	" "	
Belt, Hedgman	2d Sgt.	28	" "	
Davis, James L.	3d Sgt.	30	" "	Would not fight.
Ward, John D.	4th Sgt.	21	" "	
Fisher, George A.	5th Sgt.			
Wood, A. J.	Corporal	33	" "	Promoted to Sergt.
Hitt, Jos. W.	"	30	" "	Killed in action, June 18, '64, near Lynchburg, Va.
Bush, John J.	"	35	" "	
Ellis, James F.	"	23	" "	Died of starvation in rebel prison.
Monypenny, T. W.	"	21	" "	
Rohobough, A. E.	"	24	" "	
Montgomery, Henry	"	34	" "	
Brown, Thomas	"	31	March 31, 1864.	
Tanner, John	Wagon'r	59	Sept. 1, 1862.	
Adams, Isaac	Private	48	" "	Working on fortifications at Washington, D. C., since Nov. 19, '64.
Arbogast, Daniel	"	27	" "	
Baily, Albert	"	20	" "	
Butcher, M. E.	"	23	" "	
Bond, Levi W.	"	19	" "	Died in prison.
Burkhammer, Joseph	"	18	" "	
Burns, Patrick	Corporal	21	" "	Died since mustered out.
Brown, Jesse	Private	34	" "	
Baily, Philander	"	18	" "	Died at New Creek Nov. 1, '62, of measels.

Names.	Rank.	Age.	When Mustered into Service.	Remarks.
Bush, Henry H.	Private	21	Sept. 1, 1862.	A fine young man, starved to death at Andersonville prison.
Bowan, John E.	"	18	March 31, 1864.	
Crawford, Joseph	"	18	" "	Taken prisoner of war at Cedar Creek Oct. 19, '64.
Carney, Michael	"	26	Sept. 1, 1862.	Died since mustered out.
Cutwright, Isaac	"	25	" "	
Conrad, Geo. W.	"	29	" "	
Clark, John	"	25	March 31, 1864.	
Croul, John W.	"	25	Sept. 1, 1862.	
Davis, Lorenzo L.	"	19	Oct. 16, "	
Davis, Wm. H.	"	35	Sept. 1, "	In hospital at Sandy Hook, Aug. 1, '64.
Doory, John	"	32	" "	
Dinsmore, John A.	Regt. Armorer	26	" "	2d Sergt., but volunteered as Regt. armorer.
Dodson, Chas. E.	Private	18	March 31, 1864.	
Daily, Charles	"	19	" "	
Finster, Simon	"	39	Sept. 1, 1862.	
Fisher, Jacob C.	"	37	" "	
Garton, James	"	22	" "	
Horan, Peter	"	20	" "	
Horan, Kieran	"	23	" "	Killed in action at Cedar Creek, Oct. 19, '64.
Hanson, Chas. W.	"	20	Sept. 1, 1864.	
Hacker, William G.	"	22	" "	Wounded at Hatcher Run, April 2, '65.
Hall, Joseph	"	43	" "	Wounded at Cedar Creek, Oct. 19, '64.
Hines, Thomas	"	18	" "	Killed in action near Staunton, Va., June 10, '64.
Jones, Benjamin S.	"	23	" "	
Jenkins, Joseph	"	18	June 20, 63.	A wild youth, who would go where he pleased.
Jewell, Albert	"	46	Sept. 1, 1862.	Discharged at New Creek, Dec. 9, '62.
Knapp, Wm. T.	"	31	" "	
Laurrell, John	Corporal	27	" "	Prisoner of war at Salisbury, N. C.
Lamb, Skidmore	Private	22	" "	
Literal, James	"	18	" "	

Names.	Rank.	Age.	When Mustered into Service.		Remarks.
Monypenny, James	Private	18	Sept. 1, 1862.		
Monypenny, William	"	37	"	"	
Monypenny, Albert	"	29	"	"	
Monypenny, Napoleon B.	"	22	"	"	Died of typhoid fever at Wheeling, Oct. 14, '62.
Means, Calvin	"	30	"	"	
McCudden, James	"	23	"	"	Wounded at Hatcher Run, April 2, '65.
McManus, Patrick	"	21	"	"	
Monypenny, Henry	"	28	"	"	Prisoner of war at Salisbury, N. C.
Means, Isaac	"	38	"	"	Died of wounds received at Cedar Creek, Oct. 19, '64.
Newcomb, John	Wagon'r	43	"	"	
Nicholar, Carr	Private	19	"	"	
Nicholas, M. C.	"	28	"	"	
Osborne, Harrison	"	25	"	"	
Patten, Hinton	"	21	"	"	
Plunket, James	"	18	"	"	Severely wounded at Cedar Creek, Oct. 19, '64.
Pletcher, Jonathan	"	27	"	"	
Pletcher, Wm. H.	"	24	"	"	Captur'd at Charleston, W. Va., Aug. 10, '64.
Rohobaugh, John G.	"	19	"	"	Wounded at Winchester, Va., Sept. 19, '64.
Sheerer, Andrew	"	27	"	"	Died of wounds received near Staunton, Va.
Swicker, Manly	"	19	"	"	
Sheerer, Henry	"	25	"	"	Died of wounds received in action near Staunton, Va.
Steinback, Geo. W.	"	19	"	"	
Shoulder, Jacob L.	"	24	"	"	Died of typhoid fever at Jarvis Hospital, Baltimore, Md., Sept. 13, '64.
Sleeth, Adam C.	"	25	"	"	
Spouse, Wm.	"	25	"	"	
Sheifer, Jno. T.	"	32	"	"	Died in rebel prison, Salisbury, N. C.
Simmons, W.	"	25	"	"	

Names.	Rank.	Age.	When Mustered into Service.	Remarks.
Sneed, Achilles H.	Private	28	Sept. 1, 1862.	Captured at Cedar Creek, Oct. 19, '64.
Turner, Johnson V.	"	33	" "	
West, Charles	"	26	" "	
West, Alexander	"	28	" "	
West, George	"	38	" "	Died of wounds received at Winchester, Sept. 19, '64.
Waldeck, F. M.	"	21	" "	
Ward, Henry M.	"	19	" "	
Woofler, Albert	"	18	" "	Died of starvation while prisoner of war at Salisbury, N. C.
Wilkinson, Joshua S.	"	21	June 20, 1863.	Captured at Cedar Creek, Oct. 19, '64.